THE TRANSPORTER

DISCARD

D1522316

ALSO BY LIZ MAVERICK

The Crimson City Series

Crimson City
Crimson Rogue
A Time to Howl
Crimson & Steam

The Wired Series

Wired
Irreversible

Others

Hot & Bothered
The Shadow Runners

THE TRANSPORTER

LIZ
MAVERICK

Published by Montlake Romance, Seattle

www.apub.com

Amazon, the Amazon logo, and Montlake Romance are trademarks of Amazon.com, Inc., or its affiliates.

ISBN-13: 9781477822609
ISBN-10: 1477822607

Cover design by Jason Blackburn

Printed in the United States of America

This is for my dad, who always believed in me and used to say (with a big grin),
"Today is a day in which to excel."

CHAPTER 1

I'm not the kind of girl this is supposed to happen to.

Diesel fumes stung Cecily's nose, and her head pounded from the incessant swish of speeding traffic. It was just after morning rush hour. A Greyhound much like the one she'd arrived on twenty minutes ago zoomed past, this time having no reason to stop at the crumbling freeway cutout that passed as a bus shelter. She was the only passenger to get off here, and hopefully the four she'd left behind were still hunched in their seats, lost in their dreams of a better tomorrow; as far as she could tell, not a soul saw her drag her suitcase to the gas station through that hole in the rusting chain-link fence bordering the freeway.

Cecily coughed on another whiff of fumes and mildew, tears pricking her eyes as she tried unsuccessfully to keep the past in the past. *He said if I ever left, he hoped I'd step in front of a bus,* she thought grimly. *That's how bad a judge of character I am. I picked a guy who would rather I step in front of a bus than be happy.* She itched to call Dex again; seeing her brother on video chat was the only time she ever remembered what being safe felt like, but James had done something to her phone.

She desperately, desperately wished Dex were coming to get her himself, but no way was she going to blame him. If anything, she should blame herself for listening when that bastard told her she couldn't go visit her brother after his accident. *It would have all come out, and I'd never have come back here, and all of this wouldn't have spiraled out of control like it did.*

Cecily shook out her right hand, which had gone pins and needles from clutching the handle of her suitcase like a life preserver. It wasn't working. The throbbing patch under her left eye still hurt, but she'd done a great job of camouflaging the ugly. If her plans in New York City didn't work out, maybe she should consider beauty school. *Ha-ha, Cecily.* Anyway, by the time her brother saw her, the bruising would be gone.

Of course, that was a couple of days from now, and this was *now* now. And as a car came into view, snaking down the lonely off-ramp, Cecily grew more self-conscious. The humidity was pretty intense; tendrils of hair clung to her face, her makeup was sweating, and her T-shirt was stuck to her skin.

Her brother's friend wasn't late; she'd come early. It had seemed like a good idea at the time—get out while the gettin' was good— but maybe she ought to have picked a rendezvous point with people around.

Cecily plastered on the plucky smile she'd perfected in her bathroom at home, but it faltered as the car neared the station and pulled in, window down. A BMW. A really big-looking, really, really nice-looking BMW. And a really big-looking, really, really not-so-nice-looking man at the wheel.

Is this Shane? My brother's a total nerd. His friends always drove cars that had parts falling off at every stoplight. His friends didn't wear mirrored sunglasses and have tattoos covering well-developed muscles on arms that hung out car windows like machine guns.

Cecily took a step back, her sneakers hitting her suitcase. Her head was spinning. *Dex is too late; James has found me. He's found me and sent someone to take me back to him.*

"You Cecily?"

The car door opened, and the man stepped out of the car. Unfolded himself, really, to reveal a massive frame wearing shitkicker boots, jeans, a T-shirt, and lots more muscles.

A sob caught in Cecily's throat. She didn't know what James's worst looked like. She'd only just realized that she hadn't really known him at all. Maybe the worst looked like *this*. She froze, her world turning to slow motion as the man removed his sunglasses, revealing eyes as dark as the scowl on his face. *Oh, god. He's going to do something to me.*

Their eyes locked, something flickered in his expression, and a rush sliced through Cecily's bloodstream. *That's your survival instinct, stupid.*

RUN!

She bolted, knocking the suitcase over to buy time, even though he probably crushed it with one step, like Godzilla stomping a tiny human. Behind the gas station was nothing but abandoned decay. Cecily raced through the weed-strewn parking lot, past a mess of faded lines, smashed windows, and flapping strips of awning. There was nothing here and no one who could help her.

He was calling her name and *"Not gonna hurt you . . ."*

Sweat blurred her vision, and she stumbled on a dandelion patch poking through broken pavement.

"Hey, kid!"

Not even going to look. You look back, they always win. They nip you at the finish line. The ground literally jumped from the weight of his boots pounding behind her; she could feel his heat against her back, and then he had her, one arm around her waist, and she tripped.

"Please," she begged. "Please make it fast." Cecily closed her eyes, though absolute panic and fear already made her blind. The smell of gasoline stung her nose as the damp, jagged pavement came up to meet her, and they hit the ground and rolled. No longer fighting, she felt every muscle in her body clench as she anticipated the pain of whatever he had in mind. "I'm sorry I'm leaving you alone, Dex," she mumbled, blood in her mouth, tears stinging her eyes.

I'm not the kind of girl this is supposed to happen to . . .

◆ ◆ ◆

Cecily woke up with her face smashed into some pretty nice leather in the backseat of a car. The engine purred, and judging from the crisp temperature and swishing sounds, the window was open and they were moving fast down a freeway. She kept her eyes closed and pretended she was still asleep and took a moment to gauge the situation. Nothing new hurt, she wasn't bound, and there was a blanket on top of her.

Maybe James didn't send him; he didn't hurt me, and I'm not dead.

And then, *Points for intelligence!*

And then, *Hey, I may have lost my common sense and dignity, but I still have a sense of humor. That's promising.*

"Go ahead and sit up."

Cecily's eyes widened. Her fake sleep face always fooled James.

"Sit. Up."

She sat up, and the blanket fell to the seat beside her. It was a beige-and-black plaid cashmere blanket that coordinated with the tan interior of the car—not the sort of blanket you'd use to wrap up a dead body. This gave her comfort. What didn't give her comfort was the pair of unblinking dark eyes gazing at her in the rearview mirror. At least one day of scruff roughed up the driver's jaw, and his hair was longish and kind of messy.

Did he look like one of her brother's old friends? Hell, no. Did he look like a Shane? Definitely. But with the odd exception of a pair of brown suede driving gloves, he didn't look like the owner of this car. Maybe she was asking too much of the plaid cashmere. She should have learned every lesson in the world about judging a book by its cover. James looked like a nice, attractive, wealthy businessman. "Shane" looked like a hot badass cowboy in a stolen car. He was either an angel in disguise or he had an entirely different dead-body blanket waiting for her in the trunk.

Safe or not safe?

"Seat belt *on*," the driver said, a note of exasperation in his voice.

Being ordered around left a bitter taste in Cecily's mouth like it always did, but (a) given they were in a moving vehicle over which she had no control and (b) this would have been an unquestionably reasonable request under pretty much any other circumstance, she buckled herself in where she could see his eyes in the mirror and at least some of his profile. This gave her another opportunity to take his measure. Unfortunately, the only new piece of information she gleaned was the hilt of a knife poking out of a camouflage-patterned ankle holster where the bend of his knee lifted the hem of his jeans. *Lovely. Just great.* Cecily adjusted the belt strap and looked out the window for a useful freeway sign. Still in Minnesota. That told her nothing, since she wasn't a native and hadn't left Minneapolis much during her stay.

Okay, keep it together until you're sure. Don't panic unless it's really time to panic. "Who are you?" she asked. She hoped he was her brother's friend. She prayed he was. But she didn't want to offer up the name to this guy if he wasn't.

"You knew Dex was sending a friend to take you back to New York. Why'd you run?" the driver asked by way of response.

You didn't answer my question. Cecily swallowed hard. "How do I know you're the one Dex sent?"

Something came flying over the front seat; Cecily flinched as a worn yellow bunny planted headfirst in the seat next to her. She squealed and pulled the bunny to her chest.

"I'm Shane," the driver said. "Dex said the rabbit's name is . . ." He paused, sighed, and shook his head. "Bun-Bun. That good enough for you?"

Only my brother would know that. Only my brother would even know where that box of stuff was. A wave of tension left her body. "Yeah, Shane," Cecily whispered. "That's good enough for me. Thanks for picking me up."

The eyes narrowed, studying her as she clutched the bunny with trembling hands. Cecily was suddenly unable to get enough air.

"Just know you're safe on my watch," Shane said.

Safe. Finally out of there. Safe. Cecily buried her fingers in the bunny's fur and broke.

Through her tears, she saw Shane's eyes watching her in the mirror. He finally blinked.

CHAPTER 2

Fuck. The girl was crying. Shane would definitely not have waited an extra day in Salt Lake City for an overnighted bunny that was gonna make a girl cry. Particularly since he was supposed to get Cecily back to New York and under Hudson Kings protection as soon as humanly possible. But Dex insisted on sending it as a kind of code word for his sister, since he couldn't come himself, and it was technically on Shane's way—if you consider Utah an errand on the way to Minnesota from California.

If this kinda bullshit wasn't exactly what it meant to be loyal, Shane didn't know what it meant, because he sure wouldn't be doing it for just anybody. It wasn't just the big ops that counted; it was also the personal stuff. Dex and Roth and the other guys were the closest thing he'd ever have to family, and he wasn't inclined to lose his home for the holidays. Didn't always make it home, but he liked knowing it was there.

He sighed and adjusted his driving gloves. She was not what he'd expected.

Dexter's sister was about ten years old in the picture on her brother's desk back in Manhattan. Shane vaguely remembered a kid in overalls and sneakers, messy brown hair, and wide eyes, with her big brother's arm slung around her shoulders.

What she looked like now shouldn't have been a surprise, since she and Dex were still blue-eyed, brown-haired color copies of each other, except that Shane hadn't factored in what it would look like when that ten-year-old waif turned into the twentysomething-woman version of her younger self.

One big difference was that she wasn't smiling now like she had been in the picture. She was completely alone at an abandoned gas station, and she looked every inch a girl looking for life's nearest exit: vulnerable, nervous . . . but luckily, like maybe the last bit of fire hadn't been beaten out of her.

That fire hit him immediately—socked him in the gut when he got his first look at her trying to stand her ground. She appeared to have a lot of leg for her height, but she was tiny; a man could wrap his arms around her in a bear hug and she'd probably vanish from sight. She was pretty; he could see that even though she was a mess between the nasty bruise and the humidity. Shirt plastered against her showed she had a cute little bod that needed some extra meat. Whether she was on a diet to impress the asshole who beat her or the asshole made her lose her appetite, he knew she was far too light because he'd carried her to the car when she'd passed out.

She'd bolted before he could explain, and the next thing he knew, she was lying in his arms, her lip dotting blood where she'd opened an old cut, and her skin pale with fear except for the makeup blotches that weren't fooling anybody. It was nothing to lift her over one shoulder, grab her suitcase on the way to the car, and be on his way. But now that he was on his way, he was beginning to realize this was not even close to business as usual, and he didn't have the faintest idea what to do with her and all her . . . feelings.

This was new; this was not welcome. Typical freight didn't have emotions. Typical Shane didn't either.

Her jag ended pretty quickly, so the sick feeling in Shane's stomach at the sound of her quiet sobs didn't stick around. "Sorry about that," Cecily said, swiping at her tearstained face with her T-shirt.

Shane watched a slice of skin appear at her midriff as she pulled the fabric up; he tightened his grip and stared at the road.

"Did Dex tell you what happened?" she asked.

"He didn't give me details. As he likes to say, it's binary." *Some asshole treats you like crap, gotta get you out the mess. End of story.* He didn't need to know more. Didn't want to know more.

"That sounds like my brother," she said, and then blurted, "Short version: I told James it wasn't working. He told me it was. So then I told him I was leaving. He told me I wasn't. That's how I got this. It's the first time he ever hit me."

A long pause. Shane looked in the mirror; she was staring out the window. He didn't prompt. But it was clear she had no idea how much bigger this situation really was. She understood James was an asshole, but she didn't know the one label didn't even begin to cover it. That her entire relationship with that shit was just a setup to get intel on Dex and the rest of the Hudson Kings mercenaries.

She also didn't know Shane suspected someone was watching when he went to pick her up. Unfortunately, when he'd had to run after her, he'd lost the mark: a white beater sedan.

All of a sudden, her eyes were back in the mirror, a sad, bewildered expression on her face. "I never would have thought I'd be the type. I never would have thought something like this could happen to me. But after he cut me down so many times . . . well, I guess I started to believe him. I know Dex is surprised I believed him. And he feels shitty he believed me when I said I was fine all those times." Her cheeks flushed. "Anyway . . . do you hang out with him a lot in New York?"

"Yeah, I hang out with Dex when I'm in New York." Shane watched, fascinated as his answer sparked a grin. *Holy shit. Smile lights up everything around her. A total disaster, she's still effing gorgeous.* He ripped his gaze away, scowling. *Dex's sister. Just had a bad experience. Whole thing is off-limits, man. Even if you were up for something, which . . . You. Are. Not.*

"Is something wrong?" she asked uncertainly.

"No." He took his hands off the steering wheel and stick long enough to crack his knuckles and shake out his fingers, which had gone uncharacteristically stiff. *No good driving tense. Shake it off.* Sure, Shane's priority was the big picture, the Hudson Kings mission to take down Yakov Petrenko, a.k.a. James Peterson, a Russian handler who was acting as the middleman for a cell of Russian sleeper agents living in New York. Agents who were really good at pretending to be people they definitely were not. But, man, he wouldn't pass up the opportunity to take a shot at James just for roughing up Cecily.

"Uh, are we driving straight through to New York, or is there any chance we could stop and, you know, shower and stuff?"

Shane grimaced. He was a drive-through-the-night guy. But this wasn't a professional gig. The correct answer would be stop at a hotel on the way. That's what you do. You stop so she can shower that asshole off her once and for all. So she can rest and fix her pretty face and put on some clean clothes and stop feeling like a pile of shit.

The problem was that he'd been driving hot since California, with a delivery sitting in his trunk destined for the Chicago area. On the one hand, if he had to make a stop anyway, he might as well give her an opportunity to shower and rest. On the other hand, Shane mused as he checked his rearview mirror, his gut was telling him to keep driving and avoid noncritical detours.

"You don't really like having me in your car, do you?" Cecily asked.

"I don't like having anyone in my car." *My car is a contained space that I control. She's also my most loyal friend, my shelter from the storm, and I'm completely aware that sounds fucking crazy, so I sure as hell ain't going to say that out loud.*

"What do you do?" she asked.

"What did Dex tell you?"

"He didn't tell me anything except your first name. And that you'd be there when you were supposed to."

Good man. "That's how I like it."

"This is going to be a long ride to New York City," Cecily mumbled. She leaned back in the seat and blew a strand of hair off her face.

Shane Sullivan was a mercenary who handled both freelance jobs on his own and team missions for the Hudson Kings. He was a transporter, to be precise. One of the benefits of being a middleman was supposed to be that there weren't any complications. You don't care what the story is at Point A and you don't care what the story is at Point B. You're simply transporting information, material, or people, and then you drive away and let the chips fall where they may.

Taking on Cecily Keegan violated every code in his personal playbook. If he agreed with nothing else that came out of her mouth, he'd have to agree with this: Oh, yeah. It was definitely going to be a long, *long* ride.

CHAPTER 3

Twenty minutes. Twenty minutes it took for this guy to break the silence. "I drive around," he said, completely out of the blue. Cecily had been playing absently with Bun-Bun's ears, watching cows out the passenger side window while she processed the fact that she was really and truly on day one of a fresh start, when suddenly he said quietly as if they'd been having a conversation the whole time, "I drive around, I pick things up, I drop them off."

"What?" Cecily asked.

"Point A to Point B. Fast."

Seriously? Was he joking? "So, you're like . . . a pizza delivery guy," Cecily said, deliberately trying to goad him into revealing, well, anything else at all. Something miraculous happened: the corner of his mouth quirked in the tiniest hint of a smile. "I think a piece of rust just fell off your face," she said. That got her a whole lotta nothing.

Cecily looked around. Clearly, no pizza had ever polluted the interior, practically gleaming with burled walnut and tan leather detailing. No scraps of paper, no junk food wrappers, no pens—not a single piece of litter. A black messenger bag sat in the well of the front passenger seat, buckles in place and locked. The computer screen in the dash was off. At least six phones were plugged into a custom charging station, their cords neatly wrapped. Two unopened bottles of water filled the beverage slots. The dedication to order made the pulverized dirt on the floor mat under the soles of his boots that much more jarring.

Shane eased the car off the freeway and into a gas station. Cecily pulled on the handle, but the door was locked. *Um, did he childproof me into the backseat? Not cool.*

"You stay in the car until I finish gassing up," he said. "Then I escort you inside to hit the can, and we get something to eat."

Cecily's eyes narrowed. *Whoa, now.* He didn't even ask if she needed to use the bathroom. Or if she was hungry. He was ordering her around, and he wasn't letting her out of his sight. *Been there, done that. Done with that.*

"I'll be back in five," she said tightly, reaching to the front to pop the door lock. She pushed open her door and stepped toward the food court. How he moved that quickly, she had no idea, but before she could take one more step, she was already staring at the front of a T-shirt stretched across well-defined pecs, the top of her head not even reaching his chin.

"I'm not gonna *make* you stop if I don't have to," he said, his voice low, a menacing growl around the edges. "Because that seems like a bad idea with your history. But my job is door-to-door service. I deliver the goods exactly as promised, exactly when promised, in exactly the format promised. So I call the shots until I deliver you to Dex. When I tell you to do something, you do it."

The *goods*? Like a *package* he's delivering? Like one of James's *possessions*? Thank you, *no.* "Look, like I said, I really, really appreciate the rescue, but I'm calling my own shots now."

"Dex requested you alive and in one piece," Shane said. "I'm inclined to do these services for a brother, but let's just say that I also take pride in my work."

"We're out of the state. I saw when we crossed the border. I'm not in danger anymore," she said with a shrug. Which was sort of a bullshit thing to say, because the only thing that made her feel like she wasn't in danger anymore was Shane Sullivan's six-foot-plus arrogant self, and she had a feeling it was going to stay that way until she was safely in New York with Dex.

A muscle in his jaw throbbed; he slipped on his sunglasses. "I don't give a goddamn where we are. When you got into my car, you became my problem and my responsibility."

That word *problem* hit so hard Cecily actually sucked in a quick breath. The wave of shame and embarrassment that followed was an all-too-familiar feeling. "I'm your *problem*?" she repeated grimly. "I see. Sorry this is such a nightmare for you." Without another word, she got back into the car, shut the door, and focused on breathing deep with her arms pretzeled in front of her so he couldn't see the trembling in her fingers.

She watched Shane pump the gas, hating everything about him. Hating what a spectacle he was, with those ridiculously cool mirrored sunglasses hiding his thoughts, and how appallingly perfect his ass looked in those jeans. From this angle, she finally got a read on his tattoos and realized it was really just one, a series of ink lines winding around his left bicep, designed to look like his flesh was ripping open to reveal machinery—car parts?—underneath. Totally intimidating, totally hot. *You suck for making me feel like I'm not good enough and small in every way,* Cecily thought.

But that wasn't really true, was it? She'd made herself small. And besides, that was a James kind of thought. *James* aimed to cut her down, each and every time. Any nice things he ever said were just setups for building a high that he enjoyed cutting down to a low. This friend of her brother's, Shane Sullivan, was a bossy, arrogant, scary-quiet, possibly quite deadly machine of some as yet undetermined kind, but it wasn't the same. She didn't know what it was, other than that it was annoying as hell, but it wasn't the same as with James.

Gas pumped and paid for, Shane got back in the driver's seat and drove a short distance to a parking spot in view of the rest stop windows.

He got out and scanned the rest of the parking lot; Cecily didn't move. Shane opened the back door. "Let's go." Cecily still didn't move. Shane inhaled and exhaled slowly and then stuck his face in the open V of the door. "I'm interpreting some signals here that maybe you're kinda irritated with me."

Cecily rolled her eyes.

"But the next rest stop is in forty-six miles, and I'm not in the habit of pulling over to the side of the road mid-delivery. So, to put it bluntly, you really oughta take a piss now, because if you've gotta do it between here and there, you're gonna have to shoot in a soda can, and I'm a mite particular about my car."

He couldn't be for real. How could someone so completely inappropriate be so . . . so . . . *god, he was good-looking. Focus on the inappropriate, Cecily.* "You are a *caveman*," she breathed more than said, curling her lip in disgust.

"You're giving me too much credit," Shane said. "Out of the car."

His massive build was like a total eclipse of the sun. He was bent down, his face right in hers; she should have felt claustrophobic. And the fact that she couldn't focus on being pissed long enough to ignore the fact that that he smelled good pissed her off all over again.

He tapped the roof gently, but his "Let's go" was just another order.

She got out and went around to the trunk. "My purse is in my suitcase."

He raised an eyebrow. "Go wait by the door. I'll bring it to you." He didn't open the trunk until she was standing on the curb next to the door leading to the fast-food court.

And then he parked himself at a table, in line of sight of the bathroom door, and pointed his finger in a "go" sign.

Double ugh.

But "double ugh" was nothing compared with the infinite ugh Cecily felt staring into the restroom mirror after washing up. Ice-cold rest-stop water dripped down her arms as she stood frozen in front of her reflection. The cover-up on her bruise was useless under the garish lighting. It went very well with what had originally been a baby-blue T-shirt but was now a dirty blue-gray T-shirt. *I look like a corpse. Shane didn't say anything. Didn't even bat an eyelash, but I look like a corpse.*

But, then, why would he say anything?

Her makeup bag and hairbrush were still in her luggage, so there wasn't much she could do other than wash her face and wipe off the half-moons of black eyeliner that had failed to defy gravity. An abandoned ponytail holder on the ledge below the mirror was tempting, but Cecily just couldn't bring herself to go there, since it sat next to some other pretty dubious leftovers. At least most of it resembled known substances like chewed gum and toothpaste blobs, but still.

Cecily grabbed some toilet paper off a roll and tackled the makeup. See now, any decent woman would have mentioned this. But Shane didn't claim to be decent. And he was nothing if not *all* man.

Not to mention, if Cecily hadn't been so busy staring at his eyes in the rearview mirror, she might have noticed her own.

It said good things about her attention to detail that after all this time staring, she could say with some authority that his eyes were not merely "dark" and "brown." They were, in fact, dark and brown with a halo around the irises that registered as fire in the right light, and his lashes were *long*, something that looked particularly enticing alongside the rest of his badassery.

It said bad things about her common sense.

Ridiculous. About twenty hours prior, she'd sworn to have nothing to do with men ever again, and Shane Sullivan looked like capital-T Trouble in messy hair, fitted jeans, and tats, exactly the kind of guy she should stay away from. Of course, James was the epitome of clean-cut in his designer suit and trimmed crew cut. If the men who looked good were bad, then maybe the men who looked bad . . .

Stop it! You've known him for two seconds. Are you going to make the mistake of falling for the first guy who's even a little bit nice to you because you're used to the other side of the coin?

He's not even that nice! Ugh, Cecily. Badass super-silent mystery-package-driving hotties are NOT the stuff of fresh starts. Remember all those articles warning you that women coming out of an abusive relationship sometimes jump into intimate situations too quickly? Yeah, I'm talking to you, Cecily. You no longer have permission to stare at his eyes in the mirror. You have lost your hottie eye-staring privileges. You have—

"Cecily?"

She froze at the sound of Shane's voice. The bathroom door opened a crack. *What? No-o-o-o. You can't be serious. You are not coming in to the women's bathroom to get me. You caveman piece of—*

"You been in there awhile. Just checking."

His eyes were on the floor, like she was some dainty Victorian lady who needed privacy because she might be changing into bloomers or something. His voice wasn't impatient, just—oh, shit, he sounded—

"Need somethin'?"

He sounded *that* nice.

CHAPTER 4

She didn't need anything, so while Cecily finished up, Shane cased the area and then made his way to the food counter and ordered a bunch of different meals plus soda and water. He took his receipt and stepped aside, staring blindly at the action in the deep fryer. *I guess I am your problem,* she'd said, her face drawn and the light completely gone from her eyes. He could still see her staring straight ahead, unmoving, just waiting while he pumped the gas. *Way to go, asshole.*

For a minute it looked like total defeat. But then: "You are a *caveman,*" she'd said, her sweet cupid's bow lips curled in disgust.

Ha. She's still got fire.

The last time Shane delivered a person, it had taken sixteen hours including a ferry ride to Morocco. The guy hadn't spoken more than two or three times, and he didn't have duct tape over his mouth. Well, not for the European segment, anyway. The whole thing was so annoying Shane'd sworn to stick to cash and packages. That said, this was different. This was Cecily. Cecily Keegan. Formerly, just a little girl's face in a picture on a desk. Now a woman sitting in his car, taking up space where there'd been nothing.

His order came toward him on a plastic red tray accompanied by the smell of hot grease, just as Cecily came out of the bathroom and went to the table he'd originally chosen. He headed over and sat down across from her, selected a cheeseburger, popped the top off a water, and dug in.

Cecily stared at the pile of food and then looked uncertainly at the ordering station.

"You do get this is for two?" Shane asked.

Her answer was a burst of laughter, the sound of spontaneous joy so intense Shane stopped chewing for a moment. If that's what you get for giving a girl a sandwich, he wondered what you'd get for giving that same girl a—*shut that shit down, man. Just shut that shit down. Dex's sister, here.*

"I wasn't sure," she was saying, delicately peeling back a corner of each wrapper to peek inside.

"Woman I used to see around," Shane mumbled between bites, feeling a little shell-shocked and anxious to detour his thoughts. "Always said she wasn't hungry—always ended up eating my food, so *I* was *definitely* always hungry. Lesson learned. Buy double whenever a chick says she's not hungry."

"I don't know whether to find that gross and presumptuous or amazingly generous," Cecily said, choosing a grilled chicken sandwich.

Knew it, Shane thought.

"That said, I'm super hungry, so my conscience tells me to go with amazingly generous."

"You seriously thought I'd eat all this shit?"

"You're a big man. Your current girlfriend must have a healthy appetite."

Shane watched Cecily turn pink as soon as the words were out of her mouth, her eyes moving to make a show of focusing on the label she started ripping off the water bottle.

"I don't have a current girlfriend," he heard himself say. *WTF. Why the hell am I telling her personal deets? Less talk, more burger.*

She looked up then, her cheeks still pink. Cute as hell. Shane stuffed the second half of his cheeseburger into his mouth.

Her eyes dropped to his mouth, his bulging cheeks, and she raised an eyebrow, shaking her head. But when she spoke, her voice was soft. "You are definitely a caveman, but I think it's probably good Dex made you *my* caveman. I'm going to get home to my brother just fine, aren't I?"

Shane stopped chewing again, a lump in his throat that had nothing to do with food. *Well, assuming no one gets to us before we get to the Armory in New York, yeah. And since you're with me, it's a reasonable assumption, so, again, yeah.* He stared at her and swallowed. "Yeah, you're gonna be fine with me."

She smiled. "Thanks. By the way, I'm happy to share the driving. I know how to drive stick."

Shane looked at her incredulously. She wasn't joking. "You're touching these keys over my cold, dead body."

This time, she was the one waiting for a punch line. Which she was never gonna get.

Shane stared her down until she finally mumbled, "Oh. Um, I guess I'll find another way to help."

It took her twice as long to finish her one sandwich as it did for him to finish two burgers. They ate in silence, Shane taking note of the subtle shift in Cecily's demeanor that started about halfway through her meal. Looking out the window a lot. Wrinkling her forehead. Agitated. "What?" he asked.

She paused, opened her mouth. Closed it. Paused again and then said, "I need to ask you a favor, and I feel weird since technically all you've been doing is a series of favors, or maybe it's the same favor that never ends." She sighed, muttering, "I don't know what's worse."

"Spit it out, kid."

Another pause. *"Kid." Puts distance between us. She doesn't like it.*

"I'd really like to call my brother." Her voice started out normal but ended up bogged down with emotion. "James messed with my phone, and I don't have enough to buy a disposable or have any cards these pay phones will accept. Could I—"

"When did you last talk to him?" Shane asked.

She shrugged and looked away.

"Shit." He pulled out his phone, dialed Dex, and handed the phone over.

Cecily's eyes widened. "Is he there? Hello?" She bit her lip and took a deep breath. "Is he . . . Dex? It's me! Hi!" *And there it is. That motherfucking smile that probably gets hung on the top rung of the gates of heaven when she's not using it.*

Shane stared across the table as Cecily talked a blue streak, swiping at watery eyes, hunched over with her finger in her other ear to try to focus the sound.

He made a "time out" signal with his hands. "I'ma grab some more napkins. You don't move from this chair, yeah?"

"Yeah," she said, and went back to the conversation.

By the time he went back, figuring he'd given her enough privacy, she was looking up at him, holding out the phone as he walked back over.

"He wants to talk to you," she said. "I'm going to be right at that magazine rack over there."

Shane nodded and took the phone, his eyes glued to Cecily's tiny frame, unable to stop himself from casing her sweet figure. "She sounds okay," Dex said, on the other end.

"That's because she doesn't know I think someone was watching when I picked her up," Shane said. "That said—"

A streak of curses had Shane holding the phone away from his ear. After it trailed off, he replaced the phone. "*That said*, I haven't picked up anybody tailing us since. But I'm taking precautions."

"Just get her here in one piece," Dex said, his voice strained.

"I can do that," Shane said, watching Cecily stop in her tracks with a magazine in her hands. "You've got a plan for explaining all this to her?"

"I'll figure it out when she gets here," Dex said.

Shane grimaced. "She really has no clue. Thinks it was just a shitty ex-boyfriend thing."

"Maybe you could—" Dex began.

"No. I'm just giving you a heads-up so you know what you're getting."

"Shane—"

"Not a chance. I don't need some hysterical female freaking out on me because I tell her that her boyfriend never really loved her. This is a long drive."

Dex went silent, probably because he knew Shane was right.

"You on the mend?" Shane asked.

"I need a fucking refill on meds," Dex grumbled. "I know you don't like phones, and I'm on a project. Talk later?"

"Yeah." Now Cecily was rifling through her wallet. She put it back in her purse and then put the magazine back on the rack. *She forgot she was low on cash. A cheap magazine and she can't spring for it.* He knew that feeling from when he was a lot younger, and he hated it. He hated it for himself, and though he shouldn't have cared, he hated seeing it on Dex's sister.

"And Shane, thanks, brother. I mean, it goes without saying, she's precious cargo."

"Precious cargo," Shane said, waving Cecily back. "That's what I do."

"Why do you think I asked *you*? Later, man," Dex said and then hung up.

Dex's simple question warmed that cold place in Shane's heart. Sure, actions were supposed to speak louder than words, but there was something about hearing a teammate flat out say he was trusted with something—someone—this important that sometimes made him need to take a deep breath.

Shane stashed the phone with the others.

Cecily returned. "Does Dex sound okay to you? He sounded like—"

"He sounded fine," Shane said. He pulled his wallet from the back pocket of his jeans, grabbed a wad of crisp twenties, and pressed them into her palm and then reached to bundle up the trash.

She never closed her hand, and the bills fell to the table. "I can't take this," Cecily said, her eyes wide.

"You can," Shane said, juggling the pile of trash on the tray.

"It's too much."

"Take the money, Cecily." All he wanted her to do was to take the money and make that ugly, desperate feeling just go away. *They all want the fucking money. Most of the time, that's all they want. What the hell is wrong with her?*

"No, Shane. I can't. I don't want to owe you."

Impatient to get on the road and thrown by her resistance, Shane growled, "Take the fucking money and let's go. I don't give a damn if you pay me back or not. You're Dex's sister."

"No! I mean, ten dollars for an emergency, maybe, but this is . . . just . . . no!" She pushed the money away and sat back down at the table, obstinate as all hell.

Shane slammed the tray down on the table so hard she flinched. Slowly, he put his hand over the cash and dragged it all back save for a lone twenty, grinding out the words, "I don't have change, sweetling. Take. The. Fucking. Money."

Not a request. An order. It was like she deflated. Exhaustion and disappointment muddied her face as she slowly reached for the single remaining bill, carefully folded it in half, and stuck it in her jeans pocket.

It is what it is. Shane motioned for her to pass him, so he could look around for anything suspicious without making her nervous.

She went directly to the backseat passenger door and waited for him to release the locks. Shane opened the door for her. They took their places. Shane in the driver's seat, calling the shots, eyes between the road and the mirror. Girl in the back where he could keep his distance, keep his eye on her.

Both of them back where they belonged. Safe.

Cecily fell asleep only ten minutes back on the freeway, and the way she slumped in the seat, Shane craned his neck but couldn't see her face. It bugged him that he couldn't see her face. Hell, he should specifically not want to see her face. The fatigue in her eyes had been picking at him the entire lunch. *Fuck, fuck, fuck.* Shane put his attention back on the road and used his shift hand to slide out his phone and make his call.

No one was following them at the moment, Cecily was beat, *Shane* was beat from the drive out from California, and she had his entire focus on her care and feeding. So while an overnight wasn't part of the original plan, it wasn't gonna affect the overall goal of getting her to Dex in "like new" condition.

When Cecily awoke about eighty miles later, she popped up like a jack-in-the-box, her hair a tangled nimbus around her face, bruise moving on to a light shade of yellow. "Sorry!" she blurted. "I haven't been sleeping much lately."

"We're not stopping for another hour unless it's mission critical."

Her face started to go a little hard, and so—against his usual judgment—he did what he could to make it go soft again: "But then we're checking into a hotel. You can get cleaned up, get a decent night's sleep, then we're back on the road."

"Really?" she asked, sitting up stick straight. "Where are we staying?"

"Four Seasons."

"No, really, where?"

"Four Seasons Chicago."

Still with the big saucer eyes. Shane sighed.

"Are we getting two rooms?" she asked.

"Nope."

She went silent. If her eyes got any bigger, he'd be able to golf with them. "I don't like this," she finally said, her voice soft but firm. "I'm not trying to be a problem, and I think it's really generous of you because I obviously cannot pay, but I'm not comfortable with just one room, and I'd rather stay in a cheap roadside motel and have my own room, if it's all the same to you."

"It's all the same to me, but it's not all the same to her," he said, patting the dashboard. "You try to park a nice car in a crappy hotel lot, it sticks out like a sore thumb."

Cecily blinked. "We're staying in a single room in a five-star hotel so your *car* will fit in with its friends?"

"Yep." Well, it was at least 90 percent true. Another 5 percent was because the security was better at a Four Seasons than a motel, and the last 5 percent he couldn't explain.

"Do you think that sounds a little . . . unusual?" she asked.

"Not considering."

"Considering what?"

Shane raised an eyebrow. It was his turn to cop a moment of silence. *What little had Dex told her?* "You don't know much."

"About what?" Cecily asked, clearly perplexed.

"More than one unusual things get together, maybe you can't keep calling them unusual. Maybe it's normal. Keeping my car in five-star company is my normal." He didn't expect her to get it, and she didn't. "Do you have any idea what your brother does?"

Her forehead wrinkled. "Why would you ask me that? I mean, Dex is a computer nerd. He's a programmer for a software company. Something like that."

Shane didn't answer, which clearly made Cecily even more nervous. She was practically vibrating back there, and shit that he was, he started enjoying it a little.

Cecily sat up straighter. "Is Dex involved in something criminal?"

"I'd say Dex is more on the side of law than some of us. He's probably got some legit freelance for a day job."

"Wait, what? Legit? What? Wait. *Day* job? What's his *night* job?"

Fucking Dex didn't tell her anything. Bad enough she had no idea they were working on a mission involving a Russian spy cell connected to her ex-boyfriend. Dex hadn't even told her he was part of a mercenary team to begin with. *The little shit.* Well, he wasn't so little anymore. True enough, when Shane had met Dex, the guy fit the profile of the stereotypical scrawny nerd. A couple of years in the company of his new brothers, Dex was still a nerd but had lost the scrawny. *It is not my responsibility to break this shit to your sister, my man. That was not part of the favor.*

"If you don't mind, I'd like an answer to my question."

Girl never gave up, did she? "We're flexible with the specific hours," Shane said.

"Oh, my god. What is this all about? So your Point A to Point B delivery service. You pick things up. You drop them off. Weird packages full of . . . full of . . . weird stuff. That's really what you do, isn't it? I thought maybe you were joking a little."

"Did I laugh?" Shane asked.

"I don't think you've laughed since I got here," Cecily said, arms crossed over her chest, a surly look on her face.

That's not true. I don't think I've laughed as much in the last two years combined as I have since you got in my car. I just don't make much of a sound.

"Are you involved in something criminal?" she pressed.

"What do you mean by 'involved'?"

She gave him stink eye. "Are you . . . I think you might be enjoying this. Are you *teasing* me?"

"Might be enjoying. Possibly teasing. Not sure. What I am sure about is that this is Dex's conversation to have."

Cecily's eyes narrowed. "I need to call him," she said. Shane glanced over his shoulder in time to catch her fingernails digging into the leather on either side of her thighs. Instead of feeling irritated that she might leave marks, his mind flashed to what it might be like if her fingernails were digging into something else, like his back. *Man, where the fuck did that come from?*

"I need to call Dex," Cecily repeated. "Please don't make me beg to borrow your phone."

"Dex is gonna be irritated you're interrupting work after he just talked to you," Shane said.

"I really don't care if Dex is going to be irritated if I need to call to ask him if he's a criminal," Cecily snapped.

He sighed and dialed Dex, who answered on the first ring. "Brace," Shane said. With that opener, he handed the phone to Cecily, who wasted no time blurting out, "What is it you actually *do?*" Silence fell over the car as Dex talked first. And then Cecily said, "The *Hudson Kings?*" and glanced over at Shane. And then more silence. And then she said, "Because I care about you, and I'm worried." They talked some more as Shane watched the road; Dex must've been doling out the bare minimum because Cecily sighed and said, "Why do I keep asking why? Because I love you, big brother."

Shane glanced into the mirror and watched Cecily's face, smiling and animated as the siblings talked. *"Because I care about you, and I'm worried . . . I love you . . ."* Her emotions were bouncing all over the inside of his car, lighting it up like the sun. What would it be like to be on the receiving end of a call like that? Shane felt a stab of jealousy. Until Cecily stopped letting her brother sidetrack her and asked for more information about the Hudson Kings.

Listening to Cecily's side of the conversation when Dex started filling her in on the truth was a real treat. She was cute when she got mad, but that wasn't what grabbed his attention. She was . . . *real.* Shane wasn't used to real. He was used to one-night stands triggered in the posh bars of luxury hotels. And on the rare occasion where that one-night stand turned into something a little longer, he was used to women who were attracted to his generosity out on the town and addicted to his generosity in bed; they stuck around for the epic Os long after he made it clear he had nothing else to offer.

And the kind of women who did that weren't overburdened in the brains department and didn't give a damn about who Shane really was; they certainly weren't hoping he would interrupt foreplay with a discussion about why and how losing his parents as a kid had pretty much fucked him up for life. And if you wanted to know the man, you had to understand the kid. Since Shane didn't want anybody to know the man, keeping his past, his emotions, and his dreams locked up tight had always worked just fine.

Back in New York, Missy was the closest thing he had to a meaningful relationship with a female. Which was probably because she was really just one of the guys and didn't delve too deep into his feelings. Or at least when she did, she didn't mind when he didn't answer.

Which was why, just after Dex apparently copped to being borderline criminal on the phone, and Cecily shoved the phone back at him with a dark look on her face saying, "There's obviously *a lot* more he's not saying, but he wants to talk to you," Shane had a feeling he might be looking at trouble.

"I copped to some of my own shit. She'll understand more about the team and the big picture when she gets here," Dex said into Shane's ear, adding in a sudden rush of words, "Listen, I gotta go. Roth called everyone in. It's a scene. So, I gotta go, and I'm asking you to help make my little sister feel better about being an idiot. She's fragile and hurting, and I'm not there to give her a hug. She's kinda tetchy. Can you just, you know, defuse the situation out there?"

"Defuse the situation?" Shane repeated calmly. He made a point of not looking at Cecily. "Sorry. Bomb disposal is Flynn's territory."

A gasp shot forward from the backseat. Shane grinned into the phone.

"You just said that right in front of her," Dex said grimly. "Right. In. Front. Of. Her."

"Yup. And that's because I call bullshit," said Shane. "So, why don't I hand back the phone to your sister, and you can finish ex—"

A torrent of words cut him off: "Cece'll take the news from you like a champ. She's not drama, and I can tell she feels safe with you. Give her a hug from her big brother, man. She'll be fine until I can take over. Gotta run." And then Dex hung up choking on a laugh.

Shane's smile had vanished long ago. He stared at the phone in his hand. *He wants me to give her a fucking hug. Seriously? Who talks like that? I did not sign up for this shit.*

Like he told Dex: *bullshit.* The man just didn't want to have the bigger part of the Hudson Kings conversation with his sister. It was a complicated conversation with anywhere from a little to a lot of ugly, depending on the brother. But when one of the guys asks you to take his back, you take his back. And if he keeps asking, you keep taking it. That said, Dex was going to owe him a helluva chit for any make-my-sister-feel-better extras.

"Everything okay?" Cecily asked, big worried eyes in the mirror.

"Fine," Shane bit out.

"You look like you could really use a cup of tea right now. I'd make you one if I could," Cecily mumbled.

Shane stared back at the wonder that was Cecily Keegan in the backseat: roughed up, hurting for sleep, worry wrinkling her forehead, processing her brother's criminal activities, thinking she oughta be making *him* a CUP OF TEA.

Gonna kill you, Dex.

CHAPTER 5

Thud.

Cecily jerked as the hotel room door slammed behind her. Shane had dismissed the porter and carried her suitcase, a duffel bag, and his messenger bag without interference. Apparently, he didn't want anyone poking around in his trunk, borrowing his dead-body blanket, or whatever. Now he was busy stowing the stuff in the entry closet; she was busy staring at the single king-size bed in the adjacent room.

"There was only one room left?" Cecily asked. *It is not unreasonable for me to be irritated. It would not even be unreasonable for me to stamp my foot. This is the dictionary definition of a stampable event.* "In this entire five-star hotel? Only one available room and it comes with a single king-size bed?"

"Yup," Shane said, now by the windows, peering out and then arranging the curtains with some kind of OCD-gripped focus. Now he was at the phone, picking the thing up, checking it out. He pulled out his key chain and used one of those multitools to unscrew the bottom of the phone and poke around its innards. He glanced behind the artwork. And then he stared into the minibar.

"Are you looking for poison?" Cecily asked.

"If that's how you feel about bourbon," he said.

"Are you and Dex spies?" Cecily asked, actually finding herself wanting to giggle. No reaction from the big man over there, still sorting through minibar bottles. She was getting loopy. In part from exhaustion, in part from trying to think of her brother being organized enough to be a spy. Whoever these men were, whatever they were involved in, it was not entirely kosher. "I'm still waiting for a bigger explanation about what you guys do. You, Dex, wherever it comes from, if my life is in danger by association, I have a right to know about it."

Shane wheeled around, a bottle of booze in one hand, and what looked like genuine surprise on his face with a side order of pissed off. "You think I'd put you in danger?"

Oh, god, I think that either hurt his feelings or just made him go quietly insane. Both? "Um, well, I just can't help but notice that you're acting a little paranoid. Normal people don't act like you're acting."

"Normal people?"

"Yeah, you know. Like physical therapists and, uh, ice cream vendors or whoever. Any woman with half a brain would seriously wonder about you and my brother and this Hudson Kings organization you joined. Dex said you worked together, but I don't really understand who you work for and what you do."

"Physical therapists and ice cream vendors." He let the words hang there. Awkward. Ridiculous. Finally, he said, "It's not paranoia; it's called taking care. I'm taking care of something precious for Dex. Like I said, that's what I do."

"Oh. So this is what you'd do for any . . . package. This level of . . . care."

Shane's face stayed blank. After a moment, he said roughly, "Get in the shower. I'll order up some room service."

"What?" Cecily asked.

"You heard me. You're going to get in the shower, and then we eat." He'd already turned away, his hand first up and around the molding on the front door and then examining the lock. "After you eat, you're going to—" Suddenly, he broke off in the middle of that thought, his back still toward her, his hands stilled.

Cecily waited for him to finish telling her exactly what he wanted her to do and the precise order in which he wanted her to do it. Her jaw clamped, but she wasn't going to rise to the bait and jump all over him, even if it made her want to scream. The crazy would all be over soon. They were halfway to New York, and she'd never see him again. *The crazy would all be over soon.*

Except this was now. And *now* here Shane was, frozen in the middle of a sentence, slowly turning back around. This time when he looked at her, it was like he was really seeing her. In fact, he stared at her. Cecily realized she was holding her breath and exhaled slowly, her heart beating faster and faster under his steely gaze. "What?" she managed.

"I was, uh . . ." He folded his arms across his chest, looked down at his boots planted in a V, went completely silent for a good five seconds, and then looked up and asked, "Do you want to shower, eat, or sleep first?"

It was obvious it took some effort for the words to come out like that, all question marky and flexible sounding. Cecily stared at him in disbelief. She bit her lip, managing to keep from laughing, but couldn't keep from smiling. Shane shook his head, but he'd dropped his arms and was suddenly grinning too, one arm grabbing the back of his neck.

Shaking his head and grinning. The biggest smile on his face since they'd started this trip. *Hot. Badass. And now sweet.* "All three sound like heaven," Cecily said finally.

"If you wanna pick something out to eat from the menu, I'll order it while you shower and then it'll be here by the time you're ready," he said quietly.

"That sounds great, Shane," Cecily said. She meant to say more, wanted to say more—acknowledge that he'd made an effort to meet her halfway—but she didn't want to break the spell.

No matter. He'd tucked that smile away and was already turning away again when he said, "Sure."

◆ ◆ ◆

Steam clouded the bathroom as water poured down Cecily's face and body. She took a deep breath, almost giddy as she soaped up, inhaling the citrusy scent with a big, dumb grin on her face. It had been too long since she'd felt safe enough to close her eyes and just enjoy a hot shower.

She couldn't wait to get to New York and see Dex, but Shane was nothing if not dedicated in his commitment to keep her safe, so for the first time in forever, she felt free. Free to take the world's longest shower and slop on bath wash that smelled like pure joy hanging from an orange tree in sunny Florida. Free to jump up and down on a killer mattress. Free to change into clothes she liked, and to dial down the makeup, regardless of any man's preference. Free to just be herself, without a care in the world, without having to worry that a time bomb on the other side of her door was just waiting to go off.

Shampooing her hair with an enormous amount of suds, Cecily tried to decide if letting down her guard was a mistake.

James's agenda had been to control her and break her down. Conversely, while they didn't come any bossier than Shane, *he'd* made it clear that his agenda was to get her to New York in one piece. This suggested Shane thought delivering her to Dex in multiple pieces was in the realm of possibility, which was a little disconcerting, but then the whole situation was disconcerting.

Cecily getting caught up with a man like James was disconcerting.

Dex getting caught up with a man like Shane was disconcerting.

And judging by his behavior, Shane getting caught up with a girl like herself was also disconcerting, although outside of getting into the James mess, Cecily imagined she came off about as normal as you could be. *Like a physical therapist or an ice cream vendor,* she thought with a smile. *Well, like a graphic designer. I'm just going to move to New York and become a graphic designer and go down the path I meant to go down in the first place.*

Cecily rinsed all the soap off and stood under the hot spray, staring at the wall of steam as warning sirens went off in her head. The idea of living in New York with her brother—making a living doing what she loved, an idea that had kept her company so many nights over the last month, giving her comfort when she felt all alone—was all she could think about. And now, all of a sudden, not two days on her way to exactly what she wanted, something in her didn't want this road trip to end.

Her eyes worked through the steam and settled on the doorknob, behind which was the most enigmatic man she'd ever met. Six foot and—oh, my god—counting, with a gorgeous car to go with a gorgeous bod and a look in his eyes that could both chill and probably kill. He had a mysterious trunk he wouldn't let her near, a knife in his boot, he kept a six-pack of cell phones ready to go, and he was partial to cheap cheeseburgers and luxury lodging. That was both too much and too little to know about a man, and she hadn't locked the bathroom door. *Did I do that on purpose? Why do I feel so safe? Is this some bizarre form of Post-Traumatic Stress Disorder? Maybe it's Post-Traumatic Shane Disorder.* She giggled, and then checked herself. *For the love of god, Cecily, what James did to you is not funny, and just because you've got a personal bodyguard right now does not mean James can't find you again if he wants to make your life miserable.*

That was a sobering thought, strong enough to make her feel a chill even in hot water. She'd sworn when she got away from James that she'd be smart enough to walk away from the dark the next time she saw it, and there was Shane checking the curtains. The phone. The pictures. The locks. The doorframe. Shane was no pizza delivery guy, no ice cream vendor, that was for sure. *What are you going to ask him over dinner: "So, how dark is it, Shane?"*

Cecily watched bubbles swirl into the drain but still made no move to turn off the water. *What does it mean if I don't want to ask because I might not like the answer? What does it mean if I don't want to know the answer because I don't want to stop being around him and I don't want to have to walk away? What does it mean that I don't want to walk away because I might miss catching that tiny hint of a smile, nearly impossible to bring to life, the one that makes my heart beat faster when I finally get it?*

Cecily dripped more of the satsuma body wash into her palm, closed her eyes, let the water pound down all around her, and imagined that her hands were his hands. Shane's big hands, running perfumed soap over her shoulders, fingers grazing the edges of her back, smoothing over her naked breasts, and swirling around her nipples.

Her breath was coming more quickly now. She leaned against the back of the shower, just slowly moving her hands over her body, wondering if Shane was wild or liked to take his time, or—

A sharp rap sounded outside the door; Cecily's eyes flew open, terrified he'd caught her.

She stared at the doorknob, waiting for it to turn. *He's not coming in here; I trust him not to touch me.*

Which is such a total bummer.

She heard low voices and realized he was talking to hotel staff, that it wasn't Shane at her door, probably wasn't even an intentional knock. As disappointment seared her, all she could think was, *Oh, hell, Cecily, you're really into this guy.*

Apparently, there *was* still a time bomb on the other side of her door.

CHAPTER 6

I do not trust myself not to touch her.

I mean, of course, I'm not gonna touch her. I just . . .

Shit. If Shane were being smart, he'd go down to the bar, pick up a bored businessman's wife, and bang her in the elevator on the way back upstairs.

But Shane was not doing that at the present moment, and it wasn't just because the Hudson Kings' Russian problem was lurking somewhere over his shoulder. He couldn't take his mind off Cecily, sure as hell not while she was behind the door taking a shower.

He had to force himself to focus long enough to install devices on the front door and the windows that would alert him if someone tried to enter. Then he'd called room service and ordered steak for himself, chicken for her, plus a bottle of bourbon more his style and two bottles of wine to go with dinner—one merlot and one chardonnay since he didn't know her tastes.

The hard liquor had arrived separately. Two cheeseburgers more than two hours ago were nothing against a whole lot of suppressed lust, driving fatigue, and a generous swallow of bourbon. Shane's thoughts were beginning to spiral out of control. Never leave your glove box unlocked, he thought idly. If he was being honest, he'd have to admit that he'd somehow managed to do just that.

Now, he sat in a chair across the room from the bed upon which Cecily sat wrapped in a hotel robe after washing a man out of her hair with some kind of epically fantastic orange-scented shampoo, and the most coherent thought he could keep in his head was: *Not. Gonna. Touch. Her.* That said, if she wanted to reach her suitcase for some clothes, she'd have to step over his outstretched legs, and yet he didn't so much as uncross his ankles.

She was probably naked under the swamp of white cotton, and in order to give him something to do besides stare and think way dirtier than he had any right to, he poured a second drink. Tasted awesome, but "Not. Gonna." was quickly losing half its staying power; if dinner didn't come soon, he might just forget about the "not" and be left with the "gonna."

She smells like an orange. Never gonna look at an orange the same way ever again. I had an orange right now, I'ma take that orange. Gonna caress that orange, roll it between my hands. I'm going to peel that MOTHERFUCKING ORANGE and suck each and every part of it until her juice is running off my tongue and down my chin, and I can smell her scent all over me for days. I'm gonna—

"Shane?"

"Yeah."

"You're staring into space."

Trust me, I'm not staring into space.

"Maybe you should eat some crackers or something out of the minibar," she was saying. "Are you light-headed?"

"Just a long day, kid. Dinner'll be here soon."

Her expression told him he'd gotten his message out. *"Kid." Good as armor.*

Fuck me, I shoulda gone outside; I shoulda got a suite with a door. I shoulda taken some precaution, whatever the hell that would have been. Shane had convinced himself that he was still here, in this room, this close to her and a bed, because he was maintaining the chain of custody;

you don't leave your delivery somewhere you can't keep eyes on it. And you sure as hell don't leave your delivery out in the open when you know that what she's just been through ain't over. Hence, the "there are no rooms with doubles left" lie—and a request for a view of the hotel's driveway—down at the concierge.

And again, there was Dex, counting on Shane to do the right thing. "Handle with care," he'd said. *Do not fold, spindle, or mutilate.*

From the little Dex had to say about Cecily's opinion of James, it sounded like fold, spindle, and mutilate was the guy's specialty, mostly directed at her mind unless she was lying about that bruise being the first time.

But it was what little Dex had to say about Cecily's opinion of Shane that he couldn't get out of his mind: *"I can tell she feels safe with you."*

Here. With me. Well, she shouldn't. He leaned back in the dark, while she sat under the halo of a reading lamp. She wouldn't be able to see all of him, but he could get his fill of the wide blue eyes, the dripping wet hair and the pile of white fluff framing that heart-shaped face, all working overtime to make his dick twitch.

And that was just the surface shit. There'd been this moment, as he was coming toward her at the gas station that first time, sunglasses lowered, about to introduce himself. She'd looked him square in the eyes just before hauling ass backward, and something about her hit him in the gut. Something with a name he was still searching for.

Seeing she was what you'd call petite and seeing as how most hotel robes were made for "average" people, the fabric engulfed her. Without a single inch of skin showing beneath the neck, she was the sexiest thing Shane had ever seen in his life.

He'd had a lot of time and practice fostering a great imagination. Guy like him, people might think he didn't have it in him to be creative, but idling on an LA freeway in ninety-degree heat, he could stay calm for hours just imagining being someone else in another life on a sunny day.

And right now, from the chair in the corner, he was imagining yards of naked Cecily under the white fluff while forcing himself to look completely impassive.

Apparently, she'd just asked a question. "What?" Shane mumbled.

She bit her lip, clearly fighting annoyance. Her gaze shifted from the bourbon bottle he was gripping like a stick shift to his face, which he knew she couldn't see clearly. *She's worried I'm gonna get drunk, and I won't be able to fill her in. And frankly, that's a brilliant idea. Wish I could get shitfaced right now.*

"I said I think room service is here. I'll throw some clothes on," she said, clutching the robe together at chest level as she headed resolutely for the closet and stepped over his legs. Shane did not help her lug the suitcase to the bathroom; room service got only half his attention while he noted how Cecily's commitment to modesty at her neckline with her one free hand resulted in a nice lack of attention to covering the legs and thighs.

Room service was tipped and gone by the time Cecily got back. She was dressed in sweatpants and a tiny pink T-shirt with a glittering red heart in the middle. *You've got to be kidding me. How is it possible to be so fucking adorable and so fucking sexy at the same time?*

"Smells delicious. Thank you, Shane," she said, a little shy all of a sudden. "This is all really generous."

Shane gave a dismissive nod and was about to just pull over his warming tray of steak and tuck in, but Cecily was suddenly taking over, making sure he had a napkin, pouring two waters, removing the food from the trays, and reorganizing it on the plates he would have ignored.

He was starving, but he sat back, watching her do quiet, simple things, feeling an unfamiliar warmth spread across his chest. *How could a man have this and put a hand to her? How could a man have this and make her cry? With this one girl, that guy could have had Friday-night sexy as all hell and Sunday-night chicken dinner happy.*

With this one girl.

"Shane?" She was staring at him staring at her, holding out the breadbasket.

Shane shook himself out of his thoughts and grabbed the closest roll. "Trying to guess if you were merlot or chardonnay."

"I know you're not supposed to with chicken, but merlot, please."

"You like what you like," Shane said softly, picking up the merlot and the corkscrew.

Her eyes widened for a second, and she ducked her head down as she laid out the silverware in parallel lines, one set for each of them. "Why didn't you want room service to come in and set up?" she asked, now serving out some salad while he poured her wine.

"Habit." Shane watched her move around him, unaccustomed to sitting back and letting someone else take charge, do something nice for him. "Don't like people looking around at my kit." He indicated his bags. "Always aware of being on a job."

"Do you have anything *unusual* in there?" Cecily asked.

"No," he said, deadpan. "The unusual stuff is all in the trunk."

Cecily's eyes moved sharply back toward him, and a gruff chuckle came out of Shane's mouth.

She laughed too, but then killed the moment by asking, "Speaking of the job, Dex said you'd fill me in."

"I shouldn't be the one filling you in. How much you need to know is Dex's business." He knew he sounded as exasperated as he felt.

"But he told you to fill me in, right?"

Shane didn't like the answer so he didn't give one. Which Cecily interpreted as a "go" sign. "First, how did you meet my brother?" she asked.

"Met on a freelance job. Found we had compatible skills and didn't irritate the fuck outta each other. Now we're both specialists for Rothgar, the man who runs the Hudson Kings. Our team is former military, former gang, former white-collar badass, wherever, whatever, from all over the place. High-class, low-class, good with ideas, good with plans, good with hands . . . I guess you could say that he recruited the best, and the men who answered that call were looking for something. And though I don't know all the stories myself, and it sure as shit isn't my place to tell you, I would guess that Rothgar demonstrated that he could give them something they were missing. Either stopped them from walking alone into darkness, lent a hand at a critical time, or, maybe, just something that would seem small to the outside world, like keeping a promise."

Finally, finally, he looked right at Cecily. "That's why he commands the respect he does. The loyalty. That's why we're a brotherhood, though we don't share blood."

She nodded slowly. He figured she was trying to guess what Rothgar offered to *him* that he needed so badly. He had no plans to share that with her.

"Your specialty is . . . cars."

"In a nutshell."

"My brother?"

"Dex is the team's hacker."

Cecily bit her lip. "You mean programmer."

"I mean hacker."

She took a deep breath. "And Roth—"

"The guy who keeps everything from falling apart."

"No, really. What does he do?"

You know plenty. "Like I said, he's the glue. You'll meet him."

Cecily paused, then tried again. "What other specialists do you work with?"

"We have a money guy. A demolitions expert. That kind of thing. Others."

"The bomb thing wasn't a joke, then?"

"The bomb thing wasn't a joke, though he doesn't get as much work as he'd like."

There was a pause. Cecily cleared her throat, blinking as she moistened her lips. Shane had to look away from those lips. "You're doing well, by the way," he muttered. "Thought you'd be overreacting, freaking out around now."

"Actually, I think my head might explode. Nice to know it doesn't show."

Shane chuckled.

"Which one is Flynn again?" she asked.

Nice attention to detail. He'd mentioned Flynn on the phone with Dex.

"You'll meet him," Shane said.

"How many guys do you work with?"

"You'll meet them."

She frowned. "Right. New direction. So, who does your team work for?"

"Mostly the government."

Cecily's eyes widened. "The government? Dex made it sound kinda illegal! Oh, thank god, and here I—"

"I didn't say that," he said evenly.

She went very still.

"Not everything the government does is legal."

She swiped a piece of chicken through the sauce on her plate. "Okay, um. Mostly the government and the rest of the time . . . ?"

"The rest of the time we do what we like, take private jobs or whatever."

She didn't ask if they were legal. "And the name of the company—"

"It's not exactly a company. Girl on the team called us the Hudson Kings as shorthand. It stuck."

"There are women on your team? I mean, that's cool. I shouldn't have assumed there weren't."

You nervous about that? Jealous? "Just her. Her brother was one of our guys."

"Oh. She lost him? He died?"

"He did."

"What was his name?"

Shane didn't like to think about it, because it was a painful memory, but he liked someone asking. He liked the idea that the guys wouldn't be forgotten. Not by the Hudson Kings. Not by anyone. He liked the idea that it was clear that the loved ones left behind weren't abandoned or forgotten either. So he told her. "We've lost two guys. Missy's twin, Apollo, and Allison's brother, Graham. We were out on a mission. Things were going fine. They were partnering out in the field. We lost comms, and . . ."

"And?"

Shane stared into his drink. "They were just wiped. Gone. No bodies. No equipment. No clothes. No clues. Comms off. Cell phones off. Nothing to trace, nothing to hack. Gone. We're still watching, waiting. It's a job that will never be removed from the boards."

The room went so silent; the hum from the minibar sounded like an alarm. Cecily gazed at him across the table, eating her dinner—*God, she was a slow eater*—and not freaking out on him.

"Two girls lost their brothers," she finally said. And then: "What happened to the girls?"

"Apollo's sister, Missy, joined the Hudson Kings. She's like Rothgar's right-hand man, a full team member like the rest of us but doesn't do frontline stuff out in the field. I don't know why. She's good enough. Rothgar probably doesn't like to lose visual on her because of the past."

"What about the other girl?"

"Graham's sister. Allison. Jaysus, what a mess. Not her, I mean. She has it together. Kept it together. Just the situation. Told Rothgar to fuck off, basically. I've never seen anything like it. He hasn't made peace with that. Never will. She lives in Manhattan still, but she's got her own life. Bet you'd like her—you should see if she's still renting that sweet apartment." He'd followed up on her a couple of times early on, just to make sure she was doing okay, and the last time he saw her face, it was like he was looking in a mirror. Careful. Iced over.

"Two girls lost their brothers," Cecily repeated. "I don't know what I'd do if I lost Dex."

Staring directly into Cecily's eyes, Shane heard himself say, "I had a family once, what they call a magical childhood, before it all went to shit." He swirled the ice in his bourbon. "I could have easily been on a different path."

Cecily swallowed and said hoarsely, "I wish *I'd* taken a different path."

Shane stilled the ice, his head cocked. "You know this is not your fault. This is his fault. That James guy. You get that, right?"

"I get that," she said, but her smile was forced. Then she shrugged. "But he promised me the world, and I believed him. *That's* my fault."

What's the world, to you? Shane almost asked. Instead he mumbled, "You should see someone in New York about this shit."

"Do you see someone about *your* shit?" she asked.

An enormously long silence passed between them as Cecily and Shane stared at each other. Shane couldn't help noticing thin streaks of light gold mixed in with the brown locks. He was close enough to run his finger down one of those streaks.

He didn't try. "Point taken," he finally said. "How about I'll stay out of your shit if you stay out of mine."

Cecily tilted her head, those big blues studying his face. Women either looked at him like they had sex on the brain or were too intimidated to look at him at all. Cecily looked at him like she was digging deep into his heart, pawing through what was left of his feelings for clues. Shane didn't move a muscle under her perusal, but she was ripping him raw and didn't even know it.

"How about we do the opposite. Try being honest and open?" she asked. "And you're not going to tell Dex what I say to you, and I'm not going to tell Dex what you say to me."

Honest? Open? That is not . . . what am I . . . I need to shut this shit down. Now. Never breaking eye contact, Shane took a massive swig of bourbon, belched like a fraternity brother trying to win a contest, and said, "Sounds like a fucking nightmare."

It took Cecily a moment to process her shock. A stunned look on her face, she gently put down her fork and knife, mumbled, "Think I'm done. Excuse me," and disappeared into the bathroom.

Shane slowly pushed away from the table and went to check the view of the action in the parking lot. *Well played,* he lied to himself. *Well played.*

CHAPTER 7

Six hours later, Cecily blinked in the sudden glare, her heart pounding in her chest as Shane looked down at her in the bed. He must have flipped on the light.

"Bad dream," he said. "You okay?"

It took longer to adjust to the sight of him than it did to the light: Bare-chested, fly of his jeans unbuttoned, hair tousled, just that single magnificent tattoo twining around his arm. Holy hell, he looked good. "I actually screamed?" she said breathlessly, sitting up.

He shrugged. "More like called out for help."

She shook her head in disgust, her pulse still racing. "I am so, so sorry I woke you. I guess I didn't know where I was for a moment. I thought . . . I thought it was him. That James was here. I got scared. I—I'm sorry. God, this is all so humiliating."

"You're worried he's not going to let you go without a fight? 'Cause I'm gonna tell you something. He's not getting to you on my watch," Shane said.

"Am I worried? Yes and no. I mean, it's weird. Sometimes it seemed like he couldn't care less. But then he'd get so possessive. I honestly think that he'd never come after me if he really loved me, that he'd let me go, but the more distance I get . . ." She swallowed hard. "I don't think he really loved me. And I don't think I really loved him." She closed her trembling fingers into a fist, hoping against hope that it wasn't pity making his eyes look so fierce. "Seriously, I'm not this girl. This is not who I am," she mumbled.

Shane swiped the hair out of his eyes and grabbed the back of his neck, obviously trying to figure out what to do with her. "I'm gonna sit down on the bed for a sec," he finally said.

Cecily watched, fascinated as Shane slowly sat down on the bed next to her, keeping his body angled away as if to make it clear this wasn't a pass. She got a whiff of bourbon, a nice view of his broad muscular back, the cut of his jaw, and the palm of his hand so close to hers she could feel the heat.

"I'm not the most . . ." He frowned and trailed off, a muscle in his jaw throbbing. "I mean, this isn't my . . . Dex would . . ."

"Dex would just give me a hug and say, 'Chin up,'" Cecily said with a faint laugh.

She could have sworn he said "Fuck me," under his breath, but she couldn't be sure. Besides, Shane's gaze had flipped back to her, a curiously determined look in his eyes. All of sudden, he twisted his body, extended an arm, and tipped his head, as much of an invitation as Cecily figured she was ever going to get.

Cecily closed her eyes and leaned against Shane's torso, curling her arms up against his chest. His body tensed in her embrace, and his arm was still just kind of stuck out straight.

She opened her eyes again. *Okay, bad idea. Bad, bad, bad idea. This is definitely a pity hug. It's probably actually painful for him to be doing this.* And just as Cecily was going to pull away and apologize and maybe escape again to the bathroom and this time refuse to come out for the rest of her life, Shane's body began to relax. And slowly, oh so slowly, he lifted one arm and brought his palm up to her back and closed the embrace. A huff escaped his lips; she would have given anything to see his face, to know what he was thinking, but the sound was so tender, so sweet, she just closed her eyes, afraid to break the spell.

"Chin up," came the gruff words whispered into her ear.

Cecily broke the embrace, raised her chin, and realized her move put her mouth in line with his. And then she did something she'd been afraid to do in months, literally *afraid*: she decided to take something she wanted, without asking permission.

A flash of sudden comprehension had Shane giving a small shake of his head: *No.* He looked mesmerized, his gaze pinned to her mouth.

Stop thinking, sweet boy. Let's both stop all this thinking and just let it happen. She licked her dry lips with the tip of her tongue and leaned into him, feeling his cock press against her thigh.

"Fu-u-u-u-ck," Shane whispered.

Yes. Though they barely touched now, Cecily's skin was electrified. She swallowed hard, gathered every ounce of courage she still possessed, and brushed her lips against his. The fire of that touch made her instantly wet; also instantaneous was Shane's reaction.

"Kid. *No.*" Shane pulled back, forcing himself to literally set her away from him, and without a word, without a shred of emotion on his face, he got to his feet and he got the hell out.

Shane woke up in the hallway, against the door of their—Cecily's— hotel room. He'd been dozing on and off, not getting much sleep, as the hotel staff drove room service carts around his long legs and inevitably asked if "sir" was okay. "Sir" was not okay. To wit, he woke up thinking about her, her smile, her scent, her body, and the same thing he'd fallen asleep thinking: *I can't breathe.* I cannot breathe. *I can't do this. I can't take it. It's too fucking sweet, and nothing this sweet ever lasts. It couldn't possibly be worth the pain.*

Very not okay.

His body didn't just hurt from sleeping in the hall; it hurt from controlling every tiny muscle that wanted to organize a rebellion and push Cecily down on the bed and fuck her until management called to complain about the number of orgasms she was screaming into the night. He wanted her down on the bed, legs spread, his cock, fingers, mouth working on her until that pretty face erupted in rapture over and over and over.

He'd done everything in the book to keep his hands off her, but she kept breaking down the wall, entering his space, coming at him with that smile, that trust, that open, good-hearted nature. She just kept coming at him with everything that mattered. How the fuck could he explain that to Dex?

Let's see: "Well, Dex, your little sister is one in a million. I'm hearing myself really laugh for the first time in years; she's got a smile that makes a guy who's living life on an infinite autobahn want to park his car and come in for the night. That's why I fucked her in a hotel room less than two days after meeting her and 'rescuing' her from her abusive ex-boyfriend."

That would so not fly. If he'd had a sister he entrusted to a friend, and that guy laid one finger on her, he'd fucking kill that friend.

Rothgar's ringtone interrupted that pleasant thought. Shane took the call immediately.

"Get on the road. Stat," said that familiar no-nonsense voice. "There's a freelancer we can trace to James keeping track of Cecily's movements. Don't know if he knows who you are. Distinctive-looking guy, like an old-school thug. Pock marks on his cheeks."

"White sedan?" Shane asked.

"Not sure what he's driving. This is coming in from a source outside the Armory. I don't know if his plan is to make contact or just to watch where she goes. Bring her back to the Armory, and we'll figure out the next move."

Shane's body tensed. He looked down both ends of the corridor. Empty. "I'm still on freelance time. Got a delivery to make en route; been driving hot since before I picked Cecily up. Quick stop here in Chicago."

Rothgar went quiet; probably because he didn't have an argument. What Shane picked up must be delivered. It was his word and his honor. "You told Dex?"

"Right when he asked the favor. I assume he remembers."

"Doesn't mean it's going to sit right with him under the circumstances," Rothgar muttered.

"Not going to let anything touch her," Shane said. "I've gotta close my deal. You know how it works."

"I know how it works," Rothgar answered. "I know it's your personal business, but do us all a favor and send Missy some data about your timing and whereabouts. See you in New York."

Shane ended the call. He could hear Cecily moving around inside the hotel room. *Time to put on the armor.* He opened the door, calling out, "Kid, you rested?"

Cecily popped out from the bedroom, fully dressed. She stared at him for a moment. "Yes. Listen, I—"

"Let's get going," Shane said, pushing the door open and moving past her, his phone already on and up to his ear. "Hi, yeah, room ten twenty-three. Checking out immediately with a couple of adds on the tab. I'd like to have two breakfast sandwiches, one with egg and sausage, one just egg, two bottled waters, and a pile of napkins brought to the room as soon as possible, but leave the tray outside the door. Thanks."

He hung up, ignoring the waves of irritation coming off Cecily's person as she packed her suitcase back up. *Yeah, I'm ordering for you, and, no, I don't care what you want.* "When it gets here, pick which one you want, eat it."

As she finished getting ready, Shane got his gun out and laid it by the sink while he stripped down in the bathroom, noting that she'd taken one bar of unwrapped soap but had left everything else. After a five-minute shower, he put his messenger bag back together, grabbed everything else labeled with an orange that wasn't opened—soap, lotion, body wash—and dumped it in.

By the time he was done, pulling his last fresh T-shirt over his head, his hair soaking down the back of it, she was packed and sitting on the bed, still working through the second half of what looked to be egg only.

The gold streaks in her hair shone even more now that her hair was down and dry, hanging in soft waves just below the shoulders. A piece in front had fallen in her face; she licked the grease off her fingers and pulled it all into a ponytail. Shane's gaze shifted to her standard uniform of jeans and clinging T-shirt. He tried to focus on the puffed short sleeves, like maybe he could contain his thoughts relating to shoving his hands in her hair and ripping off her clothes if he imagined her top as the sort of T-shirt virginal English governesses would wear, but his eyes kept moving to the clinging part.

How did a girl like that get into the middle of a mess like this? Man, he didn't want to see the look on her face when they got to the Armory, and she found out what she was really dealing with.

Cecily carefully poked a bit of cheese back inside her breakfast sandwich. "Can we talk about—"

"Nope," Shane said, grabbing egg and sausage, ripping off a good third in one bite, and saying through a full mouth, "Not necessary."

Equal parts disappointment and relief warred on her face. "But we—"

"Listen, kid, there's no 'we.'" He ripped off another third, downing it in record time as he looked her square in the eyes. *There's no "we."* "Finish up. Let's go." Cramming the last part of the sandwich into his mouth, he uncapped the water and took a swig, chewing the mass in his mouth, swallowed, and then wiped the grease off with a napkin. He washed his hands in the bathroom one last time and lined up next to the luggage by the door to wait, his arms folded over his chest.

Cecily looked at him in total disbelief. "Was chewing even involved in that?"

"Food is fuel, sweetling."

She rolled her eyes but ate faster. "You're purposely trying to disgust me. Don't bother. I'm as disgusted with you as I need to be." She took a last dainty bite of her own sandwich, washed up in the bathroom, and walked out the door Shane was holding open.

"Me too," he muttered, and the door slammed shut behind them.

CHAPTER 8

The car was waiting at the hotel curb. Shane was waving off the porter again, taking a longer time than she'd expect to Tetris his duffel bag and her suitcase back into the trunk. She thought of going back to have a look, but then she saw the popped lock on the front passenger side door.

Cecily moved closer; the porter appeared and smoothly opened the door for her, and she simply got in. He didn't want to clear up last night? He wouldn't let her apologize for being an idiot? *Fine. No problem. But I'm not sitting in the backseat anymore. I'm an adult, and I made a mistake, but we're stuck together until New York, and I am not sitting in the backseat like a toddler.*

Shane stopped in his tracks as he saw her in the front seat. Cecily bit back a smile. He looked like he was processing this. He took his sunglasses off, studied her face, looked at the backseat, back at her, and then just got into the driver's seat, pulled on his gloves, and turned on the ignition.

"I thought you might tell me to move," Cecily said.

"I thought I might too," Shane answered. He opened the sunroof and looked up at the sky. Just stared at the blue sky and the clouds for a minute and then got them on the road.

"But you didn't," Cecily pushed.

"Nope."

After a pause, Cecily asked, "What's in the trunk?"

He didn't answer.

"You have something really weird in your trunk, don't you?" she teased.

He didn't answer. Her smile faded; his slowly emerged.

Oh, man. He does have something really weird in his trunk. Did he have it when he picked me up? How weird is weird, anyway? "Are we going to drive all the way to New York with this question mark between us?"

"There's no question mark for me," Shane said. "I know exactly what's in my trunk."

"Man, you're a pain in the ass," she said. She stared out the windshield, thinking maybe she shouldn't have been so quick to sit up front. *How did I get here?*

Shane kept glancing over.

"Can you watch the road, please?" she snapped. She kept her mouth shut after that, for so long, in fact, that it had the interesting effect of making Shane uncomfortable to the point that he actually said, "Last night wasn't a big deal. You should be okay . . ."

Cecily stared straight ahead. "I guess I'm not entirely okay after a completely embarrassing night during which I put the moves on a guy whose body seems to like it, but whose mind makes him turn me down."

"It wasn't embarrassing."

"Yeah, it was."

"It wasn't embarrassing."

"Oh, yeah, Shane?" Cecily said wearily. "If it wasn't embarrassing, what was it?"

"It was hot. That embarrassing? I don't think hot is embarrassing. I think hot is hot."

Which made her hot *and* embarrassed.

"Hot and stupid," he added.

Great.

"Do you get that if you were just a woman in an elevator I'd nail you in a second?"

Cecily's blush turned into a burn. "What's the difference between a random woman in an elevator and a random woman you met a day ago whom you happen to be driving around in your car?"

Shane shifted as traffic ahead slowed down, and then looked over. "You know you're not random. I'm beginning to think the reason you picked this James guy is because you don't know anything about guys. Try assuming the opposite of whatever you're thinking and go with that. I think your mileage will improve."

Cecily rolled her eyes.

"I think you're a hot little piece, kid. Now try imagining me saying *that* to your brother and maybe you'll have some insight into the situation."

Cecily's eyes widened. *A hot little piece? A hot little piece,* kid? *What do you even say to that?* "I cannot imagine why you think I'd share anything about my sex life with Dex." That was, in fact, a revolting thought.

"He trusts me to take care of you, Cecily," Shane said softly. "You're Hudson Kings family. I don't get to do whatever I want. You don't mess with family loyalty for no good reason."

What if I think having spontaneous hotel sex with you is taking care of me? What if I think your body looks like the best antidote to a terrible relationship experience I've ever seen? "Wait, you've had elevator sex?" Cecily blurted.

"I stay in hotels a lot," Shane answered blandly.

"I never really gave it too much thought, but being around you is starting to make me realize how insanely vanilla I am," Cecily mumbled.

"Vanilla is classic," he said after a while. "Nice."

Nice. Ugh. "You didn't come back to the room last night. What did you do after you left?"

"I considered going down to the lobby bathroom to jack off in a stall, but I just ended up sleeping in the hall outside our room."

God. At this rate, Cecily was pretty sure her cheeks were going to be stained pink with heat and lust.

"Not a great night for me," he finished.

"I can't help but notice that you're talking more than usual," Cecily said, getting a little desperate to change the subject matter away from elevator sex and jacking off. "I like that."

"This conversation has been a good return on investment."

Cecily looked over in confusion.

"Talking about sex makes you blush. Sometimes it makes you squirm. Just because I'm not interested in touching you doesn't mean I'm not interested in watching you."

He was smiling. And it was so excellent—that unguarded Shane Sullivan smile—that Cecily wouldn't have even minded if he'd added the word *kid.*

One of his cell phones rang. Shane picked it up: "Sullivan . . . hey. Uh-huh . . . yeah, I got you, but I'm not sure about the timing." He looked over at Cecily and then went back to his call. "Let me check, and I'll get back to you with something more precise."

After another moment he hung up, and Cecily looked over. "If there's something we need to do on the way, obviously you should do whatever you'd normally do without me in the car," she said.

"I've got a delivery to make on the way home."

Cecily watched the scenery go by, an alternating blur of green and gray. "I'm happy to wait."

"Figured you'd want to get to Dex as soon as possible."

Cecily chewed on her lip. She should, especially given last night's debacle. "Just saying that you're doing me a favor, and I don't mind if you need to detour and do your own stuff." She flipped down the sunshade and checked her face in the mirror. "Besides, you'd be doing me a favor by delaying. If Dex is really looking, you can still see the bruise a little."

Shane went silent for a while then. "That guy messed up your phone. And your face. What else did he mess up?"

"What do you mean?"

"Why did you run off without cash in your wallet?"

Cecily looked to see if Shane was joking. He did not seem to be joking. "I wasn't going to steal cash out of his wallet!"

"He treated you like shit and said you couldn't go when you wanted to. If you didn't have cash in your own wallet, it's 'cause he made it that way."

"Stealing money from people doesn't exactly come naturally to me. I knew I'd be with you—well, I didn't know it was *you*—and I wasn't thinking about how long it would take to get back to Dex, which was really stupid, now that I think about it, because now you've had to pay for everything . . ." Cecily felt ugly all over again. "I guess I should have thought about taking money out of his wallet."

After a moment, Shane said, "You're really fucking decent."

"Is that an insult?" Cecily asked.

"God, no. But you need someone who's gonna take care of you."

"I definitely do not," Cecily said, not even trying to keep the edge out of her voice. "James 'took care of me.' He made sure to remind me every day."

"You need to go find a man who understands the meaning of taking care."

"The way *you're* taking care of me?"

Shane watched the road. "From personal experience I know the kind of taking care James gave you, and from the Hudson Kings I know what kind a girl like you should look for in a man."

Cecily blinked, trying to imagine someone taking Shane's credit and debit cards and breaking his phone and hitting Shane in the face and getting away with it. She blinked again trying to imagine Shane having more than a one-time personal experience with getting hit in the face. "Who hit you?"

Shane didn't answer her question. His face was carefully blank, and Cecily knew she'd pressed a button. If someone had hit Shane, probably after his parents were gone and he was just a little kid, maybe they did it more than once. Maybe a lot to make a boy go so blank as a man. Cecily stared out the window, gritting her teeth, suddenly very, very angry.

Because Shane was Dex's friend. Shane had taken his personal time to come get Cecily because of that friendship. And now Shane was her friend too, even if she'd done her best to screw that up in the middle of the night.

All of a sudden Shane spoke, staring out the windshield. "I remember being a kid and having a pizza dinner every Friday night. It was just pepperoni pizza, you know. But it was a thrill. Everybody was in a good mood. Dad, Mom, me. We did it at the top of every weekend. We were tight. One time, my parents went to get the pizza, and some guy came in and shot up the parlor. Always thought that maybe if I'd been there, they'd still be alive." He shrugged. "Anyway, life ended, you know. Got sent around different places, but nothing stuck. Mostly because I kept running away . . . lot of people who shouldn't be around a kid will take in a kid for money."

Cecily stared at Shane's profile, tears welling up in her eyes. She wanted to touch him, comfort him. "I'm so, so sorry," she whispered instead, knowing it wasn't enough. He didn't respond.

Shane was right. He did know the true meaning of taking care. He'd had it once, but it didn't seem like anyone was taking care of him now or had in a while. "Does anybody in New York take care of *you*?" she asked gently, not sure what answer she was hoping for.

Shane looked over, puzzled. "Have you noticed I'm a fearless motherfucker with huge fists and access to weapons? Don't need it."

Of course not. Cecily turned her head back to the window so he wouldn't see her small smile. She knew better. She'd felt his body relax in the hotel room; she'd heard the sweet sound of tenderness in that one breath. He might not recognize what it meant to connect with another person, to care and be cared for, but Shane Sullivan liked the feeling, and he needed it just as much as she did.

The phone rang again. Shane took the call. "Yeah. I've got a two-hour window, but that's all I can spare, so let's keep it simple." He met Cecily's eyes, something in his flickered, he went back to his call. "The gym? . . . That's what I was expecting. Works for me."

All he said when he hung up the phone was "Gonna take that detour now."

CHAPTER 9

Shane pulled briefly off the freeway into a public rest stop, drove between a van and an SUV, and got out of the car. Cecily followed him to the front of the car, looking impressed when he reached under his bumper and flipped his plates. She followed him to the back, and he did the same and then popped the trunk. She instinctively backed away.

"C'mere," Shane said.

She peered inside. A wide grin spread over her face. "Oh!"

"Push this button."

Cecily pushed a button on the inside of the trunk, and the bottom section opened to reveal what looked like a flat garment bag . . . but it kept going and raised vertically until it was a mini garment rack.

Through the plastic window of the top garment the black satin lapels of a tuxedo were visible.

"Seriously?" Cecily said, clearly delighted by the unexpected surprise. "I guess I'm just so used to you in jeans and boots. I'll bet you look amazing in a tux."

I'd like to see you looking at me in a tux.

"I thought it'd be some kind of arsenal," she added, reaching toward a hairline crack in the bottom of the wardrobe platform.

Shane wrapped a hand around Cecily's wrist and pulled her back. Playtime was over. "No. That stuff doesn't touch you."

She stood quietly next to him while he moved the garment bags around and then opened one and selected a navy-blue sweatshirt stained with white paint on the pocket and a worn-out Chicago Bears ball cap. His tattoo vanished under the sweatshirt; his face vanished under the hat. Didn't matter how much or how little he changed his appearance. Just the act of putting on something different from his usual helped him get in the zone.

He got back into the car and started it up. Cecily stood frozen for a moment before she got in the passenger side, deep in thought.

She opened her mouth to express those thoughts, and Shane cut her off at the pass: "Next time we get off the freeway, we're going to drive and park outside a coffee shop called Bernard's. I'll be across the street. Gonna point you out to Bernard and get you a snack. You're gonna eat the snack until I come and get you."

"I'm *gonna*," Cecily said under her breath and then knee-jerked out with "I'm gonna eat the snack."

Shane found himself getting irritated. He got that she wasn't keen on being told what to do; he'd try to remember that, when it was shit that didn't really matter. Like he warned, they parked in front of Bernard's. Shane came around and opened the passenger door because she hadn't gotten out.

He held out his wallet. She sat there some more, staring at money poking out the side, and then with a big huff, she exited the car and took the wallet with an expression that suggested he'd sprayed it with some kind of contaminant. "What snack would you like me to eat, Shane?"

"I thought you were cool with me doing a quick job, Cecily. Are you cool with that, or are you not cool with that? 'Cause this is me doing a quick job. I don't have time for nineteenth-century pleasantries or whatever the fuck it is you expect from me. I don't have brain space to spend making you feel whatever it is you want to feel. If you are cool with me doing a quick job, I need you to follow orders without sass and go buy yourself a fucking snack and entertain yourself until I get back without leaving the café. Do you think you can do that for me?"

The sass had leaked out of her expression by the time he was done with his speech. Cecily's eyes widened, and then she mumbled, "I can do that for you."

"Didn't think it'd be that easy," he muttered, indicating she needed to start walking toward Bernard's.

"Sorry, Shane, it should be, shouldn't it? You deserve more respect than that. I trust you. You've earned it from me. Sometimes I forget this isn't a movie, because I don't really understand what you and Dex have gotten yourselves into. But this is real, and you've got business to attend to. I didn't mean to be bitchy." She went straight up the stairs into Bernard's and got into line, Shane staring after her.

He shook his head and then popped the glove compartment and took out a gun, which he stuck in his waistband. Then he went to the trunk, opened the compartment underneath the wardrobe module, and pushed aside the weapons and the ammunition to grab the duffel bag he'd stowed. All the while, his mind tried to process her words.

Earned it? Respect? An odd sensation swept through him. Sweetness. He was surprised he gave a shit, but there was something really special about having earned even a fragment of fucking-decent-Cecily's trust or respect. A man made it far enough with Rothgar to be given a room and a job with the Hudson Kings, that man got a certain amount of respect, de facto. Any friend of Rothgar's, and all that. Not the case with Cecily, and it was with a truly warm feeling inside that Shane confirmed Cecily was in line to get coffee before he popped into the back room to set up a guard for her with Bernard. Bernard would have Cecily's seat on his video monitor and one of the "baristas" out front keeping tabs firsthand.

He didn't acknowledge Cecily on the way out, though he could see her through the café window when he looked back. And then he put her out of his mind, because that's what he always did. He never let anything that was bothering him in real life touch him on a job, and he never broke a sweat.

Shane hoisted the duffel bag on his back and headed across the street to the gym.

◆ ◆ ◆

The front of the gym was buzzing with action. The serious guys were training in a ring lined with shiny red padding and watched over by posters of current world boxing champions. A bunch of wannabes punched bags along the sides.

The back of the building was another story. You had to walk past a set of offices to get to the old section of the gym. Here, the decor was rotting wood beams, a rusty bench press, and some abandoned exercise bicycles circa eighties Jane Fonda. There was nothing else here except Shane . . . and Shorty plus his merry band of fuckups.

"You need me to repeat it?" Shorty asked, gesturing to the money. The duffel bag Shane had brought was zipped closed on the floor next to a patriotic-looking sports bag opened to reveal Shane's client's money; Shane's cut was stacked on the bench.

"No. I *want* you to repeat it," Shane said. Neutral tone, cold eyes. He figured he got his point across.

"I said, 'You're late, and we want a discount.' That's why it's short."

Shane watched a trickle of sweat slither down the side of Shorty's nose. He felt his own pulse accelerate as the guy next to him reached down and pulled a knife from somewhere in a pair of voluminous sweatpants. He stared down at his portion of the money, which was definitely short, and raised his hand up to his jaw to scratch his stubble.

The move sent a wave of tension through the room.

"Well," Shane said, his words light, his jaw tight. "This is highly unprofessional."

He looked at the guy he was calling Shorty—for at least two reasons—and made a big, slow motion to pull out his phone. Eyes on Shorty, he dialed his Point A and let out a sigh while the phone rang once and the client picked up. "I'm standing here in a room that's at least ninety degrees with a bunch of amateurs with sweaty hands who are giving me way too many clues about what I just dropped off. I'm seeing things I don't wanna see and learning things I don't wanna learn. They don't have the money packed up and ready, and they're asking for a *discount*, claiming I'm *late*. I had a window, and I'm inside that window. If this is not resolved, you and I have a problem. I don't want us to have a problem. We've been doing happy business for a long time now. We clear?" Shane hung up the phone.

A second later Shorty's phone rang. "Is that how it works?" he was saying too loud. "Yeah. I feel ya. Yeah . . . oh. No, didn't do that."

Shane tried to tune it all out. He pulled his knife from his ankle holster and cleaned a bit of dirt out from his thumbnail. Knowing more than he needed to put him in a bad mood, and there were too many other factors here already putting him in a bad mood. He should have been back with Cecily by now.

"Oh, shit," Shorty said. "Really? Didn't know that either." Shane watched Shorty look around and gesture to a plastic drawstring shopping bag from the Gap sitting with some of the guys' backpacks and workout bags. Still on the phone, Shorty snapped his fingers and said something Shane again tried really hard to tune out. All of sudden someone was dumping underwear and socks out of the Gap bag and using the bag to stash Shane's cut of the cash.

"Jaysus," Shane muttered, staring up at the ceiling. He practiced throwing his knife into a slim wood doorframe and hit the knotty eye he was aiming at square so many times the other guys in the room took a step back.

Shane paused, his knife in his hand, his gun in his waistband, and stared down at the money. He took a moment to count it all and then zipped up the sports bag. "I'm trying to be a nicer person," he said and waited a moment to let that sink in. "The next guy will probably kill you for this bullshit."

He grabbed his client's cash bag and his own cash bag, and all of a sudden, the mood in the room changed. A couple of the guys couldn't quit arguing over Shane's cut. Two fuckers still wanted their "discount."

One of them pulled a gun. In walked Cecily, and Shane lost his mind.

"You left your wallet with me. I worried you might need it." The minute the words were out of Cecily's mouth she realized he'd left it with her on purpose, and, no, Shane definitely didn't need it. This was because at the same time she was speaking he was pulling his gun out of the back of his jeans and probably didn't need a discount card for the grocery store at the moment.

He stared at her in disbelief, in one hand a knife and in the other hand a gun. Perhaps things were not going as smoothly as Shane had hoped. Cecily's heart started beating as the six men looked at her, the old black duffel bag, a badly out-of-style sports bag plastered in stars and stripes, and a smaller Gap bag on the floor between them all.

Shane threw his knife into the doorframe, apparently to free up one hand, which he used to try to shepherd Cecily behind his back.

All of a sudden, the guy standing in front started grinning. "She why you were late?"

"Me? Oh, I'm definitely the reason," Cecily answered for him.

"I wasn't late," Shane said, looking about as pissed as she'd ever seen him.

"Delayed?" Cecily suggested.

He looked like he was going to blow a fuse, but he merely cocked his head with a shrug that said he was willing to cop to "delayed."

"Delayed." She looked back at the grinning guy. "He was just delayed. Delayed is not late. It's just later. Because of me. Yes. So, are we done here?"

The guy was giving her a once-over that felt like a hands-on airport inspection. *Gross.* She could feel herself blushing.

Shane made a sound. A dangerous sound. He looked at Cecily but apparently decided that he would play it her way.

He looked at the guy. "Are we?" Shane asked.

"Yeah, man," the guy said with complete amusement, clearly forgoing the discount.

Shane grabbed his knife and stuck it back in his ankle holster, one hand on Cecily the whole time. Then he hoisted the sports bag and the Gap bag over one shoulder. He grabbed Cecily's arm and moved her in front of his body, shielding her from the men as he marched her to the door.

He kept her pressed against him as they walked to the less creepy part of the gym where all the people were and then even still as he hustled her out of the building altogether. He was angry. Justifiably so. She could tell because his muscles were leaping and jerking and his body temperature felt like it had jumped to a hundred degrees. Or maybe it was *her* body temperature. *Oh, god.*

"On the plus side," she whispered, her voice shaking with adrenaline, "I think I did a pretty good job of defusing the situation."

CHAPTER 10

Shane was on fire. All the usual adrenaline from doing a job, all the usual ramp-up from a job getting complicated, and then Cecily walking into the middle of a trigger-happy pissing contest. If they'd touched her . . . if they'd so much as pointed a weapon at her, he would have lost his fucking shit. Forget the money. It was all he could do to go along with her ridiculous happy-go-lucky charm-my-way-out-of-it game plan, when what he really wanted to do was blow somebody's head off just for looking at her too long.

They made it outside, and Shane dragged her around the corner. For a minute, he just stood there, the sports bag over his shoulder, and the string of a blue-and-white Gap bag full of hundred-dollar bills swinging from his fist while his brain skittered between the memories of Cecily's soft body against his and all the things he'd convinced himself during his hotel-hallway "Come to Jesus" moment when he'd sworn hands off.

Apparently, no matter how easy the job or how many you've done . . . no matter how poker your face looks to the outside world . . . well, there's just something about walking out of a dangerous situation holding the take and looking into the eyes of a girl you desperately want to fuck, who you know desperately wants to fuck you, that's just going to shut down your logic receptors and make your dick hard.

Shane didn't care. He didn't care about stupid criminals breaking rules. He didn't care about Dex. He didn't care about James and the Russians. And he didn't care about time.

Cecily started for the car, Shane two steps behind her, when he turned in the opposite direction, using one arm to hook his girl and duck them both into an adjacent alley.

Against the brick wall of the coffee shop she sucked in a quick breath. Her purse slid to her feet, and her eyes went wide. "Are you—"

"Dunno," he said randomly, crushing his mouth down on hers, the bag of cash out of his grip falling between their feet.

Shane let the adrenaline feed his desire. Every iota of self-control he'd exhibited in the hotel went out the window. Cecily gasped against his mouth as he pulled her closer, but any surprise in that was blown away by a breathy *"Yes."*

That's all he needed to hear. He grabbed her, fistfuls of her collar on either side, and drove her into the wall behind her. *Gonna make you come so hard you'll never stop thinking about me.* His tongue plundered her mouth, and she answered his call, alternately pressing her body up against his and grabbing on to whatever she could to bring him closer. Sloppy, rough, nearly mindless, all Shane could think about was how much he wanted to touch her skin. His mouth trailed down her throat. Cecily arched her back, and Shane licked her nipple through her clothes.

He loosened her belt, had her fly down, his hand moving to her panties.

She reached for his waistband; Shane batted her hand away, sunk one finger into her wet pussy, pressed her firmly against the bricks, and went still. *Oh, my god, so wet. So gorgeous . . . wet.*

"Shane?" Cecily asked.

A smile curled the corners of his mouth as he covered her body with his, his fingers in her panties covered with her slick. She couldn't move underneath his weight. Her eyes widened the moment she understood, and then her mouth opened. The only thing he moved was the slight brush of his finger across the lips of her pussy.

His eyes locked on hers, his massive body covering her own. He held her against the wall, caging her in his embrace, his hard cock throbbing through his jeans against her side. And he just . . . barely . . . touched her clit.

"Oh, my god," Cecily whispered, her face flushed. He didn't have to explain or ask; she let him own her. His finger circled her bud, changing pressure only just enough as he watched her face and followed her passion.

She tried to squirm, tried to press up against him, but he held her fast, now kneading his cock against her more rhythmically as he pressed another finger into her cunt and fucked her with his hand.

"I'm—I'm . . ." Her head dropped, her face pressing into the crook of his neck. Shane whispered, "I know you're gonna have the sweetest pussy, and I haven't even tasted you yet" into her ear, and Cecily just reared her head back, her eyes closed and mouth open, and let out a long, uncontrolled shout of release.

As she recovered and raised her smile from his shoulder, Shane slowly pulled his hand away, reveling in her musky scent.

"What about you?" Cecily asked, a little mischievous as she wiped the sweat off her face. But then she looked down at whatever she was stepping on and saw the giant pile of money. Her smile extinguished, and it was like the sun had just gone down.

"That's dirty money, isn't it?"

It didn't sound like much of a question, actually. Shane pulled his defensive mask on, going dead eyes and flat mouth. "You keep stepping on it, it will be." He bent down and stuffed the cash back inside and then tried to hand her the bag. "Here. Consider it your cut."

"What are you doing? *I'm* not going to hold it!" She took a step back, and it fell on the ground again. "I don't like this. Is this what you and Dex are into? Who gave you that? Why would someone give you that?"

"How about because I did my job?" Shane suggested. "What did you *think* was gonna be in the bag? What did you think I was doing in there? Lifting weights for fun?"

All Shane could see was red. Anger, desire—he had no idea. He just wanted to knock some sense into her and kiss that mouth some more. Something. Anything. "Don't look like that. You know I'm not going to let anything happen to you."

"This is getting crazy," Cecily said.

"This is what I do."

She sucked in a quick breath.

"I didn't ask you to come into the gym," Shane said. "In fact, I set it up so none of that would touch you. You walked into *my* world. And if you'd stop to think, you'd realize that not everything that's legal is inherently good. It's generally perfectly legal for some asshole you're dating to yell at you and make you feel like shit."

"Well, I'm not taking dirty money," Cecily said. "And I'm really starting to freak out about Dex taking it too."

Shane set his jaw, feeling strangely hurt and still hopped up on the twin thrills of the take and the kiss. He pulled out his phone. "Do you need to call your brother and nag him about it right now? Or do you want to take a few more seconds to enjoy the afterglow of the orgasm I just gave you?"

"You're an asshole."

"You're a closed-minded b—"

Cecily blanched, and he closed his mouth.

A bolt of shame raced through Shane's body. He looked down at the filthy ground, shaking his head. "Sorry . . ."

She was waiting for the end of his sentence, looking about as puzzled as he felt, bee-stung lips and a faint scrape across her cheekbone from his stubble when he'd whispered in her ear. Shane shook his head, and words just exploded out of his mouth before he could think or stop them or change them into something else. "You know, kid, we've got this thing between us, and it is . . . this thing that clearly I can't stop myself from wanting to explore. You're this combination that I never thought existed, and if I ever thought it existed, I'm sure I didn't think it existed for someone like me. My hands, my mouth, my cock are all 'man, what is your problem' and I just want to touch you all the time. You still smell like oranges, and I'm still fucking hard for you, but we've got these . . . I don't know . . . *circumstances,* and I just don't see how it ever ends without us standing in an alley staring at each other like we just can't understand what the hell the other person was thinking."

Shane reached out and ran his fingers down a wave of hair resting against her stunned face. Then he grabbed the sports bag. "Car's right outside. Take your time."

When he got back to the curb, his habitual glance up and down the street produced some results. There was a car parked by a hungry meter flashing red with indignation. Shitty white sedan, Japanese make needing a wash, notable only for the last three digits of the license being 321. Nothing special except for the fact that it was the car that looked suspicious back when he'd first picked Cecily up. The driver was either ducked down in the seat or watching from afar, maybe even inside the café. Thank fuck he and Cecily had ducked into that alley for their little one-on-one.

Still. *Shit.*

Shane turned on his phone and called Rothgar back, recited the plate number, and got a confirmation that the plate and the freelancer were a match. "Guess James Peterson didn't put all that time in faking a life with Cecily Keegan for nothing," Rothgar said. "She's still a weak link he thinks has intel on the Hudson Kings. And it appears he's considering asking for a second chance."

She's not weak. But she was defenseless. Shane clenched a fist. "I'm heading straight for New York," he said.

"Haul ass, brother. You're in enemy sights."

CHAPTER 11

I still smell like oranges?

Stricken, Cecily watched him leave. He wasn't in a huff. He wasn't pissed off. He'd just told it like it was and then left the money in the alley with her, didn't seem to care whether she picked it up or not.

What just happened? What just happened? Her mind was racing as fast as her heart. That kiss. Oh, my god, the way he kissed her. He would have easily fucked her in the alley if she hadn't started freaking out about the money, which was crazy. Shane Sullivan would have easily fucked her in an alley in broad daylight, which was a complete turn-on because Cecily really, really liked the way he seemed to get slightly out of control whenever they touched.

She was starting to notice that this guy who seemed to have everything under control, who could take care of himself and anyone around him, couldn't stop himself from deviating off course when it came to her. If a man was going to have a weakness, what a completely, divinely romantic and delicious possibility it was that it might be her. She'd never felt as close to James as she already did with Shane. Somehow, she got behind Shane's walls . . . and somehow he was getting behind hers.

James cared about Cecily in terms of what she could do for him: how she looked on his arm, how she decorated his house. Shane had detoured from his own obligations, focused on her safety, and even comforted her when he didn't know her at all. She'd forgotten there was something deeper out there than just having a plus-one for a cocktail party. She'd forgotten a man could be like that, giving something of his soul—even if he didn't mean to, and even if he didn't know he was doing it.

Shane could talk the talk: *"There's no we."* He could walk the walk by turning his back whenever things went sideways and retreating to the hermetically sealed bubble he called his car. But he couldn't permanently keep his distance from her. Maybe he was attracted to train wrecks, maybe she'd just gotten under his skin, but Cecily knew it, and he'd eventually figure it out, and so the only question that could possibly matter now was whether the fact that they were insanely attracted to each other was actually a problem.

Of course, there was the question of rebound, but, honestly, no rebound she'd ever been through before had ever felt so right. Cecily sighed and picked up the Gap bag. It nearly broke from the weight of the cash inside.

Does it matter whether or not I know what he did to get it? He had a gun, but if he didn't fire it, does it matter? What if he did, but the people he fired at were like James, or worse? Cecily hoisted the cash higher, unable to see over the top, vaguely aware that bundles of money were slipping around in her arms.

One wad slipped through the angle of her elbow. All of a sudden, Shane was beside her catching the cash in one hand. "Put on your seat belt."

He opened the back door, took the money out of Cecily's arms, and threw it in the backseat. The bag burst open, sending bundles of twenties all over the place. Shane's movements were crisp, urgent. He was up to something. "I always put on my seat belt," she said.

She'd barely closed the door when he hit the ignition and started to drive. He glanced in the rearview mirror and said in a tight voice, "Yep. There he is. This is gonna be fun."

"What is?" Cecily asked.

"You interested in seeing how fast she goes?" he asked.

Cecily stared at him in wonder. Until Shane, no man ever asked her something like that. Dex certainly never invited his little sister to live on the edge. "Definitely. Yeah!"

"You're not afraid of driving fast?"

"No. Not to mention, you kind of seem like an expert. Let it rip, maestro," Cecily said gamely.

"Maestro." His face was blank, but Cecily knew better. He liked it.

Her big smile turned into a surprised *O* when he hit the gas and pointed the car toward a gap between two moving vans the size of a toaster slot.

"I thought you said 'fast,' not 'flat,'" Cecily squeaked.

"Trick is to get as close as possible but never touch," Shane murmured, his voice low and intense, eyes glued front.

How that managed to sound sexy, Cecily didn't know. "Are you talking about us or the car?" she asked.

The car flipped to the side, weight on two wheels, and they zipped between the two enormous vehicles like a motorcycle splitting lanes.

"The car," Shane said, rather unnecessarily at this point, Cecily thought.

Cecily grabbed at the armrest. The needle moved up another ten miles per hour. She squeaked and dug her fingernails into the leather. Shane didn't comment on the transgression, which was when she noticed that he was keeping tabs on someone outside the car. Maybe he wasn't just showing off for her; maybe this was for real. She didn't know whether to be pissed, impressed, or scared shitless. "Um, excuse me, but . . . is this a car chase?"

No answer. No answer from Shane was as good as confirmation. Cecily's heart started hammering in her chest.

She craned her neck around, trying to catch a glimpse beyond the headrest. "Who are we trying to get away from?"

"Who are we leaving behind," Shane clarified, hitting the brakes suddenly enough to just squeal onto a passing off-ramp before it was too late.

"Is it James?" Cecily asked. Her stomach lurched. The idea of James actually coming after her was terrifying. If she hadn't been worried in the first place, she wouldn't have asked Dex to send an escort home. But somehow, the actuality of James not letting her go without a fuss—or a fight—hadn't hit home until now. Probably because the minute she knew that Shane was on her side, she hadn't had to worry about, well, anything. But Shane wouldn't be at her side for much longer.

"Can't tell who it is," Shane muttered. He exited the freeway and headed for a series of underpasses stretched out before them like the ribs of a whale. A flicker of a frown disturbed his impassive face.

"Is he still there?" Cecily asked.

"Still there," Shane said. He shifted, and drove the car up on the side of the tunnel wall.

"Oh. My. God," Cecily shrieked.

"Hold tight," Shane said.

And then he did it again, except this time, he took the tunnel like a half-pipe and somersaulted the entire car.

They landed hard, slamming against their seat belts. Cecily craned her neck to see what they were up against. "Are we running away, or . . . ?"

Shane flashed a smile, but he was focused on the road. "That would be 'or.' Come *on*, man. You can do it."

Cecily's heart was beating out of her chest. She was glued to the seat mostly due to the fact that her fingernails were still stuck into the armrest and seat cushion. "You . . . you're *disappointed*?" She took a deep breath after noting the frisson of hysteria tainting her accusation. "Tell me you're not letting this crazy person . . . catch up!"

"It's been a while since I had some decent competition. This is more me showing off for you."

"Oh. Wow. Um, well, I'm very . . . um, impressed . . . so, we're still going . . . what"—Cecily leaned over to look at the speedometer—"like one hundred miles per hour."

"Unfortunately, we lost him. Again."

"I thought we were trying to lose him," Cecily said.

"I thought it would be harder," Shane said.

"Maybe we should let him stay lost," Cecily suggested.

"I almost think he wants to have a chat," Shane said.

"What makes you think that? I mean it seemed like he was going to ram us."

"He wasn't going to ram us."

"I really think he was going to ram us."

"He wasn't going to ram us, because he had a couple of decent shots, and he didn't ram us."

"Don't you think that's weird?"

"Not if he wants to have a chat," Shane said, his calm words at odds with the tremendous speed at which they were driving, which had them weaving through vehicles and dodging motorcycles.

Cecily watched in her rearview mirror as the white sedan made some headway and then switched to the lane next to theirs. "I think he's got hamsters instead of horses in that piece of shit. Maybe I should slow down even more," Shane said.

"Slow down? So, if he doesn't want to ram us, what's he want?"

"Like I said, I think he wants to talk."

"You're serious? Maybe he should call us on the phone!"

"I'm not giving him my personal number, are you?" Shane asked.

"Then what's going to happen?"

"I guess we'd better roll down the window and ask. I want to see if I recognize him."

"Shane!" Cecily shrieked.

The white sedan labored up next to them; Cecily could tell something had gone wrong enough with the car that a bit of ugly smoke was seeping out the tailpipe.

Shane rolled down his window as the car sidled up. He took a look and then shook his head at her as if to confirm that he didn't recognize him. Cecily took a deep breath as Shane also popped the armrest compartment between them and helped himself to a very small, very sharp knife.

A man with dark brown hair, a nose that clearly had once played football in high school, and cheeks riddled with chicken pox scars leaned over and glanced between Shane and Cecily. "Cecily Keegan," he said matter-of-factly.

Cecily sucked in a quick breath. *Oh, god.*

The man looked at Shane. "Who are you?"

"Her driver."

The man smiled at Cecily. "I'm a message. Tell your brother to lay off the pirozhki."

Shane let the words sit there for a moment. "Anything else?"

"It's five o'clock. Do you know where your razor is?"

"You've got to be fucking kidding me. Do you keep a staff writer for this shit?"

The man shrugged, his car swerving slightly.

"I don't use a razor," Shane said. He raised the hand that had lain concealed on his lap and threw the knife with a practiced flick.

Cecily yelped as the blade sailed through the sedan's window and nailed the passenger headrest, the hilt swinging left and right as the driver reared back in surprise. It was apparently all Shane had to discuss, because he put the pedal to the metal and left the sedan in the dust. After a quiet five minutes of driving at about a hundred miles per hour, he slowed to eighty-five.

It took her that long to calm down, and when she looked over at Shane, she was surprised to find he didn't look calm at all. If anything, he looked way more agitated than he had driving up the side of a tunnel.

"Shane," she said, trying to keep it together. "What's in your head?"

"Manhattan," he said tightly, shooting a glance in her direction. He looked spent. Bleak. It was like the thrill of the chase was gone and reality was setting in.

"What about Manhattan?" Cecily asked.

"It's hitting me. All of sudden . . . just . . . do you have any idea what you're . . . ?" He broke off then, shaking his head.

No, she didn't. "What did he mean? How did he know my brother? And pirozhkis? What the hell was that about? And the razor thing."

Shane stared out the windshield. "The razor thing was his way of saying he's been shadowing us. Which I already knew since he's been trailing behind since I picked you up in Minneapolis."

Too shocked to answer for a moment, Cecily sat frozen next to Shane as they continued to drive in silence. "Are you serious? Why is this happening?"

Shane gave her a look. "Ask Dex. You're going to have to ask Dex about a lot of things."

"I don't understand," Cecily said.

Shane shook his head, and then it was like he just exploded. "*Wake up*, Cecily. Why do you think it is that you know me better after two days than after a year or whatever with your ex?"

Cold fear moved down Cecily's spine. "You're different," she said.

"You bet I am," Shane said. "I'm not a Russian spy who lied to you about everything from where I went to school to what I like to eat."

"What?" she blurted, absolutely reeling.

Shane looked up at the sky through the sunroof. "Dex will fill you in at the Armory. I think I'm done throwing bombshells today. I think I'm just . . . *done*."

Cecily couldn't breathe for a moment. "James isn't Russian."

"Yeah, he is," Shane said dully. "He's a Russian spy who's been using you over the past year in a long-tail attempt to get information about Dex and his team. My team. The Hudson Kings. Which just so happens to be working on a contract to uncover Russian sleeper agents in New York City. That guy we just smoked is probably someone James hired to follow you."

"James has never even met Dex!" As soon as she said it, though, it clicked. James constantly asking questions about her brother. What was he like? What did he do for a living? How was his work going? Had she talked to him recently . . . the times she caught him looking at her e-mail and she thought he was worried about her cheating . . .

"That's gotta be on purpose. He took you to Minneapolis to isolate you, I'm sure. Probably couldn't take a chance that Dex might recognize his picture in a file somewhere, although I'm sure he makes a point of changing up his appearance."

"But everything I know about the Hudson Kings and Dex's work, I just learned on the road with you."

"James doesn't know that. And for all he knows, still, you're just a girl going to stay with her brother after a bad relationship. You're not useless to him yet. Not by a long shot."

Cecily watched Shane's face. "How long have you known this?"

He went silent.

"Shane!"

"I didn't know how it was going to be with us." He stared doggedly ahead.

"That's it? By the way, Cecily, your boyfriend James was a fake? He was a *Russian spy*? And I'm only now just telling you?" It was all starting to hit her. The crazy was all starting to hit her now. From the moment she'd gotten into Shane's car, it was like she'd entered another world. Five-star hotels and illegal deals in seedy gyms, car chases and having the best orgasm of her life in an alley with thousands of dollars under her feet . . . *this is not real life*. It was a dream that sounded a little too much like it could easily turn into a nightmare.

"Like I said. I didn't know we were gonna . . . that we . . . *damn.*" He tried again, in the same gravelly voice: "You're gonna be tough to forget."

Cecily stared at him in disbelief, trying to decide how she felt about the bombshell, as he called it. Trying to decide, as they sped toward Dex and the end of her time with Shane, how she felt about all of it. Him.

"Tough to forget" was one hell of an understatement, at least on her side. The whole affair was about to end before it had even begun, but Cecily felt like she was tied in knots. *Not even an "affair." A nonaffair. A nonevent. He's right. There is no "we." We fooled around in an alley. He didn't even get off. I'm an idiot for being even remotely sad about this.*

He's going to pull up to Dex's apartment, pop the trunk, drop my suitcase at my feet, and leave me there. He won't look sad. He probably won't be sad. *And then he'll tuck himself back into the cocoon of his car, drive off to more interesting adventures that require duct tape and secret fancy dress pants.*

Oh, god. Cecily now knew exactly how she felt. Violated by James. Scared that she'd gotten mixed up in something bad that she didn't understand. Spooked by the idea that James wasn't going away. Pissed that Dex and Shane had kept such a big secret from her. And devastated by the realization that Shane *was* going away.

They drove in silence for ages, the pastoral mountains of Pennsylvania finally giving way to New Jersey's concrete hodgepodge of buildings, punctuated only rarely by the vintage charm of white-lettered signage touting businesses shuttered decades ago.

At last, the Lincoln Tunnel loomed up ahead. Shane cracked his neck. Cecily's heart raced. She recognized the facade, with its huge arches framing inky passageways, from driving in as a tourist here once before, years earlier. When they finally passed through the tunnel, the traffic closed in on them even more. Soon, they were sitting in grid-locked traffic in the middle of Manhattan.

Shane dialed his cell phone and spoke: "Incoming. Say five minutes, if my shortcut's not blocked. Give Dex the heads-up, yeah?" Then a terse "Thanks," and the phone went back into its little charger well.

"Well, Cecily," Shane said in near monotone. "Welcome to New York. Welcome to your new life. I hope you find what you're looking for."

Cecily stared at Shane's profile. "I hope you do too, Shane."

His head whipped around. "Didn't know I was looking for something," he said.

I know, Cecily thought. *I know.*

CHAPTER 12

The Armory was one of several built over the course of Manhattan's history. A place for living, training, strategizing, and storing weapons and equipment, the one used by the Hudson Kings was as true to form in its current incarnation as it had been during the city's earliest days.

A few of the city's armories were public tourist attractions, event spaces even. Some of them had been turned over to private buyers and had been lost over time to history. Even if you managed to wind your way to the proper location and got past the massive brick walls shielding Rothgar's complex from sight, you'd still probably think you were looking at crumbling history and some nondescript warehousing unless you had the right map. Get past the barbed wire, security cameras, and camouflage, and you had something very different.

Shane's favorite part was the thirty-thousand-square-foot garage that had been a drill hall in the 1800s courtesy of President Lincoln's request for troops during the Civil War. Now it housed the Hudson Kings' vast collection of personal cars, trucks, and motorcycles in addition to a stable of mission-oriented ex-military vans, armored transports, and the odd piece of artillery or bomb squad equipment.

How Roth ended up owning this much Manhattan real estate was a question Shane hadn't asked; whatever the case, it was Roth's, and he'd opened it up to the men who formed the Hudson Kings, so Shane had a room here. It was the one place in this world, besides the interior of his car, where he felt comfortable.

And the only thing Roth had asked of the circle of men who knew the entry codes was that they keep the location on a need-to-know basis and give to the team the same balls-to-the-wall loyalty that they got.

Shane swung the car through a tunnel made out of glass and steel and came out the other side into a courtyard that still held what was obviously part of the original structure; the heart of the Armory looked like a castle. A massive brick castle.

"Dex lives here?" Cecily asked doubtfully. "I don't know whether to hug him or hit him. Same goes for you."

Before Shane could answer, Dex appeared at the top of the front steps, brace on his leg and cane in his hand. "Oh, my god, I'm definitely going to hug him first." Cecily squealed and waved and jumped out of the car as soon as it came to a stop. She raced up the steps like a bolt of energy, the gold in her hair glinting in the sun. She tackled Dex on the landing, and Shane smiled in spite of himself as she nearly took her brother down.

Watching the show, he wondered how in the hell he even gave a shit about what she did to Dex. All of Cecily's goodness was literally walking away from him, being aimed at someone else, and it burned. He had no idea how the woman had gotten under his skin in such a short time. He half wished he could go back to the way he'd been before he met her, but he wasn't willing to give up laughing with her, kissing her . . .

All the more reason to be glad she wasn't his anymore. *Shane,* he thought, shaking his head, *you crossed more than one line on this trip.*

"Hey, Shane!" Just ahead of where Shane parked, Nick was hanging out in the front courtyard watching Chase operate a drone. The man raised a hand and gave a wave, that solid-gold old-school watch of his shining brighter than Cecily's hair. Nick's screwed-up freelance gig must still have been plaguing him, because the man usually breezed in for team meetings and right back out again without so much as tweaking the polish on his expensive brogues.

"Money in the back?" Nick asked.

"Yep," Shane answered. "It's unlocked. Same percentages. Thanks."

"Good to see you," Nick said. The financier shook Shane's hand like he always did—like they were sealing a million-dollar deal—and headed for the BMW.

Chase steered the drone carefully through a maze of tree branches, lowered it to the ground in front of Shane's feet, and then took a small pad of paper from his pocket and penciled a note. Along with Shane, the guy was a go-to floater and team generalist, but his specialty was building whatever it was you could dream up. Most people didn't guess that behind the trickster smile, beat-up cowboy boots, moth-eaten Super Bowl T-shirt, and jeans so worn you could see the outline of his cell phone straight through the pocket was a serious-ass engineer.

"Yo." Chase bumped fists. "Welcome back, man."

From the top of the stairs, Cecily shrieked with delight as she roughhoused with her brother. Dex'd picked her up with his free arm and was throwing her over his shoulder. She was laughing her ass off.

Shane pulled Cecily's suitcase from his trunk and set it down, mesmerized by the sound.

"Put me down," Cecily screamed joyfully, beating on Dex's back. Shane watched her fuss over Dex's leg and point to the cane. And then she pointed to his stomach. Her brother gestured for her to hit him. She did and then shook out her "hurt" fist in mock pain, laughing, always laughing. Dex rolled his eyes at her for the benefit of the guys watching, but he was pleased.

Dex *should* be pleased. Cecily was just lit up with joy.

"Long drive?" Chase said with a grin, following Shane's gaze.

Shane ignored him. Nick walked up with the money bags and set them against the tree trunk next to the drone gear, chuckling. "His mind is on short and sweet."

Rothgar came out on the stairs, the corner of his mouth tipping up at the siblings as he breezed by them. Roth had maybe ten years on Shane, but the big man was fucking built like a ring fighter and still looked like he'd be a formidable competitor against any one of the Hudson Kings. He was wearing what the team liked to call his "office uniform": boots under dark jeans and a dress shirt that he said was to remind him that even if the Armory was his home, he was always on the job. Of course, sharp as he made an effort to look, the salt-and-pepper in the scruff on Rothgar's cut jaw made it difficult to resist the urge to tell a grandpa joke during team meals. And that said, far as Shane could tell, the guy's looks fell squarely into the asset category when it came to women. Shane had seen him work more than one bar like a magnet without even trying.

"One piece," Roth said gruffly. "Always a plus. You already got some plans we've got to work around, or can I count on you for an indefinite period of time?"

"I'll stick around," Shane said, turning away from the sight of Cecily tucking her hair behind her ears. "Gonna get the car to the garage for a tune-up."

"I'll get a meeting together," Roth said, picking up Cecily's bag and heading back up the stairs.

Shane turned and headed back to the car, feeling strangely empty. He got back into his car and shut the door, but the silence wasn't a relief, not when he could still see Cecily smiling on the steps.

You had your chance.

Dex looked over and waved, mouthing "Thank you" and flashing a hand signal that said they'd talk later.

Shane raised his chin by way of an answer, then turned the key and stared unseeing at the dashboard computer. After a moment, he touched the gas and pulled away only to have to swerve very suddenly to one side as Cecily hurtled toward his car. The laughter was gone; she just looked worried. Shane lowered the window. "What's up, sweetling?"

"You've got to get out of the car!" Her eyes were huge.

"What—"

"Get out of the car, Shane!"

Shane threw the car in park and got out, his eyes automatically searching for whatever threat had her all hopped up.

Nothing. He quirked an eyebrow.

Cecily launched herself into his arms so hard he fell back with her against the car door. His face nearly smothered in a pile of orange-scented hair, her neck warm, her body fitting perfectly under his hands. He watched Dex, still standing on the steps but now vacillating between disapproving and confused, and Chase and Nick letting the drone get tangled in tree branches as they continued to watch the show with extreme amusement.

Shane gave himself a moment to breathe in her scent, enjoy her warmth, the feel of her body one last time under his fingers, and then he gently detached her.

She stood there, eyes still like saucers, a million emotions swimming around in there like always. "I . . . we didn't get to say good-bye."

He waited. That was apparently it. "I'm not leaving, I'm parking. I live here."

"What?"

"When I'm off the road, I live here."

Cecily blinked, clearly trying to process. "Oh. You and Dex both live here."

"Yeah."

"And those other extremely huge, super-hot guys. All here?"

"Yeah."

"Are they Flynn and Rothgar?"

"No. That's Chase and Nick."

Cecily exhaled slowly, a frown creasing her brow. "So there are more extremely huge, super-hot guys inside named things like Flynn and Rothgar, who explode things and plan 'missions,' who also live with you here."

"You okay?" Shane asked, not inclined to opine about anybody's definition of "super-hot."

"I've got a lot to process. Everything you told me . . . and all the things you didn't. I think my normal just got more abnormal," Cecily said.

"I'll take that as a yes, you're okay." Shane got back into the car.

Cecily stared up the stairs at her brother. Then over at Chase and Nick, who were having way too good a time watching her show. And then back at Shane.

"Kid."

"Uh-huh?" Cecily managed.

"You're leaning on the window."

With a nervous titter, Cecily stepped away from the car.

Shane raised the window and put the car in gear, and only after he'd gone past the far side of the Armory and headed into the garage did he start laughing.

CHAPTER 13

Cecily sat cross-legged on her brother's bed, feeling spent after confessing all the details of her life over the last year with James, right up to the misunderstanding at Shane's pickup and some—though not all—of the details of the road trip.

Dex was resting in bed, a laptop at one side and his leg propped up; the recent surgery meant he was still a little messed up. And he didn't look happy.

A look of guilt washed clear across Dex's features. "As soon as I knew who James was, as soon as we put the pieces together, I called you and told you to go, and I called Shane and told him to go get you. I am so sorry, Cece. I am so sorry that me being part of the Hudson Kings got you into trouble. If I'd had the slightest idea . . ." He swallowed hard, and Cecily touched the side of her head to his.

"I know you never meant for me to be in any sort of danger," she said.

She could feel him nod. "It's that, but also . . . you know it's not *just* that," Dex said. He looked at her with worried eyes.

Cecily's cheeks burned. "I hate it when you look at me like that. I *know*. Look, I admit that it was going downhill fast, and I should have left sooner, before you called, but that was the only time he ever hit me. Right after I told him I wanted to go see you and get some space. Really. I'm better than that, Dex. I *know*. I'm so embarrassed."

It was worse than embarrassed, but she couldn't say it. That James was a Russian spy and neither an all-American boy nor a New York banker doing business in Minneapolis was so crazy it was hard to believe. But when she finally had a moment to herself after arriving at the Armory, it started to sink in. The violation of it all. She couldn't tell her brother that it made her sick to think of sleeping with James. That it made her sick to think of the time she put into building the two of them a beautiful life. And she certainly couldn't tell him that part of what made her relationship with James seem so obscene and so very hollow was meeting Shane and finding out how deep you could really get with a man, even in such a short time.

"Anyway," Cecily said. "*I'm* sorry I lied to you all those times, making excuses for him and pretending everything was okay. But I guess," she added pointedly, "we've been lying to each other for a while now."

Dex took a deep breath.

"You going to tell me what this place is, who all these guys are, what you're all doing, and if there's a possibility you could either, oh, I dunno, get arrested or die doing it? Because, I swear to god, I don't want to lose you," Cecily said.

"Didn't Shane tell you?" Dex asked.

"He told me some—probably as little as possible."

"I don't blame him," he muttered.

"You knew Shane before he was with the Hudson Kings, right?" Cecily asked.

Dex nodded. "Our paths crossed a couple of times. That used to happen with more than one guy currently on the team. I'd get hired for some *Ocean's Eleven* gig, or whatever, and get matched with somebody I'd worked with before. You start to see what a man is made of, you know? That's how I met Shane. I've been talking in his ear or listening in on his moves for a long while now. He told Roth about me, Roth hired me freelance on a couple of jobs, watched me operate, liked what he saw, and invited me into the fold."

Cecily leaned back on Dex's pillow. "Dex," she said quietly. "I thought you were just a computer programmer. You know, the guy who's going to keep the corporate website from going offline, or whatever."

Dex stared down at his hands. "You know how Mom was constantly moving us from city to city and then disappearing for a week at a time?"

How could Cecily forget?

"We'd go to the library after school because we didn't want to go sit in whatever shitty motel room she'd paid for. Unlike you, you *know* I wasn't always doing my homework. I was going online, trying stuff out, meeting people. Online I didn't have to look like the guy whose head you were going to shove in the toilet," Dex said.

"You sure don't look like one now."

"Well, if you look around at the other guys here, you'll see I had some incentive not to be the odd man out. Growing up, that's all it was, being the scrawny nerdy new kid. The nerdy came in handy. The scrawny I could do something about. And here I'm not the odd man out. And I've got friends I can count on. Brothers."

"Who are these people, Dex?"

He shrugged. "Guys like Chase, jack-of-all-trades, can fit in anywhere. He calls himself a construction worker, but that doesn't even begin to describe the things he can build. Nick knows how to get around inside the New York money business and can launder better than the fucking Clorox Company. Geo . . . well, shit. I can't tell you about Geo, and there are a couple of our other guys in the shadows who've made a decision not to surface, so they're off record. Flynn . . . explosives and custom devices. He's got the messed up face to prove it. Romeo . . ." Dex chuckled. "Romeo is a master of disguise and a smooth talker. His skills are not to be underestimated. Nothing I really want to get into with my sister. And you know about Shane."

"Not that much," she said wryly.

Dex's forehead creased. "The trip was okay, right? I mean, I know Shane's . . . different. But it was fine, right?"

"Don't look so worried," Cecily said. "It was obviously embarrassing, because he knew what happened to me. And it was weird to do a road trip with a complete stranger, but then he stopped being a complete stranger, and it was really fun."

Dex couldn't seem to process that statement. "Shane was *fun.*"

The suspicious look on his face was the same one he'd sported after Cecily jogged back up the Armory steps after throwing herself in Shane's arms. Well, she'd thought he was leaving. She wanted him to know she appreciated what he'd done. How was she to know he wasn't going anywhere? "Yeah. That's what I said," she said.

"Broody, don't-breath-in-my-space, don't-touch-anything-in-my-car Shane was . . . *fun*? I mean, Shane is cool. He gets plenty of ladies. Plays the strong, silent type. He's a good wingman."

Ugh.

"But Shane . . . *fun*? That's not really a Shane keyword."

"Yes, you've made that very clear. But he was. At times."

"I think my meds are off," Dex muttered. "I'm not hearing you right."

She studied his new look, which was basically his old look except that he was fit and muscular and had lost the never-see-the-sun pallor she remembered. Which meant that apparently he was eating well, working out like a fiend, and periodically leaving his man cave. He looked *amazing*, like a geek gone wild, if you didn't count the leg. "When was the surgery again, Bro?"

"Uh, last week," he said vaguely. "Hurt like a mofo."

She reached for a bottle of aspirin, and her brother grabbed her wrist so suddenly she gasped, suddenly back in Minneapolis, suddenly in James's crosshairs. She leaped off the bed.

"Shit, Cece, sorry!" He stared at her. "Was it like *that*?"

"No! I mean, yes, but no! Not . . . just in the last couple of weeks. He was a little . . . rough."

Dex's whole body tensed. "Rough?"

Cecily suddenly realized that the new model of Dex could probably take James in a fight. A thought that made her both proud and terrified. "Not like what you're thinking. Not that bad. Okay, let's both calm down." She inhaled and exhaled a yoga breath that was supposed to make everything better but didn't usually make a difference. "I'm just on edge. All of this"—she waved her fingers in the air, indicating the Armory—"plus leaving James. It's just a lot, you know?"

He nodded, still studying her face. "You'll get used to it here."

"I wasn't planning on staying. I've got plans. And I guess I thought . . . I mean, we never talked about it, but I thought maybe you'd like to get an apartment with me. It would be fun."

"Cecily, until we figure this out, you've got to stay close . . . or at least with friendlies."

When had her brother started sounding like a TV show? "Friendlies?" Cecily asked, trying not to huff. "I was talking about you and me."

"If you want an apartment, ask Missy to hook you up," Dex said. "Rothgar's cleared a girl who's got a place we sometimes use. I'm making good money here. I can spot you for some rent and whatever you want to do to get on your feet. Lord knows you pulled enough coffee drinks in high school to pay for my shit."

Cecily blinked. "Yeah. Allison, right? Shane mentioned her. He also mentioned her missing brother. Look, I get the appeal. Doing this stuff, it's like living in a video game. Which is one of the reasons I bet it really appeals to you, but I'm not sure it's good for you."

A pissed look flashed across his face. "What do you mean? This is the best thing that ever happened to me. You know how shitty it was." He gestured to his body. "You know what I was."

Dex had been bullied, had the crap beaten out of him regularly, even had a couple of serious scars from locker room grates and garbage can edges. It was awesome he'd remade his life, remade his body to be strong, but something about him was off.

"I know, big brother. I'm not judging. But when we talked about our future, it was always you and me looking out for each other. Living a normal, happy life. You have an option."

A chime sounded. Dex looked over at the computer screen, read something, typed in something that resulted in the printer on his bureau turning on, and said, "Listen. Rothgar wants to go over some stuff. I've gotta get going." He added under his breath, "Do *not* want to forget anything."

Cecily tried not to let her disappointment show. "I thought you and I could start fresh together."

"I don't think you get it; I already started fresh." Dex pushed off the bed and crossed to a bureau where he apparently didn't actually keep any clothes. Cecily could see that the drawer he pulled open contained a slew of computer parts, bits of metal pages from notebooks covered in diagrams. It was all organized on plastic, compartmentalized trays, where the underwear was supposed to be separated from the socks. The printer was spitting out some kind of a list.

Cecily watched his face while biting her nails as he poked through the parts and put some of them into a gym bag. Time stretched out, and he seemed to forget she was there.

On the one hand, her brother looked good; his body was buff. He had a confidence about him that she didn't remember. It was weird seeing her brother have his shit together so well, look so competent. On the other hand, his clothes were disheveled, he was way touchy, and he winced every time he put too much pressure on his bad knee. "With as much as you know about computers, you could get a really great job in Manhattan."

"I have a really great job in Manhattan," he said, checking the contents of his kit against his list. "And I'm attempting to do it."

"One that doesn't cause you to get shot in the knee," Cecily said.

He whipped around. "Who told you that?"

Dread filled Cecily's bloodstream. "A week ago, I wouldn't have guessed you were bullshitting me about a weightlifting accident. But it's been quite a week."

"Don't start."

"Shane told me about Missy and Allison. About their brothers going missing. They're probably dead. I mean, what else could it be?"

Dex's eyes went soft. "Is that what this is really about? You think something is going to happen to me?"

A week ago, she wouldn't have been worried about anything close to what he was suggesting. But after everything she'd been through with Shane and everything both of them had told her about the team, danger wasn't just theoretical anymore. It was real. "I'm not trying to get you to turn your back on this family that, it sounds like, all of you have built. But . . ." She had to speak in a hushed voice to avoid having her voice actually crack. "It sounds like those boys left behind people who loved them."

Dex took Cecily's hand and gave it a squeeze. "You don't know all the facts, Sis. You don't know how the Hudson Kings work, what we do, how we do it."

She was losing this fight. She'd had some ridiculous fantasy of coming to New York and picking up Dex and starting their lives over, and now he'd already gone and done that—with a new family that appeared to eat danger for breakfast. Cecily panicked, blurting, "I *do* know. Shane took me on a job on the way over."

Dex pushed back from his work so hard that computer parts sprayed all over the floor. "What did you say?"

Cecily stared at her brother, tongue-tied by the venom in his voice. "That was an exaggeration. He didn't want me to get involved, but I sort of . . ."

"You sort of *what?*"

"Um, walked into the situation. Listen, I shouldn't have said anything." Dex's expression had turned to stone. *Oh, god. Oh, god. I really should* not *have said that.*

"*He took you on a job* and then you got *involved* in the *situation?* Tell me what happened and don't lie to me."

"Dex," she said gently. "I—"

"Don't lie to me!"

"Don't yell at me," she ground out, feeling her blood race just like it did when James started down that path. "Thank you. Thank you for helping me when I needed it. Thank you for sending Shane to me. But I don't *have* to explain anything to you. If you have a problem with Shane—which you shouldn't, because he was . . ." *Ack. Digging a hole much? Can't say he was a perfect gentleman. Can't say he never did anything unsafe.* In a voice suddenly clogged with emotions, Cecily said, "He was there when I needed him." *In every way.* "You have no right to shout at *me* about lying, Mr. Oh-did-I-forget-to-mention-your-boyfriend-is-a-spy-and-I'm-a-mercenary-Hudson-Kings-hacker-man-person!"

Dex looked pretty close to losing his mind.

"You're really pissed," Cecily said nervously.

"Yup. But not at you."

"Don't be pissed at Shane."

There was a long silence. "Cece," Dex said in a low voice. "He's not for you. You know that. Maybe he doesn't. Do I need to have a conversation with him?"

"And say what? Are you going to pass him a note during a meeting telling him I have a crush on him? Do *not* humiliate me like that!"

Dex sat heavily down in his chair, his face a mix of disbelief and misery. "*You* have a *crush* on *Shane?*"

"What?" *Argh!* "No! I was assuming that *you* assumed that. Can we end this conversation?"

"Absolutely," Dex said grimly.

"So, you won't say something stupid to Shane?"

"I won't say anything *stupid*."

Cecily curled her hands into fists. If she'd been a cartoon, she'd have heat lines above her head.

"You don't need to protect him, Sis," Dex said, obviously working hard on self-control. "You've been down that path way too recently."

"Ugh. Are you talking about James?"

"It's not like it was that long ago. You know I'm right. You need to watch yourself. Give yourself time to heal. Listen, I need to get to that meeting. You want me to take you back to—"

"No, I can find it!" It was only because Dex was right that Cecily got so mad. Dex rolled his eyes, hobbled over, and held open the door while she flounced under his arm and down the hall.

She lost her way pretty fast in the Armory's maze of corridors and pulled on random doors for a while.

Note to self: stock up on water, trail mix—and find out where all the bathrooms are.

After about fifteen more minutes of wandering, to the point where she couldn't even have returned to Dex's room if she'd wanted to, Cecily stopped below a video camera mounted above one of the doorframes and waved both arms like a complete and utter idiot.

It took another five minutes for someone to show up. Cecily's heart started beating wildly as a door at the far end of the hall opened up and a man walked through. Her body had obviously wanted it to be Shane. Based on visuals alone, at least it was the next best thing. Shane didn't have this man's beauty, but somehow Cecily preferred Shane's rougher edges to this man's smooth perfection.

"Hi," the man said in a deep, rich voice. "I'm Nick."

Oh, come on. They can't seriously all look like heaven and sound like sin. Is that a requirement for membership?

This one was dressed like James . . . times half a million dollars . . . but there was at least one significant difference. He. Was. Huge.

"Extremely huge, super-hot," Cecily blurted. Without asking him if she could check the label in his pants—which did hold a certain amount of appeal—it was obvious he had expensive tastes. Dex had described Nick as the money guy; he definitely knew how to spend.

Dress pants and a crisp white dress shirt with a hint of light-gray pinstripe. A suit coat slung over one shoulder. No tie, so the collar was open around the neck, showing off some serious bone structure and a delicious swath of flesh. A massive gold watch circled the cords of his wrist. His hair was much shorter than Shane's, although a certain amount of neglect had left a longer piece on top. It was this piece that he swept off his face as his lips curled in a smile. "You looked like you needed a hand," he said.

"This?" Cecily asked, waving her arms in the air even more ridiculously than before. "Yeah, that would be me needing help. I'm definitely lost. I've learned an important lesson about living in an armory. If you're going to flounce out of a room, you'd better know where you're going."

"Not a bad mantra for life," Nick said, holding out his arm.

Cecily took it with a smile. "Can you get me to Missy's?"

Nick paused. "Not Shane's?"

Cecily looked up at him with narrowed eyes. "You trying to make trouble?"

"Make it? I think you brought it with you," Nick said, holding the door open at the end of the hall and gesturing to the left.

"You've got the wrong idea," Cecily said. "I'm sure you know about me, but I have to tell you I am really not about drama. The opposite."

Nick turned them to the right this time and after a minute said, "Shane looks more relaxed than I've seen him in years."

"That's Shane relaxed?"

Nick laughed.

"Sorry to say that has nothing to do with me. I think I made him a little crazy," Cecily said.

"That too," Nick said, finally stopping in front of a door that had been painted to look like a cottage entrance, complete with grass and flowerpots. He knocked then, crossed his arms over his chest, and stared down at Cecily. "Known him for a while. Saw you two when he brought you in. Talked to him briefly. Think you threw him for a loop. Think he likes it. You messing with our guy or what?"

"I'm really not the messing-with type," Cecily said, a little bewildered.

A redhead in her twenties wearing a grease monkey jumpsuit and black Nike high-tops finally, blessedly opened the door.

Missy smiled a huge, welcoming, uber-extroverted smile. Nothing about her appeared to find it strange that a woman she'd never met before was appearing on her doorstep, expecting to move in.

It was with some shyness that Cecily, still fatigued at being helped by so many people who never seemed to expect anything in return, held out her hand and said, "Hi, I'm Cecily Keegan, Dex's sister, and I was told—"

"Cool! You're here. Holy shit, you totally look like Dex! Except you're a supercute female!" She stopped abruptly and looked at Nick. "Why the escort? Something going down?"

"Just looking out for Shane," he said, his mouth turned up in a wicked grin.

Missy leaned forward like she was going to inhale a delicious piece of gossip. "Shane needs looking out for?" she asked reverently. "Do tell."

"He thinks I'm messing with Shane," Cecily mumbled. *I'm usually the messed-with.*

Nick shrugged innocently.

Missy cocked an eyebrow. "Are you messing with Shane?" she asked Cecily.

"No, I'm not," Cecily said. *But I'd like to be* messing around *with Shane.* She couldn't shake the regret that their time together was at an end. Shane's responsibility for anything to do with Cecily was at an end, and he'd been almost eager to drive away from her. Dex had already logged his stamp of disapproval. It was definitely over, and nobody was messing with or around anybody. Nick and Missy seemed to be having so much fun joking around about it they missed Cecily's gloomy sigh.

"Oh. Right, then I guess we have it." Missy faux whispered in Cecily's ear, "I like to stay in the know."

"That could have been way more fun, Missy," Nick groused.

She did not seem concerned. "Anything else, Nick? 'Cause we've got that meeting, and I know you need to refresh your makeup or something."

Nick scowled down at Missy. "Watch your step."

"I always do," she answered sweetly, pulling Cecily inside and slamming the door behind them.

CHAPTER 14

It seemed a little odd that in a place this big, Cecily would have to share a room, but she wasn't about to question the decision. *You get too many unusual things together, and maybe they stop seeming so unusual.*

If that was really true, Cecily was having the most normal day of her life.

Besides, Missy's room was fabulous. It was a huge space, with lavender curtains and big, bright windows overlooking a patio space landscaped with orange-and-yellow striped tulips. The closet door was open, and Cecily caught a glimpse of several other jumpsuits on hangers, a pair of Missy-size shitkicker boots on the closet floor and one royal-blue party dress encased in a plastic garment bag along with a pair of pumps with kitten heels dyed the same color and embroidered with flowers. What appeared to be a crossbow was perched in one corner, and some sort of samurai sword hung on the wall. Before Shane, Cecily might have assumed they were props—fakes—but, oh, what a difference a simple little road trip with a mercenary could make.

"I'm guessing you have good hand-eye coordination," Cecily said.

"Excellent," Missy replied.

A gallery wall on the right was covered with photos, a mix of tacked-on snapshots and mounted photos in mismatched frames. Two long shelves were nailed into the wall above a one-tier bookshelf. The first shelf held a massive row of cigarettes and cigars, every single one a different brand. The second shelf was full of repurposed pharmacy bottles, each one carefully labeled with a code number instead of a name, holding just a few tablets or a small amount of liquid. There were also tiny boxes full of powders and herbs—Chinese medicine?

The bookshelf anchoring the bottom of the wall was packed with liquor, organized into an artistic display by color rather than kind, most of the bottles local artisanal brands with labels like Brooklyn Distillery covered in the spidery black ink of limited-edition production numbers.

On the other side of the room was clearly Missy's queen-size bed, with a generous amount of space separating it from a twin-size bed, beside which stood Cecily's suitcase. At one point she'd apparently purchased for herself one of those bed-in-a-bag sets in purple watercolors. The girlie effect was slightly marred by the addition of a square of wooly brown that was either a horse cover or a military blanket with some stenciled numbers and letters. It was folded carefully in half atop the crisply made bed.

The twin was made up with plain beige sheets, the kind of sheets you keep around as spares when you live in a place with lots of guys who probably don't want to sleep in a bed full of purple flowers. On top of the sheets sat a Bankers Box.

"Are you sure you don't want to stick me somewhere else and keep your privacy?" Cecily asked.

Missy shrugged. "I'm the only girl for miles; I've been looking forward to this. Besides, it'll make Dex feel better."

"I don't think anybody could get past security here," Cecily said. "I'm about as safe as I've ever been."

"Now that you're inside the Armory, you've got nothing to worry about," Missy said. "But as you've figured out, it's easy to get lost. Easier to show you the ropes if you're here with me." She paused and then said, "You know about James now. Are you worried you're not safe?"

Cecily hadn't had enough time with the new information to process everything she was feeling, but she didn't feel unsafe. Not here, not now. Not behind these walls. "Yes and no. I hope I never hear from him again. And given how many times he told me he could do better, it's a reasonable hope that I won't." She didn't mention how, when James got really angry, he'd make crazy threats. But that was before he knew she knew about him. Before she knew he was a Russian spy hoping to get info through her about Dex and the Hudson Kings, she thought he was just a possessive boyfriend. He didn't know that she knew more. He didn't know that she was at the Armory. He didn't know that Dex and his friends had put all the pieces together. God, this was insane. The more distance she put between herself and James, the more she realized how little substance their relationship had ever had.

Missy nodded and started unpacking the box atop the spare bed. "Here's your new phone. Some toiletries, just in case. A pair of unused but gently washed pj's I got for Christmas last year from one of the guys, who apparently thinks every human being is at least five six and that I'm the equivalent of a thirteen-year-old boy." She sighed and muttered, "Story of my life. If any of these guys ever bothered to try and take my clothes off, they'd know better."

Cecily laughed and picked up the flannel pajamas. Little monkeys. Little monkeys all wearing different hats. "These are really, *really* bad," she said. "Particularly as a present from a hot guy."

Missy's smile lit up her face. "You *so* get me." She stuck out her hand. "Welcome to the Armory, Cecily Keegan!"

Cecily shook Missy's hand. Things were definitely looking up. She'd still see Shane here at the Armory. She could look after her brother. She had a new friend.

"Oh, shit," Missy said in mock horror. "Don't cry on me. I don't know what to do with that." She paused and then added, "Which might have something to do with why I've got thirteen-year-old-boy pajamas."

Cecily kept her warm-happy to herself and turned on the phone. "Already charged. You think of everything."

Missy smiled. "Of course. Everything's already been transferred. You're good to go."

"Thanks." Cecily looked at the voice mail list and her blood temperature dropped a couple of degrees. James was listed over and over and over. He'd been calling her all this time—even though he had to figure she wasn't getting the messages yet because he'd disabled her phone himself. Thinking of James at that level of desperation made Cecily queasy.

Missy was studying her face. "I'll make you a drink. You put it on speakerphone, and we'll listen together," she said. "What's your poison?"

"Is it all hard liquor? That's a little intense for day," Cecily said.

Missy looked over her shoulder. "Whatever you want."

"Red wine? Merlot, if you have it?"

"I have everything." Missy pulled a bottle from a closet Cecily had assumed held clothes. Of course, nobody needed as many closets as Missy had for clothes. They settled in on the couch set up in the middle of the room on an area rug with a small coffee table, which gave the effect of a comfortable lounge. Cecily pushed "Play" for each message left on her phone since the day she'd met Shane, and they listened together while Cecily drank wine and Missy sipped something from a shot glass that smelled hard-core strong.

When the messages ended, Cecily took back her phone, her cheeks flaming and her heart beating in all the wrong ways. The messages were obviously all made at a time when he still thought he had a chance to get her back, before she learned the truth. Listening to his lies now, the false charm in his voice was chilling.

"Well," Missy said. "Several recurring themes. There's 'I love you, I adore you, I'm sorry, I suck,' and then there's 'I'm working on myself, I'm fixing myself, I'll do better, come back . . .'" Missy paused and looked up at Cecily for a minute, like she was taking her pulse, and then finished with "And then there's 'I'll come find you, we'll talk, don't leave me, you can't leave me.' He sounds . . . persistent."

"He knows Dex lives in New York. He doesn't like to lose. Oh, god. So many times I wondered if I should break up with him, but I never did. I think I was waiting for him to do it, and then I couldn't wait anymore. I made myself such an easy mark," Cecily said, wishing she could close her eyes and make this all go away, wishing she hadn't been so stupid, hadn't been so superficial. The more she had time to think about it, the more surprised she was by how easily James had taken her for a ride, and how easily she'd bought what he was selling.

Now, safe in the Armory with an increasing amount of distance between her new life and the one she'd shared with James, Cecily started worrying more than ever. She'd been naïve to think she could just walk away from a personality like that. And now she knew he also had an agenda. If he knew she'd discovered the truth, would he leave it at that? Or would he try even harder? The possibility that she was still on his radar . . . might stay on his radar indefinitely . . .

She covered her mouth with trembling fingertips, walking backward until her legs hit the bed, and then she sat down and took a gulp of wine. "Thank god he doesn't know where I am."

"We'll get him before he gets you," Missy said, getting up and moving one of the bottles so that the colors coordinated better.

Cecily stared at her. The girl was serious. How was this all happening? How did Dex find these people? "My brother never started a fight in his life," Cecily said with a nervous laugh.

Missy raised an eyebrow. "I think we might know different versions of your brother. Besides, it's not just Dex alone. He's got a pack of brothers who'd be happy to throw punches at his side on your behalf."

"I just got here!" Cecily said, unsure whether she was more unsettled by the idea of her couch potato brother turned into a fighting machine or by the idea that men she didn't know would go after James on her behalf.

Missy echoed her thoughts when she said, "That's just what we do. We're in it together, Cecily. Get used to it. It's one of the things I love best about being here. Knowing that there's a family that's going to look out for me as much as I'm going to look out for them."

Cecily wanted to ask Missy about *her* brother, but she didn't want to give Shane's confidence away.

A knock on Missy's door killed the opportunity anyway. Since the door was already opened, a head peeked round the corner. "Heading over. You coming?"

Missy looked at the time on her phone and grimaced. "Should've been there to help set up." She stuffed the phone in her back pocket and headed for the door. "Rothgar's going to want a debrief of your time with James. And your messages. There might be some good clues. Can I set that up?"

"Anything that helps give James what he's got coming, I'm cool with," Cecily said.

"Back in a bit, then. Make yourself at home. Oh. Not the second shelf, though, right?"

Cecily smiled at Missy, and the redhead disappeared out the door. She was alone in the room.

She pulled Bun-Bun out of her purse and stuck him on the bed. Then she picked up her phone, made herself comfortable next to him, and checked her e-mail. A massive column of e-mails from James. That sick feeling in her stomach returned as she skimmed through the same variations of the phone calls. Some just said, "Please call me." As if he didn't remember he'd messed with her phone.

And then something that gave her even more pause.

A small group of e-mails that weren't from James. They weren't unread. Stuff from a college friend, a reminder to pay for something she'd bought, an inquiry about freelance opportunities. It could be anything. Something that happened accidentally while Missy was setting her up with a new phone. But Cecily couldn't shake the fear that James had been reading her e-mail while she was with Shane. And judging by the dates, he might still be doing it now.

CHAPTER 15

Five minutes before the meeting and it was already rowdy in there. Shane pushed the door open to find the other members of the Hudson Kings team—at least the ones who weren't either undercover or out of town—sprawled about the room. He was instantly reminded how glad he was he'd chosen to join the Hudson Kings instead of the Sixth Ward. It made for a little extra tension on freelance jobs whenever the two competing merc teams mixed, but Shane wouldn't trade away the men in this room—nor Rothgar for the Ward's leader, O'Neill—no matter how good those guys were.

"Bet you missed this," Nick said, giving Shane a nod and looking every inch the billionaire businessman in one of his many fine suits. He'd scored the oversize leather club chair.

Roth stood at the head of the room going over a list of something with Missy, who had started on the team as a proxy for her missing brother, Apollo, but had earned her place as a member in her own right.

The corner seat was occupied by Geo, wearing his signature combat boots and sunglasses, the latter to hide a pair of the deadliest-looking eyes Shane had ever seen.

Romeo was at the big sofa looking over a fistful of red files. He had dark moons under his eyes and was wearing a long-sleeved T-shirt with sweatpants—not his usual look.

Chase came in next and took a seat on Shane's right. "You sticking around long?"

Shane's mind moved to Cecily so fast he almost gave his own brain whiplash. If Roth needed him, he'd stay as long as that took. If Cecily needed him—hell, he'd stick around just to see her settle in safe. He knew he would. "We'll see what's on Roth's plate. But you can bet I'll be here long enough to take all your cash in Hold'em."

"That's what I like about you, Shane. Your blind optimism."

Shane snorted. "You know what I like about *you*, Chase? Your shitty poker face."

Dex appeared in the doorway, balancing awkwardly with his leg in the brace, and shot Shane a pissed look before taking a seat at the computer up front next to Roth. If Shane was hoping for any sort of thanks from his friend for taking care of Cecily, it didn't appear he was going to get anything close. *What the fuck?*

Cecily must've said something. That surprised him. She balked at the idea of Dex knowing anything about her sex life, so there was nothing to tell him. Maybe if any of what went down on the road had actually meant something, that'd be one thing, but there wasn't. They had a road trip. They fooled around a little. She was safe, and they were over before they'd ever really started. End of story. No use getting Dex riled up.

Shane sighed. He'd find him after the meeting and clear the air.

Once Flynn entered and closed the door behind him, Rothgar wasted no time. "Let's get on with it. It's been a while since we've all been in one place." He touched an index finger to his temple and then pointed it in Shane's direction. A murmur of welcomes passed around the room, giving Shane an oddly warm feeling, like maybe these guys really were brothers and maybe this really was home. *I should come home more often.*

When the room quieted, Rothgar said, "Some of you know all of the details, and all of you know some of the details, but let me catch everyone up-to-date. About one year ago, I took a contract from the US government to help uncover a cell of Russian sleeper agents. They were able to give me next to nothing as far as starting information. Members of our team have been laying the groundwork for a long time just to get some suspects, some names, some initial evidence to point us in the right direction. The break in the case came when we outed Yakov Petrenko, a.k.a. James Peterson. He's the handler for this cell—makes sure the agents get what they were promised and get what they need to continue their charade in this country. James is aware of us and, in fact, has been trying to get counterintelligence, if you will, on our team through Dex's sister, Cecily. But we don't think he knows that we know the game he's been playing; we don't think he knows he's been made."

Shane shifted in his chair, listening to Rothgar do the rundown. It should have felt like any other mission briefing, but this still felt personal. He wanted to flip the switch, go back to the man he was before Cecily, but he just couldn't think of her as simply a file detail in a case to be solved.

"If we didn't need to supply a healthy stack of evidence to the government, I'd send Geo in to take care of this shithead just for that."

Somebody went, "Ooooh," and everybody swiveled around and looked at Geo, who didn't move a muscle and showed no actual signs of life.

Rothgar continued. "But we took on a job and we're going to deliver. So, we're going to focus on building an ironclad evidence file against our first name. Low-hanging fruit, because she's not even trying to pass as something other than Russian. Anya Gorchakov. Like I said, we believe James is her handler, so we'll be able to pull evidence in on him at the same time, but we don't want to take him out of action unnecessarily, since he may be our link to other agents on the list."

That didn't sit well with Shane. He fumed for a minute, trusting Rothgar to make the right decision but hating the idea that they couldn't pull James in immediately, because he might lead them to the other agents.

"If it goes well," Rothgar said, "we might get the contract to work on the rest of the suspected ring. The government has specified we can use any means necessary, and, as you know, that either means they've tried and failed within the constraints of what they consider to be the law, or they know enough to know they should punt to freelancers immediately."

"Cold War's back," Romeo said with a grin. "Maybe this means action movies get good again."

"Not exactly," Rothgar said. "But we're part of the plan to keep it back in the eighties where it belongs. The Russians like to play the long game, get agents embedded in everyday life, put them into action against the United States years later. Our game is to weed them out before they even get a chance to work against us. We know they've already got spies hacking into election results, transportation hubs, corporate networks, and the like. And we know they've put people on the ground to build relationships and position themselves to gain access into areas of influence. The big bad isn't here, but that's because the government's hiring people like us to stop it before it grows."

Rothgar opened a bottled water and took a long draft.

"We're putting more of our own guys on the job than we probably need, going light on freelancers. Just to cross all the t's, dot the i's. It won't change your cut." He paused and crossed his arms over his chest. "That said, I also want to remind you that if you don't feel like risking—"

Somebody booed and then the whole room took it up. Roth cracked a smile and tried to speak again. A wad of crumpled paper hit him square in the chest amid an even louder roar of dissent. "Quit with the disclaimers, Roth. You've got our backs; we've got yours," Shane said when the noise quieted down. "Besides, I'm not the only one who still owes you."

Roth held up his palm. "Fine, then. This one's gonna bring in a serious chunk of change. Something nice for those of you working on nest eggs, and something nice for those of you who just want to blow it all."

Laughter rang out.

"Hey, Shane," Chase called out. "Which one are *you* now?"

Shane felt Dex's gaze swing over.

Rothgar continued. "Just don't get yourself killed. Not to be selfish, but you're not easily replaceable. I'm still in the planning mode, but I'll come to each of you with details, and then we'll do a project meeting." He looked up. "Oh, and an official welcome back to Shane." He looked over at Dex. "And welcome to Dex's sister, Cecily. Goes without saying she's off-limits."

"Maybe you should've said that a little earlier," Romeo said.

Nick raised an eyebrow. "Careful, Romeo."

Romeo blinked, all innocence. "You can downshift that look, brother. I'm not about to accelerate on Dex's sister, here, but you might have to put the brakes on someone else."

"Is there something here we need to cover?" Dex asked Shane through his teeth.

Shane shot Romeo a look of death.

"Let's break for twenty, and then we'll get to work on the specifics of the mission," Rothgar said, his voice cutting into the tension like a knife. He gave Shane an irritated look. *"What the fuck" is right,* thought Shane. He turned back to deal with Dex, but he'd already left.

When Shane stepped into the hall, Cecily was standing there listening to her brother, rubbing the palm of one hand with her thumb, her lower lip caught in her top teeth. Her forehead was wrinkled. She wasn't smiling.

Not his job or his place anymore. Shane walked on. *Nervous gestures. No light in those baby blues.* Without breaking his stride, he just wheeled around and headed back.

"But I hadn't read any e-mail since I left Minneapolis, and some were marked as read," she was saying. "Some of the ones that were from actual people and not spam."

"And you changed your password?" Dex asked.

She nodded, then caught sight of Shane. "Hi," she said softly.

"Hi. There a problem?" Shane asked.

"Got it covered," Dex said, *problem* written all over his face.

"James bugging you?" he asked Cecily.

Dex raised an eyebrow. "I said I got it covered. It's a computer thing."

"Right. Got that," Shane said evenly. "I was just asking Cecily if James was still bugging her."

"I don't know," she said. "It's weird. I think maybe he's reading my e-mail even though I know I changed my password just before I left."

Damn. That was definitely Dex's territory. "You need anything from me, you just ask," he told her. He gave Dex a nod. "I still got your back."

Dex stared at him and then looked at his sister, who looked slightly maniacal, what with her big, bright, fake smile.

Shane left in flames, itching to talk to Cecily some more, feeling the strange barrier of Dex's protection, like his chance was gone, the opportunity over.

Seemed like she didn't need him for anything. Not anymore.

In a week, job done, it will be like we'd never met. Like we never kissed. I'll start going invisible again. And I'll be relieved. I'll miss the feel of the road, the steering wheel in my hands, the power of my car under my control. And I'll disappear.

CHAPTER 16

With Dex less than receptive to clearing the air about Cecily, Shane went back to his room in the officer's quarters. He still hadn't unpacked. Just left his stuff in the middle of the floor. He didn't own much, and the place was Spartan, at best. Some of the other guys had put in the time to make their rooms a home; some of them had even combined more than one room to make a sweet pad.

Cecily would be good at that. She'd probably take one look at this place and roll up her sleeves, and the next thing he knew the tin ceiling would be polished, the walls cheerfully painted, that stuffed rabbit she'd been carrying around in her purse would be hogging the blanket, and art would suddenly color the walls.

Shane paused a moment, weighing his thoughts, waiting to feel annoyed by this imaginary impertinence of hers, waiting to feel violated. But in that moment, all he could think was that he was used to Cecily's presence next to him in the car, and the right side of his body suddenly had too much fucking space.

Knock-knock. "Shane, you in there?"

Shane opened the door, and Missy barreled in, phone in hand, index finger ready to take notes.

"Your phone's off again," Missy said. "How the hell do you do business with the phone off?"

"Not taking any jobs right now," he said. "And I'm in walking radius of anybody else who needs me."

"I don't get it. Most people can't pull themselves away from the phone. Most people sit at their boring old office jobs and think of things they don't need to do with their phone and do them just so they can sit and poke at their damn phone. You, you go around doing the most dangerous things you can think of and don't even wonder if your phone's on for backup. Anyway, I think it's brilliant you're finally home. Hope you stay for longer this time." She swiped a fingertip across the empty top of the bureau and grimaced. "Oh, jeez." Then she turned and looked around. "Do you want stuff for the fridge?"

"Bottled water would be great."

"Snacks?"

"A box of those energy bars."

"I know the ones. Booze?"

"A bottle of red," he said without thinking.

Missy raised an eyebrow, waiting for . . . clarification? She wasn't going to get any. "A bottle of red wine," she repeated, fingertip hovering. "What kind?"

It doesn't matter. Right? It doesn't matter, Shane. "Um, merlot or . . . whatever," he heard himself say.

"Merlot." She stared at him. A small smile played on her lips. She was dying, dying to ask more questions. Because he did not *do* merlot. But Shane'd known Missy since the inception of the Hudson Kings, and if she knew anything was sacred to him, she knew it was his privacy. "And your usual?" she finally continued.

"I'm trying to cut back."

She waited. "I'll bring a small," she finally said. "You okay?"

"I'm fine."

Missy scratched the tip of her nose, studying his face.

Nothing's off about me. I'm nothing if not consistent. I'm exactly the same as always. Nothing has changed.

"I guess you're always a little weird coming off a long road trip. Especially when you've had bodies in the car," she said. "So what's up with you and Dex? He was shooting daggers at you at the meeting."

Shane wasn't exactly saved from answering by the sudden pounding on his door.

Dex apparently didn't give a shit about Shane's legendary privacy. He'd hobbled over on his bad knee, fire in his brains, looking like if he'd brought a weapon with him he'd have used it. Shane's door opened so hard it slammed against the wall inside the room.

"Holy . . . ," said Missy, moving away from the inevitable crossfire, but in true Missy style, not actually leaving.

In lieu of bullets, Dex fired words. "I asked you because I trusted you."

"And?"

"You took a job on the way. And Cecily was *there*. What the fuck happened to 'Point A to Point B'? Are you fucking insane? Do you have any idea how stupid that was? What if it went wrong? That's my *sister!*"

Holy fuck. He's pissed about the job? "Is she here? Is she safe?" Shane asked.

"That's not the point. You were supposed to rescue her from that piece of shit, not set her up with a criminal record or a sheet in our enemy's database! What if someone was watching you?" Dex said, getting up in Shane's face.

"If you have a problem with someone watching me, you probably shouldn't ask me to drag your sister into frame. Not to mention, she was there because she put herself there. Or maybe, I should say, she was there because *you* put her there. She was with James in the first place because he figured out you were part of the Hudson Kings team and thought he could get to you through her."

They both knew what he was suggesting: Dex was a weak link. Dex put his sister in danger. A look of pure guilt passed across Dex's features . . . before it switched to pure anger. "Fuck you, Shane."

"You're welcome, Dex. Are we done, or did you want to share a pot of tea and some scones in the kitchen?"

"*Fuck you*, Shane."

Shane stared at Dex, debating his next move, oddly territorial about Cecily. "Missy, get out. Now."

Missy walked out the door and closed it behind her.

"Your hands shake, Dex," Shane said.

"What?"

"I said, 'Your hands shake.'"

Dex stared at him, then looked around wildly, trying to figure out the connection, and finally looked down at his trembling fingers. He didn't get it. "My sister mentioned that she had *fun* with you. I'm still trying to figure out how that word applies to you. You get that she's on the rebound, right? She's in a space where she'll do things she'd never otherwise do, right?"

Shane did not like the implication of that. And he had to wonder what exactly Cecily had told her brother about what they'd done on the road, if she didn't tell him about her sex life.

Dex flared up again—"You've been a good friend to me"—and then broke off like he suddenly wasn't sure about the ending to that thought.

"Yeah, thought we were good enough friends not to just drop it all at the first challenge," Shane said, surprised at the amount of hurt he was actually feeling. See, all this shit, *this* was why he did better staying blank.

"We're talking about *Cecily*," Dex stressed.

"This convo is over," Shane said, officially shutting down. "You are not yourself. Haven't been in months."

Dex shook his head in disgust and turned to the door.

"I don't think you're listening," Shane called. "If you're smart, you'll get someone to check your code."

"What the hell, man! This is not about me. Nice deflection."

"Your other option is to detox."

Dex's face went white. "If you so much as touch my sister, I will take you down."

"Tell her not to make it so easy," Shane shot back. *Fuck! Not okay, man. What are you doing?*

But he didn't make it right, and a long, long, long silence was the only response his rude accusation earned.

"Wow," Dex finally said, looking stunned.

Shane braced for the inevitable punch. He'd let Dex have it. Wouldn't lift a finger in defense. But Dex was still staring at him, and the shock and hurt on his face stung worse than his fist ever would.

"What did you do?" Dex asked, too quiet, too grim.

"Cecily's an adult. Why don't you talk to your sister, see if she's got any concerns?"

"What. Did. You. Do?"

Just as quiet, just as grim, Shane said, "I didn't do anything to her. Far's I can tell, I've only been doing things *for* her. Since the day I picked her up." *You gotta apologize for that earlier crack, Shane. Out of line.*

The two men stared at each other, Dex clearly trying to decide his move, Shane still a little surprised he hadn't already made one—with his fists.

Footsteps and voices down the hall got louder. Beyond relieved at the interruption, Shane opened the door to Nick and Chase passing by.

"Break's over," Chase said.

The tension in the room was not lost on anybody. Chase and Nick looked around and then looked at each other.

"Guys," Nick urged. "We got a job to do."

Shane and Dex followed him out, neither one speaking; Shane fell in with Chase while Nick fell back with Dex.

"Not going to ask if you're fine," Chase said.

"Good call," Shane said curtly as they passed into the meeting space, already occupied by Rothgar and the rest of the Kings.

Cecily was sitting at a desk in front of a bank of computers with Rothgar, like it was the most normal thing in the world to be hanging out in the war room of an armory full of confidential material talking to the leader of a mercenary team.

"What the hell is she doing here?" both Shane and Dex asked in unison. They gave each other annoyed looks and then both of them stared at her. Dex hovered over his sister; Shane took a seat.

I am not fine. Not at all.

It didn't escape Shane that it didn't escape Rothgar that something was messing with Shane's mind—and that the something was probably Cecily—but he did his best to focus on the plan at hand.

"Missy put together the blueprint for the first part of our mission," Rothgar said. "We believe we can gather enough evidence to prove that one very beautiful model named Anya Gorchakov is operating in New York City as a Russian sleeper agent. We also believe we can bolster that evidence—and evidence that James is at least one middleman at the hub of the entire cell—by getting audio and video of them together. We've got an opportunity to do just that tomorrow night, so we're going to take it and then move back to the details of Anya over the next two weeks."

Shane's gaze moved back to Cecily. She didn't seem freaked out. She seemed . . . interested.

Missy stood up and flipped a piece of paper over the top of her clipboard. "We believe that James Peterson likes to meet with the agents in his care at a restaurant called Madison 57. He's a regular at a corner table near the pianist and an extremely healthy ficus plant."

A snort of laughter sounded from somewhere in the chairs behind Shane.

Missy looked up with a grin. "I'm just sayin' we've got sound and sight obstruction."

Flynn gave a salute, touching his hand to the permanent damage on his face with a teasing expression. "Appreciate the heads-up. I'll wire things up with that in mind."

"Yep. There's a great balcony table that will give a clear aerial view but has a rail you can hide behind. Which reminds me . . ." She looked back at Rothgar. "What are we doing about Romeo?"

Shane looked around. Sure enough, Romeo was missing. Normally, he'd be the natural choice for hanging out in a fancy restaurant pretending to be on a date or whatever.

"He's sick," Nick explained. "It's been going on and on."

Rothgar raised his chin in their direction. "Right. So, Nick, we need you here in the room with Dex and access to a computer in case one of them pays with a card of some kind. Follow the money, yeah?"

"Nothing better," Nick said, rubbing his thumb and index fingers together.

"So, of Shane and I, who's the floater and who gets to have the fancy meal?" asked Chase.

Rothgar opened his mouth to answer.

"I get to have the fancy meal!" Cecily blurted.

Shane sat up in his chair, saw Dex drop his forehead to his hand, and suddenly everybody was talking, hooting, laughing, or hollering.

"Yo!" Roth barked.

Cecily barreled headfirst into the silence saying, "I deserve the chance to help bring him down. More than anybody."

"You're a little light on experience," Dex said through his teeth.

Cecily flushed. "I know what I'm getting into." She glanced over at Shane. He winced as her look was caught and catalogued by every person in the room. Missy managed to suppress a smile, but nobody tried to hide his amusement. Well, except for Dex. He wasn't even close to being amused. "A couple is just another couple. A hot guy eating alone is noticeable," Cecily added.

"She talking about you or me?" Chase said with a shit-eating grin, nudging Shane's shoulder. "I'm the hot guy, right?"

Dex was protesting, using every argument in the book: She wasn't experienced. James might see her, and they'd be outed. She was putting herself in a potentially vulnerable position any time she went near James.

For some odd reason, Shane felt . . . pride. Pride and more. It was a definite turn-on, a *definite* turn-on, confirming that this slip of a woman who looked so vulnerable was so damn game. He shifted his gaze to Rothgar, wondering how long she'd been trying to convince him and, most of all, which aspect it was that had won the big man over. Because Rothgar was the furthest thing from a pushover. And no way could she convince him to run a mission in anything but the way he 100 percent wanted to run it.

"I'm putting Shane in with Cecily on this one," Rothgar actually said. For some crazy reason, Shane's pulse sped up. "They have a familiar working relationship . . ."

You could say that.

The guys in the room were whispering to one another. Rothgar put up a hand and the room quieted. "I know what you're thinking—especially you, Dex. But Cecily, here, made some pretty reasonable arguments." Rothgar paused and looked down at his feet, a sign that he was trying to be delicate, something that didn't happen very often. Then he added, "Cecily had a point about being a wronged party in all of this. Not just her time with this man. The fact is, if she didn't have ties to the Hudson Kings, she wouldn't have been targeted. She's asked to be part of righting this wrong." Rothgar looked over at Dex. "I'll accept a veto from Dex, though."

"Dex, I—" Cecily began.

Rothgar silenced her with a look. "There's one more thing Dex needs to factor in. I've asked Cecily not to shut the door on James."

"What the fuck!" Dex said.

Shane said exactly the same thing in his head.

"She's been getting phone and e-mail messages since she left him. None of it suggests he thinks she knows who he really is. All that James knows is that he hit your sister, and she left him to join her brother in

New York. He doesn't know that he's been made as a Russian spy and a fake piece of shit who sold Cecily a bill o' goods."

Shane watched Cecily struggle with shame. He hated feeling powerless. He wanted to cross the room, go to her, make it okay. But she wasn't his. She was Dex's.

"He doesn't know the Hudson Kings are all over his ass," Rothgar continued. "For all he knows, she's just a girl who left a bad relationship and went home to a brother he's probably seen in pictures but never met. If Cecily leaves the door open a crack, makes James think he might be able to fix things, we have a far easier road keeping tabs on him, what he knows, and what he's going to try."

"What exactly are you asking her to do?" Dex asked.

Rothgar shrugged. "Change her language from 'never' to 'need space and time.' Have her answer an e-mail or two. Have her sound unsure of herself. Keep the possibility in his mind that he can reconcile and complete his plan of getting intel on us through her."

"I asked Rothgar to put me in the restaurant, Dex," Cecily said. "Please don't veto this. I have a right to help take him down." She lifted her chin and said defiantly, "And I keep a cool head in the field."

Fuck, Shane thought.

"Well, Dex, what's it going to be?" Rothgar said.

Dex stared at Rothgar. He stared at his sister and immediately looked away with a guilty look. "This is messed up . . . but no veto." And then he shot a dirty look at Shane.

Rothgar's eyes narrowed as he followed the dirty look home.

Shane stayed blank.

"No veto from Dex. Cecily's with Shane at the restaurant. Done. Let's move on. That means Chase will be working home base throughout the rest of the mission, so the continuity works for me there too. Anyone got a problem with the bones of this plan?" Rothgar asked, his voice a little sharp.

Shane looked over at Dex, who practically had smoke coming out of his ears.

Rothgar crossed his arms over his chest and leaned back against the desk. "Okay, ladies, let's fucking kiss and make up. Whatever your beef, we do not have the time."

Aw, shit. He should've made his apology back when he had the chance. Shane lifted his hand in the air like he was turning himself in to the cops in some bad Western. "I said something to Dex about Cecily I shouldn't have said."

Cecily's eyes widened, and what sounded like the entire team said, "Whoaaaaa."

Shane looked at Dex. "And now I'm apologizing." He took it like a man, gaze straight on Dex. "You gonna make me say what it was, with *her* here, in front of everybody?"

After a moment Dex said, "We're fine. It's fine. We're fine. Sorry to bring it into the war room, Roth. Everything's fine."

"No bullshit. If it's not fine. Air it. Otherwise, it's done. Understood?"

"Understood," Dex said.

Rothgar's gaze shifted back to Shane.

Jaysus, but it was not pleasant to get momma-henned by Rothgar. Worse than a sucker punch. He could see the other guys holding back their laughter. "Understood," Shane echoed. "It's fine."

Fine enough to get on with shit, but not fine enough to feel the same brand of comfortable they used to have. But since Shane now realized Cecily hadn't quit his system, he suspected things between him and Dex weren't going to get comfortable again for some time.

Thank god Roth called an end to this tweaked version of group therapy; he was sending everybody out. As they left, Missy handed out her "blueprints" for each man's part in the job. Shane got the one with Romeo's name crossed out: a list two pages long.

Missy had also drawn a smiley face on top alongside the scrawl "Don't get made."

He was halfway down the hall before it occurred to him she might have been talking about something other than the mission.

CHAPTER 17

Cecily was sitting cross-legged on the bed in Missy's room, surrounded by brochures decorated with color palettes, when Shane walked in.

She tried not to look too happy to see him, but, damn, there was a lot to be happy about. He was wearing a T-shirt he probably kept in the closet here, because she didn't recognize it, and she *definitely* would have recognized it. It was a little more fitted than his usual fare and made the most of showing off the cut of his chest, his tattoo, and the muscular slopes of his arms.

She greeted him with a smile.

"This your graphic design stuff?" he asked.

"It sure is. I thought I'd start with a few classes and then focus on getting an internship somewhere, but my long-term plan is to get a certificate and then a full-time job." Cecily took a deep breath. "But you're not here to hear about this stuff. Are you here to tell me you don't want me at the restaurant with you or to tell me what you said about me to Dex?"

Shane stared at her for a moment, moistened his lips, and without changing expression replied, "I basically called you easy."

Cecily sucked in a horrified breath.

"Not as such, but it read that way. I said it because I was angry, and I threw you under the bus to score against him. It was bullshit, but it's kind of still out there for the moment. I apologized, but I'm going to have to give Dex some space for a while."

Easy. "Oh." She could feel those two bright red spots burning on her cheeks. "Okay. That's not what I expected. Yeah. So, this is embarrassing." *Note to self: Stop throwing yourself at him. Just STOP.*

"Understandably, Dex wasn't happy. That's it. I fucked up. And Cecily, from the bottom of my heart, I apologize for what I said. I let it get to me."

"Let what get to you?"

Shane looked out the window. "It's more than the job or the danger. He doesn't like me for you."

Cecily understood it then. Shane might be good at telling himself there was no "we," but he couldn't make himself feel something he didn't feel. She gazed up at him. "You're so together with everything except me. Why?"

"I don't know."

Cecily folded her arms across her chest. "When you finally get around to it, you have an uncanny need to tell me all kinds of truths I'm not sure I want to hear. Do you ever have a confession that isn't some kind of bombshell? I can't decide if you're trying to push me away, and dressing it up as this kind of crazy point-blank honesty. I don't think I've ever dated anyone as honest as you." She flushed. "I mean, not that we're dating. Or anything. I mean, we've never gone on a date, so . . . anyway, with your dedication to the truth, you'd probably tell me that I *do* look fat in my dress."

"I've never seen you wear a dress," Shane said, giving her a very sexy once-over. "You got a dress here?"

A bolt of laughter burst from Cecily's lips. "You basically just told my brother I was a slut, and now you're *flirting?*"

Shane's face went dark. "Just to be clear, I told your brother you were . . . game . . . because I'm an idiot, and I felt backed into a wall, and I made a shit decision that I'm copping to and trying to fix. I said something I didn't mean. It wasn't true. It won't happen again."

Her laughter disappeared as quickly as it came. She studied him, realizing she'd been close enough to him to read him better than he could imagine. And what she was reading was a whole lot of contradiction. And a whole lot of a man trying not to let himself have something he really wanted. And she thought about how much she hated all that and how she wasn't going to let herself get away with it and how she wasn't sure she wanted to let Shane get away with it.

"For the life of me," she finally said, "I can't figure out why we do and say the most ridiculous things to each other, and all I want you to do right now is kiss me."

"For the life of me, I can't figure out why I'm fighting that so hard," Shane muttered.

"We should stop fighting," Cecily said.

Shane stared down at her, not saying anything, so much tension in his body she could almost hear a dull roar building in his brain. "The Armory is always a stopover for me," he finally said. "I'm not a long-term play."

And yet, you're still standing here in front of me like you can't bring yourself to leave. "When you actually bother to communicate, everything makes a helluva lot more sense, you know. Doesn't mean I like it, but it makes sense. And I get you, Shane. I get that you're not a long-term play. Is that what you think I'm looking for? Because I'm just looking for happy. I haven't had that in a while, and I don't care what size box it comes in. The thing is, you're here *now*, aren't you? You're here for a little while working on Rothgar's job."

Shane stayed quiet for a moment. "You got a dress here?"

Cecily cocked an eyebrow. "Maybe. Not sure I should waste it. Depends on how easy you are."

"Turns out I'm pretty fucking easy when it comes to you," Shane said.

"Then I got a dress here," Cecily said.

"Be in the garage at six forty-five. The mission starts at seven."

A Friday night date with Shane? Cecily didn't care if it was fake and designed solely to bring James down. Knowing that would probably make the food taste better. "It's a date," she said totally deadpan and turned back to her brochures.

The door closed behind Shane's back.

Cecily threw her brochures into the air and watched the rainbows all fall around her.

CHAPTER 18

Of course, she didn't have a dress. She'd left all her good stuff with James—he'd paid for it. Since buying a dress on short notice was a no go, enter Missy. Again.

Cecily looked in the mirror and felt good about what she saw for the first time in a really long time. Apparently, nobody in this line of work had regular storage. You couldn't just have a trunk or a box or a closet. Your trunk had to have a secret weapons cache, your box had to have a false bottom, and your closet had to lead into a special tunnel containing a very wide selection of clothing for a variety of identities, occupations, and economic statuses.

Unlike Shane, however, Missy had no qualms about sharing her stash, probably because it was to her credit how freaking organized the woman was. Anything you needed to be, anything you wanted to do, anything you could dream up was probably there on a rack with an identification tag and its own little packet of cedar chips hung around the hanger hook.

By the time all was said and done, she'd snapped the tag off a gorgeous Von Furstenberg wrap dress, unboxed two sets of strappy sandals for Cecily to choose from, and tossed over a fancy little wristlet that pulled the whole thing together.

A dressing area the size of a Neiman Marcus VIP boutique made trying everything on a simple matter; Missy might look like something out of a Dickens musical half the time, but she had vision.

Cecily exhaled an unsteady breath, remembering how looking like this was an everyday occurrence with James. And how uncomfortable it felt trying to keep up. This felt different. She felt special now, like she was presenting Shane with something special.

"Want jewelry?" Missy asked, eyeing Cecily in her outfit like she was trying to decide where to put the next dab of paint.

Cecily wasn't big on jewelry. She had tiny diamond-chip studs she wore every day, and that was pretty much that. Missy preempted with a sigh, obviously reading the situation. "You're only, like, the second female who's been in this place, and I tell you there are two guys tops who even entertain an appreciation for this shit, but I don't wanna make you late. Your makeup looks nice, by the way; Shane'll flip. You think he looks at you now, just wait."

Cecily had decided on soft pinks and neutrals, a light gloss on her mouth, the focus on her eyes and hair, and, well, a bit of cleavage, courtesy of the dress. "How does he look at me?"

"Are you kidding? I could *still* feel the way he looks at you if I was standing behind a door."

"I hadn't really thought . . . I mean, I know how I look at him, so I guess I just figured that that feeling was coming from me."

Missy was moving Cecily around by the shoulders, giving her a hell of a critical once-over. "You know, on paper, I can't say you two make any kind of sense. But off paper?" She let Cecily go and smiled. "You're going to have a great night. You got any questions?"

"I think I've got it. We pretend we're on a date. He'll get a couple of photographs, maybe some video . . . Flynn is bugging James's table, and Dex is back here at the Armory with Nick trying to get some financial data from James's credit card or whatever he uses."

"Yeah. It really is that simple. Just have a good time. Give Shane the heads-up if you see anything he should know about." Missy lowered her voice. "And enjoy the date."

"Pretend date," Cecily clarified.

"Pretend date. Right."

"Thanks, Missy. Thanks for everything. For opening your door to me." She hoisted the expensive wristlet with the bracelet cuff and gave a wicked smile. "Particularly, the closet."

Missy laughed. "What time is he coming?"

"I'm meeting him at his car."

Missy's eyebrow hiked.

"What? Is that weird? I mean, it feels a little weird meeting him at your room."

"A, it's your room too as long as you're here. B, Shane coming to pick you up here in my room for your first date? I'd eat that shit up." Missy sighed. "Oh, well. With those heels, take the east wing freight elevator down. It'll save you a hike."

She heaved the door open, and Cecily stood up, suddenly nervous. Missy's thumb jerked upward in a "win" sign, and then she literally pushed Cecily through the door. "Go get 'im, tiger." And then the door slammed shut.

Missy's elevator tip was a good one, given that the lights were motion sensor only, and a swath of darkness lay in front of her. She made her way down to the garage without seeing anybody and walked to the stall where Shane's BMW slept barely visible in a shaft of light coming through one of the high windows.

The garage was impressive, to say the least. It looked like a hangar that could house three jumbo jets, but this one looked like it only held one small private jet. The rest of the space held a variety of motorcycles, cars, and armored vehicles repurposed from various international wars, if the markings were accurate. An intricate car elevator displayed at least eight different cars, a selection of vans and trucks, and a rack that actually held an assortment of scooters, bicycles, and hauling equipment. The walls were covered with tools and accessories, and another version of the dry-cleaner pulley system from Missy's closet, full of what looked like costumes. She couldn't see past the first row, but the top layer held several sets of motorcycle leathers, police uniforms, armed services, and service-industry suits.

It felt weird standing in the drafty, cavernous space. Too much time and space . . . Cecily shifted her weight from one foot to the next, trying to relax, trying not to make this a big deal, when—oh, boy, did it feel like a big deal.

She heard a door open, but no shaft of light appeared to give her any sort of clue, reminding Cecily again that she wasn't dealing with normal.

Shane approached her, a completely deadpan expression on his face.

He's going to cancel. No, he can't cancel. This is not a real date. This is a mission.

"Hi," Shane said quietly, his eyes starting at her toes and moving carefully and systematically up her body, where they stalled out at the cleavage revealed by the deep V of the dress and then finally wrenched free and proceeded straight to her mouth for a tense second before they took in the rest of her.

Shane brought her back with a soft "You look . . ." He shook his head, not rushing his words, being deliberate when he settled on "incredible."

"So do you," Cecily blurted, all nervous laughter and shaky footing. No lie. No lie at all. Shane looked like he usually did but like he deliberated, like he took a moment to smooth the edges. For one thing, he was wearing new jeans, ink black; a black blazer pulled up at the sleeves; and a button-down shirt. He'd taken a razor to his face, cleaning up his shadow but not eliminating it, for which Cecily said a silent thanks. He wore black boots under his jeans, the black shiny enough to suggest he saved them for nicer occasions, and he considered this one of them.

"Would it be inappropriate to ask you to turn around in a circle?" Cecily said on a tease.

Shane answered that by hauling her into his arms and lifting her off her feet. Cecily gasped, and he was all over the opportunity, his mouth taking hers for a searing kiss. She wove her fingers into his hair, even as he trapped her hard against his chest—all solid-as-fucking-hell man—and then he whirled her around in a circle.

His lips slid to her neck, leaving a trail of heat as he pressed Cecily down on the hood of his car.

"Never too early to get in character," Shane said.

"Maybe you should do that again," Cecily said, coming up for air, trying to control herself even as she arched her back, searching for his body. "For the sake of the mission."

"Love that," he said, his hands sliding under her back, his mouth back on hers, biting, sucking, claiming.

So, so good. This was different. This was Shane taking what he wanted for himself, his brain not full of shouldn't, can't, or won't.

And Cecily could feel the delicious burn on every inch of her body. *Jesus,* he could kiss.

When he finally broke away, leaving her panting and thinking that few things short of bringing down James Peterson could possibly be worth the interruption, Shane's dark eyes captured her gaze. He stared down at her, holding her in his arms on the hood of his car in the silence of the old drill hall.

The blankness was gone, absolutely erased. The same hot, bad boy was holding her in his arms, the weight of his body capturing her in his embrace. But something had unlocked. Maybe not everything, but the doors were starting to open, and Cecily just loved it. *Loved it.* Because it meant there wasn't so much distance between them after all.

"If I walk halfway and you walk halfway, we meet in the middle," she said quietly.

"Yeah, we do," he said forcefully. He shook his head and then added, "Hate to say it, but we've got to get on the road."

"Of course," Cecily murmured.

Neither of them attempted to move.

"Fuck," Shane finally said. "You know how to kiss. Got a hint back in Chicago, you just touched your tongue to me. Sweetest thing I ever had, and I still thought I could shake it. Had no idea what was waiting, though."

"I can't help it," Cecily said lamely, staring at his mouth, wishing they could just do it some more and ignore the part where they analyzed it. "You just bring it out in me. It's like there's a bigger, brighter version of me I've been holding back on."

"No holding back anymore, yeah? I can't believe you convinced Rothgar to let you do this."

"Well," she said with a grin. "I look innocent, but I guess I know how to get what I want." *No more holding back. On anything.*

Shane hadn't figured out how the hell he was going to handle Rothgar and Dex with this "no more holding back" business. The team worried all the time about distractions; the more complicated jobs couldn't handle distractions, and each didn't hesitate to point out when someone gave less than 100 percent. Dex's leg, Flynn's face, Nick's situation. . . there was plenty of proof to show that it wasn't a minor concern.

If he was really going to let Cecily into his heart, he'd have her on his mind all the time now, not only as a distraction merely because he'd like to get her into his bed and claim her once and for all but also because he worried about her becoming collateral damage.

She had no interest in committing to the Hudson Kings life. She'd made it clear that she wanted to be normal. Take classes. Get freelance work that involved a computer and a mouse instead of a weapon, a hacking device, or a bag of unmarked bills. But by being here tonight, he knew without a doubt that there was something about this life that spoke to her, appealed to her, and she was willing to meet him on that halfway line. He suddenly wondered if she understood what that meant to him.

Shane thought of the moment she'd walked into the gym, straight into the sights of Shorty and his pathetic band of brothers. He'd never had to worry about somebody he loved getting touched by that kind of dirt.

Stop thinking, sweet boy . . .

Nothing this sweet ever lasts . . .

Madison 57 was your typical tony New York eatery. Modern chandeliers dripping with crystals were paired with gleaming wood tables and striped velvet-upholstered seats. Not Shane's atmosphere of choice, but the food was probably excellent. Missy'd made the reservation, so Shane was confident they'd be at the right table, but he tipped big in case James and Anya were late and they needed to hang around awhile. As they headed up the stairs, Shane shielded Cecily from sight with his body, making it look like normal PDA. They settled in to their table at the edge of a gold-railed balcony.

It had a clear view of James's favorite table on the mezzanine but was a little too high for the perfect camera shot if he wanted a clear view of their faces. He'd have to come up with something on the fly for that.

Shane stuck his hand in his pocket and used the wireless remote to unmute his comms device. "Nice table," he said to the hostess, and then muted it again.

She smiled and gestured for their server to bring water and menus.

"We're a go," Chase's voice said through the comms to the whole team, confirming Shane was in place and the mission was on. Shane imagined Rothgar standing in the war room with his arms crossed over his chest, silently monitoring the screens and the traffic coming over the comms.

A sharp streak of static warped the line.

"Sorry," Flynn muttered, and the sound cleared up. Shane pretended to scratch an itch and adjusted his earpiece slightly.

"You going to order for me?" Cecily teased.

Shane's gaze shot up from the menu, taking in the flicker of heat in her eyes. "No."

"I think you should. You know the food better."

Shane grinned and gestured for the server. As he ordered a whole host of small plates, he reached out and took Cecily's hand. When he finished, the server took a matchbox from his long, monogrammed apron and lit the white candle between them, which he then moved off the table to the wide balcony rail. "Gives you a little more space," the man murmured.

Cecily bit her lip on a smile and looked down.

"Anya's settled in the bar, ordering a drink . . . ," Chase said.

"Oh, yeah, baby, and using a credit card to start a tab," Flynn whispered into the comms. *"Dex? You siphoning that info for Nick?"*

"On it," Dex said.

With his hand covering hers, Cecily was blushing—happy blushing—her free hand fiddling with the neck of a dress that had started out real closed up but was kind of easing up with time. Cute. And hot. It also did not escape Shane's notice that the dress seemed to be held together by a single string that went around Cecily's waist and tied in front.

A single string keeping that dress on her body.

"James is picking up Anya in the bar," Chase said.

"They aren't miked until they're at their table," Flynn said.

Shane's gaze went over the balcony and then back to the string at Cecily's waist. It was gonna be a long night.

The dishes started coming out, one after the next, enough so that the server had to get creative with a little multilevel stand. Shane looked at the tapas with total amusement. He'd have to eat about a hundred of those little plates to make a meal. "I don't actually eat out much," he said. "On the road, it's fast food or hotel food. Here in New York, I usually go to a place called Bianchi's. Romeo's got a big family, and they own a seriously kick-ass Italian restaurant . . ."

He stared at the ice cubes swirling in his glass. "Like I told you, I wasn't very old when suddenly it was just me. No relatives. I stayed on couches, basements, relied on friends. Tried out the streets, learned a lot of things I use today and learned a lot about things I need to stay away from. Figured out how to dodge social services, because everybody knows that shit's a crapshoot. Never got too attached. Known Romeo's family a long time. They invite me to every holiday known to man. Used to go when I was younger, but I always kind of felt like I was borrowing a family. Seriously, if you're going to borrow a family, the Bianchis are it. But it wasn't my family, you know? I couldn't put it together in my mind. Ma Bianchi's always had an open door for me, though. And later, Rothgar. But in all these years, no matter what I try, I don't feel like I'm home."

He looked up at Cecily then and pierced her with his gaze. "Thing is I'm beginning to think it's because I never really tried stepping over the threshold. Kept my distance to be safe, but just like everything else, where there's no risk, there's no reward."

Shane reached out across the table and tucked a piece of Cecily's hair behind her ear, letting the lock slip slowly through his fingers, and said quietly, "Sometimes when I look at you, you look like that reward. I never looked for someone like you, Cecily. Never wanted it. Because love that gets taken away is the most painful experience in the world. Nothing close. For a minute there, I thought maybe we could just be like the rest. Just physical, because, sweetling, my body cannot get enough of you. I've had so many moments when I had to fight myself over wanting to fuck you, for many reasons. So many moments. But you're different. You're special. There's no answer to what I just said. I just wanted to say it. I wanted you to hear those words. Because no matter what happens with us, I have your back, and nobody, *nobody* is ever going to hurt you again."

Cecily sucked in a breath and let it out slowly. And then the huge smile he'd put on her face slowly vanished as James Peterson and Anya Gorchakov were led through the floor of the restaurant and seated in the corner by the piano and the extremely large ficus plant.

CHAPTER 19

Cecily had totally underestimated what her reaction would be to seeing James again for the first time after leaving him. She stared at him; her jaw dropped until Shane had to gently remind her that they were pretending to be someone else in a world where she and James had never crossed paths.

The level of revulsion she felt was extreme. Her hands were shaking, her heart was thumping, and it was all she could do not to lob the candle over the balcony in the direction of his head. "What was I thinking?" she whispered down at her plate, too embarrassed to meet Shane's eyes.

He didn't answer.

"Maybe this was a mistake. Maybe I should go."

"You don't abandon a mission, Cecily," Shane said softly. "You're in it now, and you're better than that."

She looked up at him, awed by his belief in her. And then she allowed herself to look one more time over the balcony before she decided that even if this date was for show, it was still an opportunity to be with the man who *had* shown her what it really meant to take care of someone. And she wasn't going to waste one more second wishing away the time she'd spent with James. Not with Shane right across from her looking like that, looking at her like that. He wasn't judging; he wasn't embarrassed for her; he was just matter-of-factly saying that he knew she could be tough, and he was asking her to be tough.

"Listen. I just got word they're jamming the bug, and between that and the piano, the audio down there's no good. I need to get some pictures," Shane said. "Can I count on you to hang tight? Finish this like we started?" He added with a growl, "Because I like to see my missions through from start to finish, and this pretend date is far from over."

When he got that look in his eyes, she could feel it between her legs. Cecily took a deep breath. "Did it just get hot in here?"

Shane grinned and stood up, tossing his napkin to the chair before he headed for the stairs. She suddenly recalled the morning Shane had come for her. Everything was so different now. The face that looked back at her when she was getting ready tonight didn't have a bruise or dark circles. Now she looked happy, healthy, and she felt more confident about herself than she had in a long time. Some of that was just learning from life's lessons. But some of that was learning what love really could be like. If Shane went all in, love really could be something special. If she could find it in her to go for it, maybe he could too.

It was five minutes before she saw a man pass by James's table on the way to the restroom. Same build and hair color as Shane's, but the nondescript man who headed straight past the targets was wearing Buddy Holly glasses, hair parted to one side, and a tweedy pullover sweater. She tried not to stare but wasn't 100 percent sure it was even Shane until he got back and tucked a pen that probably wasn't really a pen back in his pocket. Somewhere between upstairs and downstairs he'd changed back into his regular look.

"Photo's in," Shane murmured to the team, and then he turned his attention back to Cecily.

"What happened to your, um, outfit?" Cecily asked.

"What outfit?" Shane asked too innocently.

"God, you guys are pros," she said, shaking her head in absolute awe. "The more I see, the more I think Dex was right. I have way too little experience to be messing around in your business. I don't know why Rothgar let me do this."

"It's your business too. That's the point. That's why Rothgar let you do this. He's only got brain space for one thing: work. But for him, work and honor go hand in hand."

"He's more than just a boss, isn't he? All the men, they really believe in him. I can tell."

"Can't speak for the others, but I'll tell you that Roth saved my life."

Cecily's eyes opened wide.

"Roth stopped me from killing a man when it wasn't necessary. Bunch of different guys intersected on a job one day, about a decade ago. He was there; I was there. I was a trigger pull away from blowing this guy's head off. Didn't care. Roth stopped me; put his hand on my gun arm and talked me down. Way I see it, he stepped in and stopped me from following a path of mindless, pointless destruction. After my parents died and I was thrown around—nobody stepping up to be family, always giving, never getting—I stopped giving. Just felt angry. Just felt pain. Don't know what it was, but he saw something in me and offered me a chance with the Hudson Kings. He gave me an option, and he showed me that I was worthy. He offered himself up as a brother when I had no one and didn't believe family was something I'd ever have a chance at again. He saved my life. Because I was just a punk-ass thug with dead eyes and a death wish. I was nobody a woman like you would ever want to know."

"Oh, Shane," Cecily said softly. "I'm so sorry."

"Well, look where it got me. Sittin' here across from you. Would definitely not have guessed that would be my path, but I'll take it."

She smiled. And then her smile turned into a grin.

"What are you thinking?" Shane asked.

"What you said earlier about Rothgar giving you a place, but it still didn't feel like a 'home.'"

"Yeah?"

"You should make it a home. Take the time to make it a place where you feel happy."

He stilled and then said almost too casually, "You should decorate my room."

"Oh, my god, how delicious," she squealed. "I know exactly what to do. I'll go shopping on the weekend. I was planning to take a class, anyway, so I'll be out and about."

"Delicious is not for decorating rooms, Cecily."

"Oh, yeah?"

"Yeah. Delicious is for the perfect chocolate cake and for how your pussy tastes when I put my mouth on you."

Shane took a gulp of bourbon, his eyes locked on Cecily licking her bottom lip, her eyes liquid heat. Well, what did he expect, saying a thing like that?

He leaned across the table. "And after you finish off that dessert, we're gonna find someplace I can finish off you."

Cecily leaned in to meet him in the middle and whispered, "I think I've had enough dessert."

Shane unmuted his comms. "Shane here. Pix in custody. We out?" he murmured.

"You two are good to go," Chase said. *"Have a fan-*fucking-*tastic night."*

Nice one, Chase.

Cecily's eyes were wide. "The guys can't hear our regular conversation, can they?"

"They can't hear this. And they can't see *this*." Shane's hand moved under the table, sliding his palm up Cecily's thigh. The fabric of her skirt rippled away; he hooked a finger in the side string of her panties and tugged. Just a little, but his fingers fluttering lightly over her skin was almost too much.

A huff escaped Cecily's mouth, and she parted her legs slightly, already wishing they'd left half an hour ago.

He must have read her mind. "The car should be out front," Shane said, moving in for a soft kiss, his tongue lingering against her lips.

When the kiss ended, the server made the most of the moment to return the check. He whispered a little too loudly in Cecily's ear, "He's hot. Lucky you."

Cecily bit her lip, her heart going warm. Shane didn't say a word, just finished the transaction, said his good-byes, and hustled them to the front of the house, where the hostess swapped Shane the keys for a thick roll of cash.

Which was probably why Shane's car was still parked in the loading zone right outside the restaurant where he'd left it.

Shane's eyes locked on hers, a mischievous grin on his face. He came to her, but instead of opening the door, he pressed her against it. His hands moved quickly, shoving up the back of her dress and cupping her ass.

"Shane!"

"It's New York. No one cares," he murmured into her neck. "We'll get going in just a sec."

Heat from Shane's jeans seared through her silk panties. Cecily clung to his shoulders as he kissed her hard, both of them pressing against each other, their bodies desperate for more.

And then he pulled away, the car keys jingling in his hand.

"You keep taking it away. You're the ultimate tease, Shane." She pulled hard on his shoulders. "Stop taking it away."

He grinned down at her. "I love seeing you hot for me."

She grabbed him by the front of the shirt and pulled him back. "I've been hot for you for a long time," Cecily said into his ear and then licked his lobe. "If we're going to get out of here, let's get out of here."

"Jesus," Shane said. "Man, there is so much I want to do with you. So many things . . . this dress is making me *crazy*." He hooked his finger in the string at her waist that was supposed to be keeping the wrap dress wrapped. If he so much as breathed on the loop of tied bow, her entire dress would come undone.

He did the opposite, pulling on the sides of the fabric to cover her more and opened the passenger side door. "Get in," he said gruffly.

Shane started the car and pulled them straight into the city's bloodstream. Lights illuminated the way like a sky filled with hundreds of stars. The windows were down, and as they moved slowly through the streets and changed neighborhoods, the music coming from the bars and boom boxes, from the shouting and laughing, and from the swirl of Manhattan nightlife changed like a playlist too.

Shane's shifting hand moved from the stick to wrap around her fingers. Cecily had never felt so alive, never felt so much like the person she wanted to be in the life she wanted to have.

"The president is in town," Shane finally said into a silence that felt perfectly comfortable.

"Yeah?"

"They block off certain roads, depending on his itinerary."

Cecily looked over. Shane was up to something. "Really? Have you perchance seen this itinerary?"

"I have," he said, his lips parting as a chuckle escaped. *"Perchance."*

"The nice thing about your particular brand of bad, Shane, is that I really have every confidence you will get me out of any mess you get me into."

He turned his head, the teasing gone. "You serious or you messing with me?"

"I'm serious," Cecily said, processing the weight of her own words. It was true; she knew he'd keep her safe. That wasn't exactly new. What *was* new was her willingness to walk toward fire with him at her side. Getting out of an unusual situation was one thing. Walking toward an unusual situation was another. But she had a new kind of backbone now. And unusual didn't mean wrong. And unusual didn't mean stupid.

It was just the Hudson Kings. Whatever it was that kept Missy and Dex at the Armory. "I mean it."

It took him a while before he answered. "Helluva compliment coming from you." His hand moved from her palm to the split of her dress, exposing her leg. He ran his fingers featherlight across her thigh again, caressing her skin until the light turned green and his hand vanished.

Cecily sighed on a smile, looking forward to the moment when his hands were all hers.

Shane focused on driving for a while, cutting a series of corners and coming out to a side street lined with sets of orange-and-white roadblocks as far as the eye could see.

"Guess the president's not here yet." He stopped the car and then hopped out and moved the barricade. Moments later, they were on the deserted West Side Highway.

"Ready?" he asked.

She looked at Shane and smiled. He smiled back.

And then he hit the accelerator.

No music, no talking. Just the speed of the car, lights streaking around them, the moon reflecting off the Hudson River.

And at the peak of speed, the feel of Shane's hand closing around hers.

Cecily's heart was pounding. Absolutely pounding by the time Shane brought the car to a crawl below the Manhattan entrance of the Brooklyn Bridge. They turned into a grassy space isolated from view. He didn't say anything. Just parked, threw off his seat belt, popped hers as well, and was around in a flash, pulling her out of the car and throwing her down on the hood.

His mouth came down on hers, claiming her. She took his weight, her body restless under his.

He slipped one finger through the loop of her string belt, pulling the tie apart with a jerk of his wrist. "Hell, yes," he said as the fabric pooled on either side of her nakedness. Just panties and a bra now, the light breeze caressing her skin almost as good as the sensation of Shane's hands on her body.

"Shane," Cecily moaned.

He bent down, his hands parting the sides of her dress, his mouth trailing against her skin to the V between her legs where he licked her through her panties.

God. *God.*

"What . . . ," she breathed. It was all she could get out because he'd suddenly flipped her around so that her palms were flat on the hood and she was bent over. He used his knee to spread her legs and then pressed forward against her ass, his erection huge through his jeans. Cecily groaned just thinking about it, wetness slicking between her legs across the silk.

He pulled her panties down. Two of his fingers slid into her while his cock pressed against her. Shane began moving his hips like he was fucking her from behind, and Cecily nearly lost her mind.

"'S good," she managed to say as he worked his fingers, flicking her clit, then pressing his erection slow against her.

They'd found a rhythm, the two of them; Cecily's orgasm began to build. Shane's breathing went rocky, and she knew he was on his way to losing his mind along with her.

Suddenly, his fingers slipped away.

"I want—" she blurted in alarm.

"You'll get," he growled. And the fingers came back, bringing her to a high again . . . and then once again taking it away.

"Don't stop!" Cecily gasped, even as his work made her hotter, drew out the tension, teased her body to new heights.

"Just beginning," Shane said. His free hand curled around her breast, rolling the nipple between his fingers. His body was all around hers, in charge, taking her everywhere, his delicious weight keeping her close, running the show.

He fingered her more deliberately now, still building the pleasure higher. Cecily lost track of everything except Shane's urgent voice whispering in her ear, the feel of his hard cock moving against her ass, the fingers working her clit.

"Give me—" blurted from her mouth.

She broke hard, her cry of ecstasy long and drawn out, but she didn't care. She just rode the wave and let the orgasm move through her body.

Shane held her still as the pleasure washed over her, as she came down from it, as she came back to reality and looked at him over her shoulder. And then he released her and turned her around.

He circled his arms around her and held her and then said, "I'll give you whatever you want."

"Whatever?"

"Name it."

"Your turn, then," she said, gesturing with a nod to his belt buckle.

"Uh-uh," Shane said. "Not done taking care of you."

"You know I get kind of embarrassed talking about sex," Cecily said.

Shane cocked his head and looked down at her. "Cute and hot as hell."

Cecily laughed, steeled herself, and then practiced her new policy of saying what she wanted . . . and taking it.

"I want . . . I want to watch your face while I suck your cock. I want to see you lose control over me," she whispered and then buried her face in her hands. "Oh, my god, did I just say that?"

"Holy shit," Shane said.

Cecily dropped her hands in a panic. "Too much? Too blunt? Too—"

"Shut up, beautiful. Too perfect. You say what you want, what you like. That's the kind of normal I want for you."

Oh. Holy shit, in a good way. Wow.

"Now, my turn to be honest. You've told me you wanna suck my cock, you've got about one second to get down to that, or I'm gonna make my own decision about what comes next. Between those sexy little sounds you make and the way you move your body for me when I so much as move my finger near your pussy, I'm so fucking hard I can't see straight."

Cecily got down to business, and Shane's eyes pooled like liquid night looking down at her as she made quick work of belt, button, and fly.

"Holy shit, in a *really* good way," she said, as his cock sprang free from his jeans. Gorgeous. God, he was huge. Her body ached to be filled, but, more than that, Cecily wanted to watch him come with his cock in her mouth.

Shane groaned as she took him in her hand, velvet skin against her palm. She kneeled and touched her tongue to the tip, going wet between her legs again as her tongue tasted salt. Her heart raced when he bucked.

"Fuck, sweetling," he said, more a prayer than anything else.

Down on her knees, sucking and licking, she cupped his balls, watching his face the whole time. Now she had all the power. All the power to make him feel like he was flying.

"Fuck. Fuck. Nailing it . . ." His hands gripped the car beneath him. She looked up and could see the muscles in his arms bulging and shifting as he held himself in place, just the slightest rhythm in his hips.

He was holding himself back from fucking her face. He was standing on the edge and holding himself back from taking over, letting her work, trying so hard not to take over.

The slight rocking of his hips pressed his cock farther back in her mouth; the tension in his body was so fierce it fired Cecily up even more.

"Gonna . . . *god* . . ." He looked down into her eyes as she took him deep. "God" was all he could say. His eyes went hazy. His hands reached out; his fingers raked through her hair. He groaned. Tension rippled through his body. His head went back, and on a powerful yell, he shot down Cecily's throat and fell back against the car.

Shane's chest heaved as he stared up at the stars.

Cecily wiped her mouth, and Shane righted himself. Suddenly, her feet weren't touching the ground, and Shane was hauling her to him, and he'd tucked her in the crook of his arm. They lay curled on the hood of the car.

"Hi," he said.

"Hi," she said, trying not to feel shy.

"That was fucking insane," he said, his arm around her, his gaze still up in the sky. "Can't believe I waited that long for that."

"Me neither," Cecily said, feeling a hell of a lot better. Suddenly, his hold loosened. "Hey, where are you going?"

"Not gonna leave you hanging. Look on your face with my cock in your mouth . . ." Shane slid off the hood.

"You don't . . . hey . . . where are you going?"

"To find that sweet spot between your world and mine," Shane said, flashing a cocky grin as he pressed her knees apart and lowered his head between her legs.

CHAPTER 20

Cecily didn't buy Shane a plant. She bought him three. Two of them involved flowers.

Flowers and plants. In his room.

Shane obviously didn't give a shit about interior design, but he liked the idea of Cecily leaving her mark on his living quarters.

So, yeah, she'd been busy since Friday night, and thanks to living in Manhattan, the deliveries were already arriving.

So far, the take included a new set of sheets and a new comforter and a slew of pillows, most of which had immediately ended up on the floor on Saturday night when Shane was done with his team planning session, and Cecily stopped by to set things up. And then, because he always made it a point to test new equipment in the field, he tried it all out—with Cecily on the bed, of course.

Girl done good. She'd designed a room for a man where a woman could be totally comfortable. She'd designed a room for the two of them.

The two of them.

Us.

A familiar rap on the door was followed by the immediate entrance of Missy, wheeling another cart full of boxes.

"Where's Cecily?" Missy asked. "I'm guessing that a box from a place called Gracious Home is not something you ordered."

"Hanging out with Dex."

"How's it going with him? You guys make up?"

Since he hadn't talked to Dex recently and wasn't planning to talk to him soon, he didn't answer. Missy pulled a scissors from a holster hanging off the front of the cart and started opening boxes.

"You serious?" Shane asked.

"What, am I being inappropriate?" Missy asked, continuing to run the scissor blade down the tape seams and opening lids.

"Sometimes I worry about you."

"I wouldn't worry. I've got, like, a baker's dozen of big, strong men who will take care of little ol' me in a pinch." She said this as she wielded the scissors in a final flourish, swung the handle loop around her finger like a gunslinger, and tossed them expertly back in the holster. And then: "Huh."

"What?" Shane asked.

"It's a *blankie*. Awww."

Shane looked. "That's not a blankie. It's a blanket. It's clearly a very nice, adult blanket."

"You're getting testy," Missy noted, with a grin. "I like how you defend her. Is this the real deal?"

"Missy, don't start. We're not a *thing*," he said. At least not a public thing. They were a private thing. And it made sense to keep it that way for now.

"I wouldn't shout it out either, if I had Dex and Rothgar breathing down my neck, but you gotta admit to me, anyway, that you are finally having feelings for a sister instead of a sedan."

Shane winced at that one. "Got nothing to say." He pulled the entire blanket out of the box. It was a big two-person-friendly blanket in gunmetal gray, like his car. He tossed it on the bed. "Have no idea what she had in mind with this stuff."

"Oh, I think we know what she had in mind, pal. It's a *blanket*."

Shane crossed his arms across his chest. "If you think you're welcome to stay here and open any more boxes, you got it wrong."

"I'm going, I'm going."

Nick stuck his face through the crack in the door. "Everybody decent? Oh, it's just you and Missy."

Missy made a face on her way out.

Nick walked in.

"What is this, Grand Central?" Shane asked, stacking the rest of the boxes on the bed.

"Went to see if Romeo was up to getting back to work, but he's busy puking, and these are new shoes."

Shane laughed.

"So, you continue to be the primary in the field," Nick said. "Chase is backup."

"No problem," Shane said. He took the documents and studied a graph with so many lines it looked like a mutant spider from hell. Closer inspection revealed it was actually a trail following bank accounts with lines labeled with circled letters that pointed from one page to another, around, and back again.

Nick pointed to one of the account numbers. "That's the account Anya's credit card tapped. It's being fed both by James, who's pulling dough from wire transfers out of Russia . . . and by Anya's boyfriend, one Vlad Sokolov. For the record, I don't know that Sokolov is a spy, but he's definitely doing some shady business with the mother country." He hesitated and then added, "I've worked with him."

"Well, that's some sweet intel," Shane said.

"Not exactly," Nick muttered.

Shane watched Nick carefully for a second and then decided not to get into his business. He trusted his brother to share whatever needed to be shared. He looked back down at the papers. "We adding Vlad to our watch list?"

"Rothgar's on it." Nick handed him a receipt. "And that's your latest freelance. Money's snug in bed."

Shane glanced at it to make sure the right amount had gone to his Point A. As usual, it was correct. "You take a cut for yourself?"

Nick shrugged and took a seat in one of two new guest chairs that had shown up that morning.

"Jaysus, man. You're doing me a service. Take your cut." It wasn't like Nick needed the cash; he had more money than anybody on the team, including Rothgar. But that wasn't the point.

Nick reached over and grabbed one of Cecily's new buys from a side table, a fancy candle done in gray with gold lines, and started tossing it in the air like a baseball. "I'll donate it to the SPCA."

"You ever get a dog?"

Nick's face went a little dark. "Not yet."

Shane studied his face, second-guessing his decision not to pry. "How long have you been staying at the Armory?"

"Long enough to watch on videocam one of my fish jump the tank in an ill-fated quest for a life with a better pH balance." Nick didn't look over; kept his eye on the candle.

Nick was keeping up a good front, but Shane could tell he was in some kind of pain. "You need help with that problem of yours?" Shane asked.

Nick stopped tossing the candle. "I'm starting to think about asking Geo," he said with a grin that didn't quite hide his discomfort.

Shane raised both eyebrows. He knew that Rothgar had a few guys he considered members of the Hudson Kings who had never been to the Armory, never met the rest of the team, and were essentially placed undercover in locations throughout the world. Geo was a man on the borderline of that group. Geo was also a hit man. And that was as much as most of the men on the home squad knew about him.

Before Shane had a chance to ask anything else, a voice full of piss said, "I tried, man. I really did try." This, from Dex, walking in. Shane sighed. Yeah, this was definitely Grand Central. Piss and all.

"Take a load off," Nick said to Dex, gesturing to the other new guest chair still wearing its plastic protective cover.

Dex didn't sit. "I tried to be a team player. Rothgar said put her in with you. I didn't veto. Now she's being asked not to cut ties with the guy. Leave the door open so we can keep James on a string. The fact is we're basically using my sister as bait, and you're not only okay with it, it's like you're fucking inspiring her to get involved even further in this shit."

Shane forced himself to relax his body. Nick starting tossing the candle again, but he sat forward, his body alert, ready to play referee.

"I'm not making her do anything, but I'm sure as shit trying to support her choices," Shane said. "Maybe you should try it."

"Maybe you should leave her the fuck alone." Dex looked pointedly over at the plant. He reached out and grabbed the candle from Nick in midair and held it up for Shane's inspection. "I know my sister very well," he said tightly. "I also know she's rebounding from a really bad relationship. Don't make her think there's something where there's nothing."

There was a long silence. *It's not nothing. It wasn't nothing from the moment I saw her.* "You don't seem to know just how smart she is, or how capable she is," Shane said.

"Oh, I know. I just don't think she needs to put her skills to use in a way that could get her killed." Dex looked at Nick and added, "And I'm not sure how I feel about the rest of the guys being okay with it either. Would you have put her in the restaurant, Nick?"

Nick leaned forward in his chair. He looked at Dex. He looked at Shane. "That's not my zone. I don't even carry a gun," he said. "I know how to cut off someone's air supply, but I've never had to try. I can ruin your life from my seat at a desk in an air-conditioned skyscraper, without getting a scratch on either of us. I have the cleanest shirts you've ever seen, and there's not one pair of boots in my closet. I do serious damage, but not like the bruisers on this team."

Nick made a fist, squeezing hard and then releasing. "Well, that's how it used to be. Suddenly, I find myself lying awake in an unfamiliar room in the Armory trying to figure out how to get back to normal. So, Dex, if you're asking me, if I had normal back and I cared about a woman . . ." He paused, a muscle in his jaw throbbing, and then continued. "Would I let her go into that restaurant like your sister? Would I tell her to make James think there's still an in if he asks? Nah. Not a chance."

He looked at Shane. "Sorry, buddy, but that's just my opinion. You know I always give Rothgar one hundred percent, but being loyal doesn't mean you have to agree with every decision."

Nick got up and squeezed Dex's shoulder on his way out, but he looked back. "Didn't get a chance to tell you that this shit you're doing to your room looks good. Glad you decided to rejoin the human race."

Dex stared at the floor. He looked up at Shane, and then he just followed Nick out.

In the quiet of the room, Shane ran a hand over the new blanket. *What am I forgetting? What did I do to deserve her, and how long is it going to be before someone or something takes it away?* Takes her away. His woman. A woman he was losing his heart to in a way he never knew was possible.

The last knock of the night sounded at the door, and the person behind it did not feel the need to barrel in. Cecily. *Thank fuck.* He slammed the door shut behind her.

"Sweetling," he said hoarsely. He dipped his head at the same time he hooked her around the waist and pressed her hard against the door.

Cecily moaned into his mouth. Shane kissed her thoroughly, and when they came up for air, she asked, "The stuff for the room, you happy? Any thoughts?"

"Only dirty ones," he answered, kicking hard with one boot to get the boxes off the bed, an inelegant solution Shane didn't give one fuck about.

CHAPTER 21

When the Hudson Kings were working on a big case, Rothgar made it part of Missy's job to remove external distractions. Part of this meant getting the team fed and back in the war room as soon as possible each day.

Team meals involved a lot of food, a lot of noise, and a lot of good old-school "family" time; Cecily could see more and more why Dex was so drawn to this life.

Unfortunately, Dex was too busy glowering across the table at Shane to enjoy much of Missy's truly stellar breakfast or make much conversation with said family.

Shane avoided Dex's stink eye by focusing almost exclusively on shoveling in his food. But every once in a while, his eyes would meet hers and sparks would go flying, and Dex would look pissed, and the rest of the guys would exchange amused looks.

Except for Rothgar.

Rothgar watched over the table like a man whose mind literally never stopped for a break. Cecily noticed him take in the discord at his table. His eyes met hers, and he hooked his chin toward the side counter lined with at least five different methods of coffee-brewing equipment alongside a pyramid of mismatched mugs that varied in design from kittens hanging off branches to absurdly offensive slogans.

Cecily swallowed hard and mumbled something about a refill, and then she got up and headed his way. Rothgar was just huge, and though he sure as hell didn't remind her of her father, between the intensity of his expression and his 24-7-alert body language, she had the distinct sense she was in some kind of trouble.

"Hi," he said turning to the espresso machine and spending a long time concocting a very specific cappuccino complete with a precise tap of cinnamon. "You and I need to talk."

"It's okay," Cecily managed. "I get it."

Roth's mouth quirked. "Maybe. Know that I back Dex one hundred percent, so I back you. You played it cool at the restaurant, and I've got no complaints about your abilities in the field as a novice . . ."

My abilities in the field? *In what universe am I having this conversation? And why am I so pleased I might actually be good at some of this stuff?*

"But you asked me for a favor to give James a little payback, and now the mission's over. So if what I'm hearing—that you're interested in getting on with your life—is true, don't be offended if I tell you I think that's a good idea to make that happen sooner rather than later." His gaze pierced her. "I consider you one of ours, and that means I look out for you now, but it also means we talk straight. Do you have a plan? Do you need a job? Is there something holding you back you need help with?"

*Something holding me back? God, yes. Well, some*one. Of course she still wanted to follow through with her original plans for a new life in New York City. It wasn't like she was going to up and decide to become part of a mercenary team instead of a graphic designer. Not that Rothgar was offering. What if he actually did offer? Suddenly the idea didn't seem bat-shit crazy. Maybe just regular crazy. Of course, regular crazy was still doable . . . oh, man, when had things gotten so complicated?

But Rothgar didn't offer. He simply said, "You got an answer for me?"

"Oh, no." Embarrassment had Cecily beet red; she knew this because she could feel the heat all over her face. "You don't . . . thanks, but I've got plans on the outside. I actually had plans to check out some classes tomorrow. So, I'm, um, making progress. But, really, thanks, Rothgar."

"You hear about Ally?"

"Allison? Yeah." Cecily nodded.

"Go meet her. If you like her, like the apartment, get it done. You might be off Armory territory, but you're still in our sights, and I'm not going to let anything happen to you. And that means making sure you log out with Missy before going into the wild. Don't think you're out of here, you're on your own. We're keeping tabs on James; we're keeping tabs on you."

Considering he was throwing her out, he was doing a good job. The way he said it, it *was* almost like he was asking her to take on a mission. Not the kind of mission that had as much appeal as maybe it should have. *Your mission is to get Shane to stop looking at you like he's starving. Which means you should probably go live somewhere else.* She glanced back at the table: Shane and Dex still throwing daggers; the other guys riling them up. "You've got a big job to do."

"Yes." Roth took a gulp of cappuccino, which seemed to empty the mug by half, at least. "This is what I do. It's important. And when something clouds the picture, I move the clouds. I try to make it a big win for everybody, but I'll settle for making it a big win for just my team if I have to. You get me, I think."

"I'm sorry—"

"You don't have to be sorry. But right now I need him thinking about the job, so there are decisions to be made, and like you pointed out, we're in the middle of something big. We've all got to do what we've come here to do."

Cecily took a deep breath. "Is it that you don't think it'll last anyway, or you don't want it to?"

"Does it matter?"

Cecily flinched but held her ground.

If she and Shane found their sweet spot, some place where they made sense in spite of their differences, a place without drama and distraction, why couldn't they have it all?

She just nodded. "I understand," she said softly, biting her lower lip with her teeth.

"Give my regards to Ally, if she'll take them." Rothgar raised his mug by way of dismissal and headed to Shane's place at the table. "Anybody got questions about today? Mostly same old, same old we've been doing for a week now."

A lot of head nodding. No questions. Cecily knew they were on to the next phase of building a case against Anya Gorchakov. That meant Shane would be out in his car a lot, which also meant that Shane wouldn't be rolling around on every available surface behind closed doors with Cecily.

"Shane," Rothgar continued. "Got something to add to your plate. Keep going with the usual today and tomorrow but add Romeo's night-time shift." He looked around the table. "I'm taking him off the roster indefinitely."

Shane's eyebrows flew up. Cecily had to wonder if Rothgar was giving Shane extra work to keep her away from him.

"Grab blueprints from Missy after lunch. You can hit me with any questions in an hour." Rothgar paused. "You got a problem with that?"

A faint snicker pierced the silence. "Aw, Shane, it'll be all right. You can be charming when you want to," Chase called across the table.

As Cecily took her seat, she made a mental note to ask Missy for a few more details about Romeo's specialty.

"I don't want to," Shane muttered.

"But you're good for it," Rothgar said.

Shane glowered at him, like he was pissed Rothgar had to ask. "You know I'll do what needs to be done."

"Glad you're good for something, bro," Nick called.

Shane turned to glower at him too and just missed being beaned by half of a bagel.

"Don't worry about Rothgar," Missy whispered to Cecily, licking the butter dripping from her English muffin over the back of her hand.

Missy said this a lot. Cecily wasn't planning to worry, but it did inspire her to get her ducks in a row with respect to her new career path and an alternative to living in a fraternity house with a band of mercenaries. It said something that she was feeling secure enough about things with Shane to think about what she wanted for herself during her own time. "I'm fine. It was super awkward, but it's not that big of a deal, since I'm not angling to move in permanently. I'm trying out some classes tomorrow. Rothgar's the one who shouldn't worry."

"Oh, yeah? You're planning to leave soon? I thought it was going well with Shane."

"It *is* going well," Cecily whispered, hoping Missy would take the hint and lower her voice.

"Aha!" Missy grinned. "I knew there was a reason you bought him a blankie. So do tell. Is bigger really better?"

Nick looked over, his eyebrows hiked.

Cecily buried her smile in her coffee cup.

CHAPTER 22

Cecily Keegan stood at the top of the steps leading into the design academy, shuffling some papers. Framed between two enormous Grecian columns, she looked up, smiling like she was making sure to spread enough sunshine before heading down.

A sight for sore eyes was putting it mildly. Shane, from his vantage point in the car, parked illegally next to a hot dog vendor he'd just massively tipped, thought it was the best city view he'd ever seen.

All he could think was, *How did this happen?*

He'd never harbored false expectations about his future.

First, he'd been a punk on a path that was supposed to end in jail. Rothgar pulled him out of that, and then he'd had the Hudson Kings, a family of brothers who made him think about more than just his own survival.

Maybe having an adopted family like that wasn't everything a man could ever want in life, but it was solid. And there were plenty of women around who didn't care that his heart was a block of ice, as long as his dick gave it to them hot.

And then one day, that man takes a drive. It starts the same way it always starts: key in the ignition, foot on the gas. But this time a woman named Cecily ends up in his car, and when the door closes behind her, Shane's entire life changes.

How did this happen? How did he go from nothing to feeling like all this beauty was only the beginning?

You're falling in love with her. Or maybe he already was. Since he'd never felt anything like this, he had no fucking idea where he was. But he'd take it. Life handed around enough shit. He was smart enough to know that unless you had a really good reason, you take it when the good stuff finally comes around.

A parade of people went up and down the building steps as he watched, some of them sitting down on the broad stairs with a cup of coffee, some standing in groups holding backpacks and portfolios.

Shane's practiced eye moved to a man heading for the stairs who didn't seem to fit the mold of either arty student or dressed-down faculty: expensive suit, all-American haircut, watch flashing too much in the sunlight. The guy put a tray holding two iced teas down on the ground and stepped to the side of the stairs to wait in the shade.

Definitely James. Adjusting a gun in the back of his waistband.

Shane pulled the keys from the ignition, barked at the hot dog vendor to watch his car, and fucking hightailed it to the side stairs on the far side, where James couldn't see him coming.

Cecily started down the steps. James picked up the tray of iced tea and called out to her.

Shane watched, his heart pounding, trying to figure out his move. If he revealed himself as one of the Hudson Kings, he'd know the team was onto him for what he really was. If he said nothing and just pulled a gun, it would probably imply the same thing.

Cecily stood frozen, staring at James, clutching her papers.

James was talking, holding out the iced tea, taking small steps backward; Shane figured the game was to lead her back into the shadows.

Cecily followed, slowly, uncertain.

Watching it happen made Shane want to be sick. *What the fuck are you doing, sweetling?* Then Shane remembered Rothgar had told her not to let James think she was 100 percent sold on getting clear of him. *Fuck!*

James's hand crept back toward his gun; Cecily looked back over her shoulder as she took another hesitant step. "I don't think there's really anything left to say, do you?" she asked James. "My brother doesn't want me to see you anymore."

That's *the answer right there.* Shane sprinted forward, and intercepted James before he could raise his gun, literally lifting James by the scruff of his neck. Tea splattered everywhere. Shane bodily yanked James into the darkest shadows behind the rows of columns, scraping the tips of his expensive wing tips across the concrete.

"Hi, James," Shane said into his ear as he pressed his face against the cement. "I'm feeling . . . oh, let's just, say, very unhappy."

"Who the fuck are you?" James managed to say. He wasn't a small guy, but Shane had the jump on him, and his arms were trapped beneath Shane's.

Shane squeezed tighter.

James grunted, struggling for air.

Shane jacked his right arm, about to punch James in the gut, a move that would have merely been an amuse-bouche to the complete process of showing the fucker exactly what Shane thought about his treatment of Cecily.

"She's not your girlfriend anymore, not after all the shit you said to her. Sure as hell not after you hit her," Shane clarified. "She's nobody to you anymore. I'm going to make this very clear. You don't ever bother her again. You don't call Cecily. You don't text, e-mail, walk, run, drive, nothing. She doesn't see your face. Ever. Again. Because if I find out that you've tried to contact her again, I'm going to damage you in a way that you will never come back from. I'm not even going to describe what happens if you actually try and *touch* her. She told me you were good with numbers; does what I'm saying compute?"

Shane loosened his hold but didn't let him turn, so the guy never saw his face; James fell to his knees, wheezing for air.

Shane jammed the toe of his shitkicker into the side of James's stomach and pressed. "Man, I would sorely love to beat the crap out of you right now, but"—he gestured to the sunny area out front where a young family was adjusting a baby in a baby carrier—"what I have to give you I just don't think this is the place. Now, you catch your breath, and this time I want an answer so's I know we have an understanding. *Does what I'm saying compute?*"

James tried to look up, one hand at his throat, one hand at his stomach. Shane wouldn't let him turn his head. The fucker nodded and whispered yes.

Shane looked around for Cecily. She'd turned white. His stomach dropped. She'd seen only a fraction of what he was capable of, and she looked horrified. *Can't change this part,* Shane thought. *This is what I do, who I am. The Hudson Kings.*

With one hand keeping James's face pressed to the ground, Shane used the other to grab his keys from his pocket and toss them at Cecily's feet. Her eyes widened, her entire expression a question, a shock. She looked down the steps toward the street, undoubtedly saw his car there, driver's side door still open.

Yeah, I want you to drive my car, sweetling. He signaled to her using his fingers. *Drive away.* James struggled in his grasp, and for a minute Shane thought she wasn't going to get it, but then he saw the light go on.

She grabbed his keys and ran down the steps, not sparing a glance for James cowering on the ground.

The minute Cecily was out of sight, Shane slammed James's face into the ground. The blood spatter from the guy's nose was a nasty reminder of just how much more he'd like to do to him—and just how stupid that would be in the big picture. *Keep your eye on the big picture.* Pretend you don't see the gun. He couldn't let on that he knew that

James was something more than a girlfriend-beating shitbag banker, and those kinds of men didn't generally carry loose weapons around New York City.

"You keep your face down, eating shit for a ten count, got that? I go, then you go, and we don't see each other again. You don't see Cecily again. Clear?"

"Clear," muttered James.

"One," Shane said, starting the count, then he disappeared himself into the shadows and ran. He pulled out his cell phone and dialed. His heart pounded, his head clouding with paranoia and fear. *It was too much, what she saw me do. She's gonna hand me the keys and get out and walk away.*

"I just kept driving," Cecily said, her voice nervous and thin. "I'm double-parked outside a place called Gray's Papaya. Seventy-second and . . . um . . ."

Shane started laughing. "The hot dog joint on Seventy-second and Broadway."

Cecily actually giggled. "Yes. I was looking for a landmark, but nothing obvious. Guess I figured cops like doughnut shops, mercenaries prefer hot dog joints?"

"I'm already on the way," Shane said. "Hold tight."

"Don't hang up!" she blurted.

Shane softened. "I'm right here," he said, running past the old-school cobblers and dry cleaners tucked in next to the newer chain stores that dotted the Upper West Side. "Not going anywhere." His throat was on fire from running, but he booked it until he could see the distinctive yellow Gray's Papaya sign and the slogan No Gimmicks! No Bull!

Truth, that.

And then there was the car, double-parked outside, Cecily craning her neck out the window. She saw him, flipped open the driver's side door, and moved herself to the passenger seat.

He jumped in, fire in his lungs.

She held out her hand, the keys in her palm; she had to have no idea what a lifeline that was. He took the keys and she leaned over. Holding trembling fingers to his jaw, she kissed him.

Jaysus. She gets it. She gets me. "You okay?" he asked.

"Not even a little bit," she confessed. "What about you?"

He knew she meant physically; she couldn't know he was ripped up inside in a way that didn't draw blood but hurt all the same. *I thought he was going to take you.* He shook his head.

"That was—"

"Just about killed me not to tell him I'm your man, but I didn't want him to connect any dots. We need him to still think Dex is only on him because he's a candidate for Worst Boyfriend of the Year. If he realizes other Hudson Kings are in on his business, he'll suspect we know who he really is."

Cecily's eyes widened.

"Couldn't out the mission, couldn't let him . . ." Shit, he couldn't say what he thought James might be capable of—that he worried James might actually kidnap and try to get Hudson Kings intel out of her. It was just too much to put on her. "I couldn't let him be around you. Tell me next time if you're leaving the Armory," Shane added, trying not to let on how seriously torqued he was over this. "You know, just until this thing settles down. He drop any hints in voice mail or e-mail that he knows you're with us?"

"No," Cecily said. She looked bewildered, glancing into the rear-view mirror, then the side mirror. "I used to talk about taking classes here, though. If his side has what your side has, they could hack into the registration computers and see the classes I'm trying out."

"Listen to you," Shane said, shaking his head.

"I know," Cecily said. She bit her lip and looked out the window.

"What's wrong?" Shane asked.

"I'm trying to figure out when it's going to be over," she said quietly. "It's not over until James thinks I'm not useful anymore. But how do I know when that will be? I'm more useful to him now than I ever was."

"He doesn't know that," Shane said, praying it was true.

Cecily's hands were clasped together so tightly he could see white at her knuckles. "The only time I feel safe is when I'm standing next to you."

Shane loosened her hands and took one in his. "I'll be standing next to you a lot. You're not moving out of the Armory right now. Listen, I know you hate being told what to do. I know you want that normal life out here. So you do what you want to do, when you want to do it . . . and I do what I want to do to make sure you're safe doing it. I decide what that means, and you gotta fill me in on stuff like this. *And* you gotta stick with the Armory for a little longer."

"Okay," she said, not giving him a lick of sass, which confirmed just how much James's visit spooked her. "I won't move out of the Armory right now. But Rothgar—"

"He was the one who gave me the heads-up you were going into town."

"Oh." Cecily took a moment to absorb that piece of information. "Well, he did say he was planning to keep me in his sights." She bit her lip, smiling, and added, "All the same, I think he'd just as soon I go ahead and move in with Ally."

Shane went silent for a minute and then said, "Not surprised. He's used to extending the invitation, not to mention that having a civilian around is always added security risk. You being in the Armory is unusual."

Cecily frowned. "Now I *really* feel like I'm staying in a house with a host who doesn't want me."

"It's not like that. You *are* a liability, but that just means that there are people inside the Hudson Kings who . . . care about you. Understand?"

Cecily didn't answer.

"Think I told you I went through a time so dark I didn't mind if I died. Every day I'd wake up and try to figure out what the point was of getting dressed, and if I got dressed, all I had to think about was what nasty shit I was gonna get hired to pull off. And then Rothgar asked me to be part of the team he was building, a fully formed mercenary team. Said he had something to offer me I hadn't ever really thought about."

Shane squeezed her hand. "Loyalty. A sense of family. A sense of honor. You want to be part of it, live on the inside, you play Rothgar's game with Rothgar's rules. Someone like you wants to live on the outside, it's probably easier for him to keep things smooth in the Armory, but you've still got family to come home to, and he's still going to be looking out for you. Liability's maybe not the right word. What I mean is you've become someone who matters. To Dex. To Rothgar." Shane took a deep breath and finished with, "To me."

"My man," she said softly.

"Damn straight," Shane said.

He kissed her, watching the sides of her mouth curl up and wondering if her toes did the same. "And Cecily?"

"Yeah, Shane?"

"You drive a mean getaway car."

Cecily gave him a full-on grin. "I know."

CHAPTER 23

The handouts from the classes Cecily was sampling before committing to a study track were cool. But not as cool as she expected them to be. Or maybe as she wanted them to be.

Missy sat at the desk next to her, working on a blueprint for the next piece of surveillance to bring down a Russian sleeper agent.

Cecily's school material was about how to layer a picture of a customer service agent, complete with headset and irritating smile, into a photo of an office desk chair.

The Hudson Kings were also trying to locate James, who had gone quiet since Shane's little talk. Rothgar wasn't too happy about that, but Cecily got the idea he accepted it was the better of two bad outcomes. She didn't like to think what the worst outcome was in their mind, because she suspected it had something to do with the fact that James had been carrying a gun when he came to see her at the school.

Cecily lay on the twin bed thinking about how her classes were becoming something that just gave her an excuse to leave the Armory. Maybe she didn't want to leave as much as she thought she did. They only had one girl on the team, and, obviously, sometimes they needed a girl just to be a girl, regardless of her other skills.

She looked over at Missy, who was enthusiastically pounding spy-catching plans into the keyboard. "Why didn't you go with Shane or Chase to the restaurant to take pictures that night?" Cecily asked.

Missy looked up.

"How come no one ever suggested you go with one of the guys?"

Missy blinked.

"They know you're the shit. So, why didn't your name come up?" Cecily rolled over onto her side and leaned on her elbow. "Don't tell me Rothgar thinks you aren't good enough to go out in the field because you're a girl."

"Rothgar *knows* I'm good enough," Missy snapped.

Cecily sat up. "I'm sorry. Did I just push a button?"

Missy visibly forced herself to stand down. "He had a bad experience."

He did? Or you did? Cecily waited for her to continue. She didn't. And then Cecily recalled that she'd never seen or heard about Missy actually leaving the Armory.

"Shit! What time is it?" Missy asked, looking relieved to have an excuse to divert the conversation. She answered her own question with a flick of her phone. "If we're gonna cheer you up, we need to get going."

"I'm not sad!" Cecily said, laughing.

"I'm not either, but believe me, we're gonna be a helluva lot happier if we make it to the garage on time."

"On time for what?" Cecily asked.

"Car wash, my friend. *Car wash.*"

Cecily should have had more faith.

The garage was as amazing in the day as it had been on their date night, but nothing Cecily could see trumped the spectacle of Shane and Chase standing half-naked and dripping on the garage floor next to a bucket of soapy water, and a table holding a mess of beer empties.

They were wearing nothing but jeans.

Cecily knew this was going to be good for more than one reason, but certainly because from what she'd heard from Dex and gleaned from observation, Chase was a prankster, seemed to have few inhibitions, and liked to . . . perform.

This was also going to be good because Chase was used to building things, lifting things, making things, and moving things, which did very productive things to the region above his waistband, at least.

This was *also* going to be good because, well, *Shane*.

Music blasted from speakers. Missy put her finger to her lips and Cecily nodded. She had no intention of interrupting the show.

And what a show it was. The guys were talking about something she couldn't hear over the beat, and they were doing exactly what Missy'd promised. Washing cars. From their view on the side of the bleachers mostly hidden from sight, Shane's tattoo looked more badass than ever.

His body was a thing of beauty, muscles rippling as he worked. He turned away and sucked down the last of a bottle and then turned suddenly and leaped like he was shooting a three-pointer. The bottle smashed hard into a recycling can.

When he turned back to the car, Chase caught him with the spray hose and then followed it up by nailing Shane in the chest with a massive soapy sponge.

A string of curse words followed, punctuated beautifully by the end of the playlist. In the sudden silence, Chase said, "Lost your edge, Shane? Never turn your back, eh?"

Shane looked pissed. He grabbed his sponge and plunged it down into the bucket, sending soapy water everywhere. Chase backed up. "Come on, dude, let's just finish up."

"We'll get right on that. Let me shove this down your throat first," Shane growled. He jumped. Chase dodged. Shane attacked. Chase's foot hit the bucket, and both guys went down in a mess of water, soap, and hotness.

As they wrestled it out on the garage floor, Missy muttered, "Thinkin' maybe I'd like to be reincarnated as a Hudson Kings towel."

Cecily snorted, a little too loud.

"Shit, we've been made," Missy yelped.

It wasn't clear who'd won—other than Cecily and Missy—but the men were off the floor, looking up at them. "You two going to stand up there staring, or are you going to help?" Chase called out.

Cecily stood up, her hands on her hips. "I'm wearing a white T-shirt."

"I won't complain," Shane said.

"How 'bout you, Missy?" Chase asked.

"Washing cars is like the one thing that is definitely not my job around here. But, by all means, don't let us put you behind schedule. Keep on soaping and . . . yeah, just keep with that . . . touching and wrestling." Missy crossed her legs and settled back into the bleacher rack.

Chase messed with the music, and a new song started, one that was undoubtedly linked to a playlist called something like "Get Some."

"I know this song," Missy murmured. "I know this song *well*."

Cecily only had eyes for Shane. He was looking up at her, a spark in his eyes, a quirky set to his mouth. She wanted to kiss that mouth so badly.

"Oh-h-h-h, I think something's gonna ha-a-a-appen!" Chase swiveled his pelvis.

Missy's eyebrows flew up. She shifted in her seat, part fascination and part discomfort. "I've seen you do amazing things with tools, Chase, but this is new."

"You know my momma was a dance instructor."

"You going to dance for me, Shane?" Cecily called down.

"My momma was definitely not a dance instructor," Shane said.

"And yet," Chase said, adding a moonwalk and running his fingers down the arrow of chest hair leading south. "I believe every single man on this squad knows a particular routine of mine."

Missy burst into peals of laughter. "I remember that job. I think that was the best day of my life."

"The guys had to pretend to be dancers? Strippers? You are not serious," Cecily said, her jaw dropping.

"Serious," Missy said. "I auditioned them so Rothgar could make placements. Shane impressed, but in the end we needed him in the car, so I never saw his performance. All that talent just . . . wasted." She gave an exaggerated sigh. "There's surveillance vid somewhere with Romeo, Nick, and Chase."

"They couldn't handle this," Shane said, completely expressionless, but motioning to his body. "Woulda broke the tape."

When they'd stopped laughing long enough to breathe, Cecily asked, "How many beers are you in, anyway?"

"Just enough," Chase said.

Cecily watched Shane. He didn't appear to be having difficulty controlling his liquor, but Shane was definitely loose. Comfortable. Something had changed as a result of their big date. She knew it had for her, and now she thought she could tell it had for him. There was something freer about him, and it wasn't just the alcohol. Less tension in his body, not so obsessive with the highly focused concentration . . . it was like he was remembering how to live or something. *Well, so am I,* thought Cecily. *So am I.*

"Hey Shane, show Cecily what you'd do if you had to do it for a job."

"He wouldn't," Cecily breathed more than said.

"He would. He'd have to," Missy said. "Wouldn't you, Shane? If a job depended on it, you'd drop trou and dance, wouldn't you?" She baited him further by adding, to Cecily, "He's one of the most loyal guys I know."

Shane's eyes were on hers when she said, "Yeah, show me what you'd do for a job."

Shane looked at Chase. Chase looked at Shane.

"Come down here, then," Shane said.

168

Missy and Cecily exchanged glances and then rushed to the garage floor. At which point, very deliberately, Shane ran his index finger down his bare chest the way Chase had, but this time following his treasure trail farther down into the waistband of his jeans, where he cupped his balls.

Cecily's mouth dropped open.

"Oh, shit," Chase said. "He's all in!" He tweaked the music again and took a place next to Shane.

"Holy, holy, holy . . . ," murmured Missy, looking more out of her element than usual, reaching down and grabbing two beer bottles from the ice chest and handing one to Cecily. "I should have brought over a blender. I need a blender. Fuck, I don't know what I need . . ."

"Shane, my man, you ready?"

"You put any part of this on fucking social media, you're both dead to me," Shane uttered. "This" being the way he and Chase danced over to them, with Chase taking the bottle Missy still held and Shane taking Cecily's from her hand. With a nearly synchronized flick of their wrists, they slammed the bottles down on their belt buckles, sending the tops flying, then handed them back, continuing to air fuck the girls from a distance so short that Cecily thought she could feel the heat coming off their bodies.

"Oh. My. God," Missy said. She was blinking a lot, and the hair at her temples was damp, and not just from water flinging off the men as they danced.

Suddenly, Chase pulled Missy in, and the two of them started a wet sponge fight; Shane grabbed Cecily's hand, and everything slowed down.

Bubbles drifted through the air as he pulled her close to his body, walking her backward, away from the others, until they were blocked from sight behind a Humvee.

The music continued playing. Cecily giggled, and he just kept moving, dark eyes rimmed with eyelashes spiky with water, his lips curled in a knowing grin. As Shane's mouth found hers, she let her fingers roam his taut body, slipping through the soap on his skin.

She had on a white T-shirt with a pearl-and-rhinestone Peter Pan collar, topped with a cream-colored cardigan. She was wearing jeans and sneakers. The rhinestones caught the light, and Cecily reached out, laughing, trying to touch the rainbows dancing across Shane's skin.

Voices faded. Someone hit the dimmer switch, and the space went dark save for the muted rays streaming in from a couple of large skylights.

Cecily started in surprise; Shane hauled her back into him. "Not going anywhere," he said.

He captured her hand, sending it skidding, making a soap trail across his pecs.

"Too hot," she said, panting, struggling with her sweater.

He pulled it off, and his mouth was back on hers, his tongue sweeping against hers, fire, gorgeous fire. With a soft mew into his mouth, Cecily felt the wetness slippery between her legs. She unhooked her bra and let it fall to her feet.

"God, the way you fire up for me . . ." Shane's voice was a study in control. Control she was looking forward to smashing completely with her mouth and fingers and body.

"Figured the first time I'm inside you, we're back at the Four Seasons or something," he said. "Not on the garage floor. Fuck you properly."

"Fuck me improperly," Cecily said, tracing her finger over his tattoo. That got a laugh. "You're laughing a lot more than you used to," she said.

"I know," he said, drawing a lazy circle around one nipple, bringing it to a point with his index finger. He leaned down and sucked her nipple through the wet T-shirt until Cecily gasped from the sheer pleasure. *God.*

She moved her hand down to cup between his legs. His erection was huge; she could feel the heat of him, the strain beneath the wet denim.

He groaned. God, it was fantastic, the way he reacted to her touch. "Take them off," she said into his ear.

His eyes seemed to get even darker. He slowly disengaged, and then went to work on his jeans, pulling them off as he locked onto the sight of Cecily slipping her T-shirt over her head and then shedding her jeans.

His briefs were plastered to his erection. Cecily swallowed as he moved in and put his arms around her. Being surrounded by Shane's body was divine. Flesh on flesh, finally. *Finally.*

With one hand he reached back and upended a cart filled with moving pads and blankets, pulling her down with him.

"Cecily, I want you," Shane said. "You with me?"

"Yes. Yes. *Yes.*"

There was a pause—just the rough sound of Shane's breathing. In the dim light, she saw him grab his jeans, go for his wallet. Then his lips were back on hers, pressing her gently to the ground again. The sound of ripping tinfoil, and after a moment, the tip of his cock gently pressing between her legs.

Oh, god, yes, I want this, yes, yes . . . "Want you inside me," she managed, gripping his arms.

"Yeah, baby. I'm yours." Taking his own weight on his forearms, he pushed his cock slowly into her, so slowly she could feel her body open up to him. God, he felt so big, but she was more than ready. Slick, wet, pulse pounding, she threw back her head, arched her back, and took his cock to the hilt.

"Jesus, fuck, yes, baby, yes!" Shane gasped.

He pulled back and then drilled in, this time a little harder, a little faster. So fucking fantastic Cecily couldn't verbalize the pleasure. "Still with me?" he asked around the tongue licking her ear.

"Always with you, Shane," she murmured, squirming underneath him, desperate for more.

"What do you need?" he asked.

"Need you to fuck me hard," she begged.

His mouth smiled against her neck; she could feel his hot breath and the way his lips curled against her skin. "Hot little piece," he said.

And then he started to fuck her hard.

Cecily held on as his cock worked her, the pleasure building until she thought she couldn't take it anymore.

"Not yet," he whispered. "Like to take you higher." One hand slipped down to work her clit, his thumb stroking softly even as he drove hard inside her.

Cecily whimpered. "Oh, my god."

Sweat dripped off Shane's back as he thrust, owning her with every powerful stroke. "Jesus, this feels so good," he said. "Everything feels *so good* when it's with you. Go with me."

As if she could control it. "I go where you send me, Shane. I can't help it."

"When I touch you like this, when we're in that place . . ." He shook his head, his fingers teasing her clit, his breathing ragged. "There's just nowhere else that makes any sense. I don't get it. I don't get it. You just make me so fucking *okay*. That saying about being comfortable in your own skin? I feel like that when I'm with you."

"Oh, Shane," Cecily cried out. His words, his body, the look on his face. "I'm *coming*."

"Right with you."

Cecily held on to his shoulders as he fucked her to the end, her own orgasm brought to new heights as she watched him throw his head back and find the pleasure he'd been waiting for all this time.

CHAPTER 24

Shane's brain was skilled at compartmentalizing, but when you had someone like Cecily on your mind, it was hard not to let your thoughts drift.

Yesterday was like the kind of dream he'd never dared to dream. It wasn't just the moments where he simply held her in his arms, and it wasn't just the moments where their bodies joined, on fire, taking them both to higher ground. Nope. Not just the physical stuff. Because the way his body ignited when he fucked her, made love to her, even just fooled around with her—that was all due to something more. How he felt, how she made him feel. How, because of her, he could believe in something better for himself, for his life.

Shane took a deep breath and brought his focus back to the job at hand. Anya Gorchakov. If you had to be on somebody's tail, Anya's was not exactly a hardship. Thing was, Anya's ass didn't have the same kind of appeal it might have had before Cecily had rocked both his body and his entire belief system.

It was Wednesday, and, so far, this Wednesday was exactly like last Wednesday. Anya's Mondays were always like her Mondays, her Tuesdays like her Tuesdays, and so on. She was either lacking in imagination, completely OCD, living under James's thumb in the worst possible way, trying to look very predictable to camouflage something very unpredictable, or some combination. She'd perfected resting bitch face. She spent a god-awful amount of time making herself look nice, which was helpful in terms of Shane's surveillance, because it meant fewer hours outside of her posh bathroom at home. For a so-called model—and one who was sure tall enough and beautiful enough—she'd not been called on any go-sees, and she'd not participated in any shoots. As far as Shane and the guys surveying her house and her boyfriend's world were concerned, she had exactly two equally aimless friends who also appeared to spend a god-awful amount of time focusing on being beautiful.

Maybe that wasn't resting bitch face. Maybe that was quiet misery.

Shane ran his fingers over his lips as he watched Anya receive the same Waldorf salad at the same table from the same server in the same restaurant as last Wednesday.

He'd been wearing resting bitch face for a long time, only nobody called it that when a guy was wearing it. And now that he had Cecily, he realized it wasn't even RBF. His was just quiet misery. He watched Anya cut the first chunk of apple with her knife. No fucking salad could make a woman that sad.

Maybe being a Russian agent wasn't all it was cracked up to be. He wondered what she'd been promised in exchange for her services. He wondered if James delivered.

Anya would spend forty minutes eating that salad. Shane kept the restaurant window in his peripheral vision even as he walked a distance to the flower kiosk he'd been eyeing the last couple of times he'd been on watch.

He'd pulled out his wallet as they came into view: a bouquet of mixed pinks that made him think of so many things. So many things he wasn't used to having rattling around the inside of his brain. The glittery heart on Cecily's shirt as she lay on the bed in the hotel, her lips against his tan skin, the freakin' underwear she was wearing last night.

He checked the time, confirming again Anya was still eating. *Jaysus, this was fucking serious. It's serious when buying a girl flowers felt more intense than a gun pointed in your face.*

"Help ya?" the florist asked, trimming the stems off a pile of yellow roses dripping down the corner of a piece of newsprint by the cash register.

Shane ignored the question, his gaze just stuck on the pinks. What if there *was* more? What if a beautiful life wasn't just an idea a kid once had a long time ago?

I can try. I can try out this thing we started. For some reason, even though we shouldn't make any sense at all, she brings peace to my crazy.

Shane bought the pinks, told himself to remember they were peonies if she asked, and headed back to the car, checking his cell phones for good measure. Which should have been a warning, right there and then. He didn't need to check his cell phones. They would have rung if they were gonna ring. But he was out of his element, off his game, in another world.

And in the world he just toyed around with in his brain, Cecily's world, you missed things you weren't supposed to miss. You lost your certainty about things that should have been 100 percent clear.

In that real world Cecily lived in, your car gets hit, and you don't even fucking notice because you're busy memorizing the word "peonies."

Shane just stood there on the sidewalk, the water leaking from the bottom of the bouquet down his fingers to the street wasn't half as cold as the trail icing down his spine.

This had never happened. This had never, ever fucking happened. Sure, he'd been bashed, but not without ever seeing a thing. Not ever.

The right front bumper of his BMW was scraped up, red paint and white streaks where another vehicle had grazed it. Had someone done it on purpose to send a message? Shane knelt down and ran his finger over the damage; the red peeled off under his touch. Not the white, though, seared into the chassis like claw marks through his own flesh.

Worse, it was fresh. Hot fury replaced the ice. He stood up and looked around. He'd been sight distant and sound distant—*this* close—to his car the entire time and hadn't seen it happen. He'd missed it buying Cecily flowers. *He'd missed it. He wasn't there.*

Was this what it meant to work in a dangerous business and have that business touch everyday life, so you couldn't take a minute to get flowers for your woman for fear you'd miss something, or worse, that something wouldn't miss you? *Oh, man. This is not going to work.* Maybe it stood a chance with someone like Missy or Allison. Someone who was part of the life, like it or not. Cecily was not part of the life, and he wasn't going to force a square peg into a round hole and then worry about her for their entire relationship. That sick feeling, that bone-chilling fear he'd felt watching her walk toward James on those steps that day . . . she wasn't meant for this kind of life. And he couldn't handle watching her walk up to danger time and again just because of her association with the Hudson Kings. It couldn't possibly be worth it. He couldn't do it. He *wouldn't* do it.

Nothing this sweet ever lasts.

"What the fuck am I doing?" he muttered. "What the *fuck* am I doing?"

Shane dumped Cecily's flowers facedown in a nearby trash can and blocked it all out, everything. If he wasn't the best at what he did, he had no idea who he was. He had nothing if he didn't have his place at the Armory. That place was only as strong as the men who were part of it, and Shane wasn't looking to make it or him weaker.

He turned off the phone he'd reserved for Cecily. Anya walked out of the restaurant. He turned on the engine and followed her with his fucked-up car to the exact same places she'd gone last Wednesday. When his shift was up, and he turned her over to Nick, he dialed the Four Seasons and checked into the hotel twenty minutes later. In his room, he scrolled to Keegan, ignored Cecily's name, and dialed Dex.

Dex barely got his name out when Shane started to lose it. "I did not get it, man. I did not get it. Thought you were full of shit. Thought you figured I wasn't good enough for your sister."

"Wait a—" Dex tried.

"You had it pegged, and I didn't see it."

"See what, Shane?"

Shane hated the tone of Dex's voice. Dex was supposed to be pissed. Dex was supposed to have essentially unfriended Shane. But Dex just sounded worried and concerned, and it made Shane want to throw the fucking phone through the hotel window.

"In my head I assumed I'd be right there when she needed me. I'd be close enough. But I forgot. It's too easy, isn't it?"

"Where are you, man?"

Shane stalked the room, his chest heaving. "I wasn't there when my folks died. I wasn't there. I can talk the talk and walk the walk, but sometimes, you're just not there. I was at home. Didn't want to go in the car to get the pizza because I was playing video games. *Grand Theft Auto.* Thought it was fun. Guns and cars. Having the time of my life."

"Where. Are. You?"

"I'm fine. I'm gonna be fine. And Cecily's gonna be fine. I'm stepping out of frame, okay? Tell her to go hang with Ally. Tell her to find her normal. I'm not going to bring her close to danger and then not be there when they come for her."

"Shane?" Dex said something else then, but his voice went tinny as he talked to one of the brothers in the background.

"Do not trace my call. I don't need anything. Just wanted to tell you it's done. That's all I gotta say. I'm done with Cecily. She is not going to come to harm because of me. We cool?"

"Shane—"

Shane hung up, a flood of memories crashing through his brain. Then he grabbed his card key and headed for the bar.

CHAPTER 25

Shane wasn't at the Armory. He wasn't staying in his room. He wasn't on the job. And he definitely wasn't answering his phone. Cecily knew all this because she hadn't heard from him in two days. Not since they'd made love on the garage floor.

Or maybe she'd got it all wrong. Maybe they'd just fucked.

They'd gone from zero to sixty and back again. More than sixty, since it was Shane. Sure, he'd once told her that he wasn't a long-term play, but everything they'd shared since, the things he'd said . . . he couldn't still mean that.

Missy didn't know where he was. Rothgar might know, but no way in hell was Cecily going to ask. Dex said he'd try to track him down if she wanted, but he hadn't come back to her with anything.

So, she was in Missy's room, her thoughts spiraling down along with the tears on her cheeks, waiting for a man.

So, so stupid, Cecily. Didn't you learn anything?

The phone rang. Cecily grabbed at it. "Shane?"

There was a pause. "I can't protect you," Shane said over the line. "And I don't think I can live with that."

Cecily gripped the phone. "What are you talking about? You protected me from James."

"Lucky I was there." His voice sounded hollow. Detached. "I'm not always around."

She knew then. She knew he was going to make a point of it. Not being around.

"Nothing scares me anymore. Nothing."

What was he talking about? "Come back and talk to me in person, Shane Sullivan," she ordered, her voice shaking.

Silence.

"We were finding happy!" Cecily yelled into the phone. "Why are you doing this?"

There was nobody on the line to answer that question.

After an excruciating night that saw Cecily alternately clutching Bun-Bun and her cell phone for comfort, Dex stopped by the next morning, looking like he was forcing himself to do it.

To his credit, he handed over a box of bonbons. Pale-orange apricot ones and pink-covered coconut ones. Cecily knew that the orange ones were apricot and the pink ones were coconut because they were her favorites, and she generally only ate them with a slightly revolting wild abandon when something had gone wrong. She'd eaten a lot of them in the last couple of months.

Thank god you could get them in New York City.

"I messed up again," she whispered to her brother. She knew her face looked puffy and red.

"I thought I'd feel better about this not working out," he said. "I really don't." He tipped his head to one side and opened his arms wide. Cecily shuffled over, and he closed her in a bear hug. "Sorry, Sis."

"Me too," she muttered into his shirt. "But I'll be better soon. Because bonbons. Thanks."

"It's kind of a peace offering," he said.

"I know. It's a good one."

He smiled, and Cecily stepped back to grab another apricot sweet from the box and sunk her teeth in. She chewed, studying her brother's face. "Did you talk to him?"

"He called. It was brief. Just told me you were done." Dex scratched his face, looking uneasy.

"It's a little crazy Shane bothered to tell you. You probably got more phone time than I did. How very . . . Hudson Kings. Did he—"

"Um . . . you guys should really talk directly to each other. Listen, Sis . . ." Dex started in on a gentle speech about how things would be better soon and that this was probably for the best and now she could concentrate on really moving forward, blah, blah, blah. She stopped listening and focused on eating.

When he was done, Cecily pushed the box of bonbons away and simply said, "I know."

He cocked his head. "I thought you were more into him."

"Actually, I was falling in love with him."

Dex reeled back. "Whoa . . ."

"Yeah. So, I'm finishing up my meltdown, and I'm finishing up an entire box of candy—thank you, very much—and Missy's got some sort of Manhattan cure up her sleeve, or so she said, and then I'm coming home to cap the day off with some hot cocoa, and then I'm going to go to sleep and wake up and just . . . well, go have a life. A normal life where I don't make colossal errors about which men I spend my time with."

Dex opened his mouth a couple of times as if to speak but wasn't sure how to respond. "You were falling in love with him?" he finally asked.

Cecily looked at her brother, who was clearly feeling so awkward it was adorable. She would have answered, really, but she just couldn't get the words out without tears.

Dex's forehead furrowed. "Never should have sent him."

"You were having surgery. It's not your fault. You sent him to get me out of there. That's a good thing. The rest is on me."

His gaze moved across her face. "You cried pretty hard."

"He made it seem like we were something special, and then he just ended it," she whispered and then shrugged. "So, yeah, I cried pretty hard."

"But you're gonna be okay?" Dex was turbo gnawing that nail now.

"Focus on your work, big brother. I'm heading for normal." *Where nothing ever happens, and nobody's going to make me cry.*

Cecily watched him work through that idea and then watched as his face changed and he started getting pissed. "This is really . . . you know . . . I'm not sure what to do here . . ."

"There's nothing to do," Cecily said. "He played me. He's done playing. That's it."

Dex scratched his scruffy chin. "Listen, maybe it's not quite—"

"My favorite brother-sister team!" Missy chirped, pushing through the door.

Dex didn't shift his gaze from Cecily.

Missy raised an eyebrow.

"When you said he told you it was something special and, um, 'played you,' are you saying . . . ?" Dex asked. He made a vague wriggling motion with his fingers that Cecily could only assume was meant to indicate sex.

Oh, no. No. My brother is not asking about my sex life. No. Uh-uh. We are not. Just . . . not.

A massive silence filled the space.

Missy cocked her head, her hands on her hips. "She's really blushing. She's really blushing *a lot.*"

"I'm right here!" Cecily yelped. "Not to mention . . . whose side are you on?"

Dex's face was the definition of stormy. "I'm gonna go now," he said, still frowning as he turned and walked away.

Missy closed the door behind him, noticed the bonbons, and beelined to the box. "Nice."

She held up a set of keys, and with a mouth covered in pastel sugar announced, "Get dressed. Today, we ride."

CHAPTER 26

Missy was driving a deep-green James Bondian Aston Martin, and she was doing it substantially faster than any posted speed limit they'd flashed past. Yet Cecily was somehow not feeling her old knee-jerk instinct for exercising caution. If anything, she'd like to smash her foot down on Missy's and accelerate even faster. Feeling this pissed off, this aggressive was oddly empowering. She felt strong. That said, it was good that Missy was the one driving.

"You checked your messages?" Missy asked.

"You already asked me that," Cecily said.

"You looked for a note? Maybe he left a note sometime after he called."

"You and I are roommates. Did *you* see a note? I didn't."

"No," Missy said. "I looked everywhere. For a note, for a gift. For anything. I'd tell you that there must be a plausible explanation, that it doesn't sound like the Shane I know, that it doesn't sound like the Shane who's got stars named Cecily burning out his eyeballs, but . . ." Missy shrugged, her hands lifting briefly off the steering wheel. "I've gotta say, I'm having a hard time understanding why he's being this stupid."

"I'm having a hard time understanding why you're surprised he's being this stupid." And then Cecily giggled. "'Stars named Cecily burning out his eyeballs'?"

Missy fiddled with the music and found a Prince album. "He's into you. I don't get it."

"I get it; he's a man. That's all there is to get." She flipped down the passenger-side visor mirror, raised her sunglasses, and began applying a new layer of lip gloss over the one she'd licked off. "He's a man, and I'm still a shitty judge of character."

"You don't sound like yourself." Missy glanced over again. "I can't believe a couple weeks in the Armory have corrupted you this far."

Corrupted? It didn't feel like that at all. If anything, a couple of weeks in the Armory had made her feel stronger than she'd ever felt before. "It's just me. It's my life. It's time I grew up and stopped pretending there's such a thing as a happy ending."

Missy muttered something curselike under her breath, an unhappy frown marring her face, and then more loudly: "If you can't find it, what's to become of *me*?"

"Why do you always sell yourself short?" Cecily asked.

"Do I?" Missy asked. "I thought I bragged too much."

"You sell yourself short when it comes to men," Cecily said softly. "I'd say it will happen for you eventually, but I think I'm having trouble convincing myself it will happen to *anybody*. That said, we're in a sweet ride, heading into the heart of Manhattan, with a single errand and a pocketful of spending money. I vote we look on the bright side."

Missy gave her a look that said Cecily's positivity wasn't fooling anybody but that she was happy to fake it. Then she went back to driving.

"Is this your car?" Cecily asked.

Missy'd accelerated out of the garage so fast it was a wonder they didn't strip the paint off the side on the way out.

"Sort of," Missy said. "It's technically Romeo's."

Cecily's good-girl reflexes went haywire. "He doesn't get mad?"

"Well, he's never gotten mad at *me*," Missy said, reaching into the glove compartment and shifting past a sheathed knife, a pair of binoculars, a pack of condoms, and a bottle of eau de parfum to get to the

Scarface sunglasses, which she popped on without a second thought. "Rothgar's the boss and all. But just try and imagine what the Armory would be like without all the little comforts. You want something, I get it for you." She flashed Cecily a grin. "Romeo likes his comforts."

"Breaking rules feels better than I ever thought it would," Cecily said. Shane had been kind of a shock to the system in more ways than one, but little by little, Cecily had learned to enjoy a kind of freedom she'd never before known.

Cecily felt another pang, thinking of Shane. So he wasn't the man she thought he was, and getting over him was going to be a bitch. But she didn't regret her time with him. And it had helped her understand her brother better. She could see so many reasons why Dex would be attracted to his new way of life. She really could. The guys who worked for Rothgar weren't just coworkers. They were brothers-in-arms, as different as they all were, Missy included. They gave one another the latitude to do what they wanted in the moment, apologies accepted later if lines got crossed.

Unless, of course, it was a case of putting your hands on someone's sister.

But that was almost completely behind her now; Missy was driving her back through a tunnel, and on the other side was everything you'd ever file under the word "normal." This Allison everybody seemed to know was probably the most boring person on earth. And probably another case of somebody never to be touched.

Very suddenly, Missy busted out in falsetto, "I just want your extra time and your budda-budda-budda-buh *KISS!*" and then asked, without missing a beat, "Why'd you stay with that other jerk so long? No offense, but I don't get how that happens."

Cecily took a long, deep breath and just let the truth come out. "The money. I stayed too long because he had money, and I told myself things that made that sound like a good enough reason. He told me not to go ahead with my plans for design classes because I didn't have to work. I mean, it's so ridiculous. I love doing arty stuff. It wasn't just about work. But he was all into this idea that I shouldn't have to work and I—I just went with what he wanted. I'm not going to pretend that's not just completely gross and so stupid, but I just got so confused about . . . well, everything, to the point where it seemed like maybe I *couldn't* take care of myself without James and the money. It was all *so* stupid. The money doesn't matter at all. *At all.* I just . . . he could buy things I never thought I could have. I ignored that he didn't care if I was happy, if I was doing the things I liked. It was so seductive."

Missy nodded.

"Dex and I never had any money," Cecily continued, her cheeks flaming. She couldn't read Missy's face, but she didn't mind being honest, really honest. "I didn't know what it was like to have all that stuff. I got caught up, and if this makes any sense, I think I stopped liking him way before I decided to stop loving him."

Missy nodded and then raced into a karmically placed parking spot right in front of a really nice duplex and said, "Just press the first one. Ally's the only one who lives here now."

"Aren't you coming? This is the first time I've seen you leave the Armory since I got here. Don't you want to make the most of it?"

Missy's smile faded. "I'll stay with the car," she said softly, staring up at the windows of the duplex. "You'll love her. She's great. She can say dirty things in, like, twenty languages."

Cecily laughed and looked down the street—it was a fabulous block hosting a line of willowy trees, with petunias planted in square plots around the trunks—and just shrugged.

With Rothgar's earlier words in her ears, Cecily buzzed into the mysterious Allison's apartment, coming out less than twenty minutes later in a daze. Yeah, she liked her, liked the apartment, and was about a second from agreeing to terms when the wound in her heart called Shane started hurting again.

Maybe this was all a dream. Maybe Shane was captured by pirates, and it took him a couple of days to swim to shore and explain to her that it wasn't a game, and he wasn't done with her, just because he'd finally taken her for a test drive.

Missy started the car. "Nice, huh."

"It's fantastic. I said I'd get back to her tomorrow."

Missy's hand stilled on the gearshift. "You didn't seal the deal? Interesting choice."

"What the hell," Cecily said, suddenly annoyed.

"If you're worried about James at all, don't. The guys will be looking out for you. Rothgar made it pretty clear he preferred having you clear of the Armory. He needs Shane's complete attention," Missy said.

"How is that my problem or any of your business?" Cecily burst out.

"I thought we were being honest," Missy said. "And just so you know, everything to do with the Armory is my business." Then she added in a quiet voice, "I'm not trying to be a dick. I'm sorry. I don't know you that well, and I know you don't know how things work."

"I think I just fell off Shane's radar anyway," Cecily mumbled. "I'm pretty clear of him."

They drove in silence. "You must think I'm really weird," Missy said after a while.

"Unusual," Cecily said. "And I absolutely mean that as a compliment. The things I've seen you do, how you run that show even when the boys think they're in charge . . . that doesn't even count the things you can probably do with a crossbow and a sword."

They smiled at each other. And after another pause, Cecily said, "Let's stop talking about Shane. He doesn't want to pursue anything. He doesn't—" Cecily's voice cracked. "We're obviously attracted to each other, but you've already caught on that we're total opposites. I'm not unusual at all. I'm about the most normal person you'll ever meet. My mistakes are about dating stupid men or caring too much about affording a Prada bag. Shane's mistakes would be more like grabbing the wrong enormous weapon from the trunk of his car or filing documents under 'Bad Russians' when they're supposed to be under 'Drug Dealers Who Pay Using Twenties' or something. I don't think that Shane can live in my world, and vice versa. Since he seems to be done, I guess he doesn't want to, so it really doesn't even matter anymore."

"Then why are you coming back to the Armory?" Missy asked, gently, though.

Cecily felt her face burn. "I guess I just want to see him in person, say good-bye. Know it's real and not a mistake or a stupid misunderstanding."

"Shit," Missy said, studying Cecily's face. "This is really tearing you up. I was hoping there was a possibility you still just wanted to fuck him."

Cecily blinked back tears and looked out the window. "It's not like that."

"Fair enough," Missy said. "Let's not talk about Shane anymore."

"By the way, Rothgar told me to give his regards to Allison." Cecily looked at Missy. "I did, and she said she wasn't sure she remembered which one he was."

Missy's eyes got really big, and she swallowed like she had a lump stuck in her throat, but she didn't say a word, not for a while. Just gripped the steering wheel extra hard and drove until finally she just blurted, "Doesn't remember Rothgar, my *ass*."

CHAPTER 27

Cruise control. Shane was definitely on cruise control. Not a state that was completely unfamiliar, and in fact, he did some of his best work after completely blanking out his emotions. So it really was going to be okay. It was going to be how it should be.

He had no choice but to head back to the Armory after a few days working out of the hotel. Dex was going over his blueprint with Missy in her office when he came to pick up his own.

Shane waited in the hall until Dex came out. He'd never gotten a response to the e-mail he'd sent describing how he and Cecily had unexpectedly rendezvoused with James, so he didn't know what to expect.

Dex calmly took his measure of Shane and said, "You look like shit," which was somehow a big fucking relief given what he might have said.

And Dex was right. Shane hadn't slept a whole hell of a lot the last couple of nights, and it didn't look like that was going to change now that he was subbing for Romeo on top of his other work.

"Feel like shit," Shane said. "Listen, Dex." He hesitated a moment and then came out with it. "Told you what went down with James. Doesn't matter that Cecily and I got no future. When the team's done with James, I'm gonna find and deliver the full message I didn't get a chance to deliver. I'm gonna look out for our girl and make sure he doesn't bother her again."

Dex stared at the floor for a good while and then said, "When that time comes, looks like I got plans to join you." With a curt nod, he was on his way.

Missy held out Shane's blueprint and pushed a box across the desk, looking like she was waiting for him to start a conversation he was certain he was never going to start. Which is why she started it for them. "Can I give you a piece of advice for future reference?" Missy asked, filling the box as Shane began systematically checking that she'd included everything he needed: ear wire, a chauffeur's cap, a solid black necktie, and a gun.

"No."

"I think you'll appreciate what I have to say," Missy told him.

Shane gave her a look that said he doubted it.

"It's a good idea that when you finally fuck a girl you like, you maybe do something nice after. Like a phone call. A note is fine too. Something that says, you know, 'Hi, I'm aware you're not a blow-up doll. Have a nice day.' No matter what you read in those men's magazines, breaking up with someone right after fucking them for the first time does not belong in the 'something nice' column."

Shane did not need this shit. It had taken him days to get himself back in Hudson Kings headspace after breaking things off with Cecily, and now that he was in the zone, he intended to stay there. "Gonna pretend you did not say at least three unbelievably ridiculous things just now. Holster, please."

Missy made a disgruntled sound but shut up and tossed exactly the kind of holster he liked into the box.

Twenty minutes later he met with Roth and Flynn and Chase, who were doing the break-in portion of the job. Shane would rather trespass and burglarize a Russian mobster's girlfriend's house than sub for Romeo's gig, but at least he got to be in a car. And he couldn't remember the last time he'd argued with one of Rothgar's assignments. This didn't rate to be the first.

After the meeting, he headed to the garage to check out a piece of shit from the latest rotation of disposable cars. He got into one he didn't remember ever driving and headed to Kimper's, reviewing the rest of the to-dos as he drove. Address to, address from, backstory, the stall in which the prepped limo was parked at Kimper's, Anya Gorchakov's very sexy picture, which looked like something from a boudoir shoot of questionable taste, and the rundown of his story line. Officially, he didn't know anything about anything except that the car service had called him as a sub; he was an out-of-work construction worker moonlighting as an Uber Luxury driver who also subbed for Patricia Kimper's Upper East Side car service.

Gussied up, ear wire tested, and story absorbed, Shane parked his own ride in the back and then headed into Patty's stable. She was at the desk exactly as he remembered her from a few other gigs in the last couple of years: two yellow Dixon Ticonderoga No. 2s propping up a mess of dark curls and her eyeglass-framed face nearly pressed down to the green-lined ledger she was writing in.

"Hey, Romeo," she grunted more than said, not looking up. Then it must have hit her: the different cadence of his walk or his smell or something. Because her hand reached slowly under the desk, stopping only when he said, "It's Shane. Sorry to scare you. Roth put me on sub."

Her eyebrow arched, and a laugh slowly erupted. "Really." Just *really*. And then she aimed the car keys at his bicep instead of his hand and said, "No offense, but I really try to talk as little to you guys as possible. Ciao, *bello*."

Fuck, thirty years old and she can barely fucking see. He almost asked if Roth had someone watching over her. But Roth had someone watching over everyone who mattered. "Ciao, *bella*," he said gently and went to retrieve the limo.

With the earpiece on, Shane listened to Hudson Kings chatter as the rest of the team prepped for the break-in. Everything seemed to be going according to plan. At the time specified, he parked in front of the skyscraper housing Vlad Sokolov's real estate development company and several floors of incredibly expensive condominiums, called his position in to HQ, and waited.

Anya was early, and Shane was a little surprised to see she was escorted out the door by her boyfriend this time, as the logs from their surveillance had never suggested that was his MO. He called that bit of information in too.

The boyfriend must have weighed three hundred pounds and looked less like the successful—if crooked—financier he actually was and more like he'd been holed up replaying Bobby Fischer's greatest moves, without a decent shower or a vegetable side dish to be found.

Shane took a deep breath and tried to inhabit his role, making an effort to look stupid and unremarkable if anyone happened to glance a little closer. This didn't stop him from observing the way Anya held her body away from Vlad's and quickly bussed both of his cheeks, the idea apparently to let as little of him touch her as possible. Her distinctive purple handbag with brass knuckle handles was strategically placed between them, and the flyaway fur on the collar of her coat seemed to be shedding into his mouth.

Shane got out of the car and went around to open the door.

Anya gave no sign she recognized him from any of his surveillance activities. She paused as her boyfriend disappeared back into the lobby and Shane held the door. "You're new," she said. Thick Russian accent. Smoky, appraising eyes. Her black hair was slicked down, and her hot-pink lipstick was perfectly applied, almost angular in its application.

Her eyes flicked back to the skyscraper door, which had already swung shut, and then ran the length of Shane's body. She was hot just eating a salad, and Shane was discovering that when you actually had her full attention, she was even hotter. But she wasn't close to what he wanted. Funny, he never thought of himself as a guy with a type until Cecily. Glitter T-shirts molded to her tits, jeans and sneakers, that gorgeous hair and those perfect legs, tight little ass and a thousand-watt smile. A hot little piece and a big warm heart.

Fuck. Don't think about Cecily. Just the job.

"Just a sub," he said with a shrug, forcing a polite smile, staring at her mouth. It would be more suspicious to pretend he didn't appreciate her looks. He just wished the effect wasn't comparing how much more he wished she were Cecily.

He settled Anya into the car and got them moving. "On our way," he said for the benefit of both Anya and Rothgar on the other side of his earpiece.

"Shane, it's HQ. Snag. We need more time."

"There's not much traffic," Shane said casually. "I'll have you there in no time."

"Find some traffic," Rothgar said into his ear. *"You know what we discussed."*

Yeah, Shane knew what they'd discussed. But that kinda shit was Plan B. His mind was full of a bunch of questions he could not verbalize with Anya in the car. Questions like "Come on, guys, what the fuck is taking you so long to get the goods?" and, oh, maybe "What the hell is going *on?*"

"I'm not in any rush," Anya said, watching his eyes in the rearview mirror just like Cecily had.

Shane silently requested a slew of red lights and then had to ask himself why he was making this a big deal. He dealt with the unexpected all the time. That was part of his job. Why was he letting the thought of Cecily get in his way if he'd already given her up?

Shane hit another green light. "We'll be there soon."

"Find some traffic, Shane. You know what she likes," Rothgar repeated, his voice edged with tension.

"I'd really like a drink, but there's something wrong with the minibar. Could you pull over and have a look, please?" Anya asked. Shane glanced in the mirror; Anya had not actually tried to get anything out of the minibar.

Cecily is not your girlfriend. She is not your girlfriend, and you've already confirmed that you don't make sense. Do not fuck up a job for an idea that doesn't have legs.

Speaking of legs. The rearview mirror revealed Anya had gone commando. "Driver?" she asked.

"Solve this," Rothgar said coldly into his ear.

Shane turned into a cul-de-sac and eased the car to a stop.

He paused for a moment, staring through the windshield, knowing that if it came to it, he could make his body betray him just the way Rothgar wanted him to.

Close your eyes and think of oranges. And then go home and rip Romeo a new one.

CHAPTER 28

Cecily knew she had to make a decision. Fast. In the real world, Allison had e-mailed a follow-up, saying she was welcome any time. In the world of the Hudson Kings, Cecily had dined alone on overcooked ramen noodles and a seltzer because almost the entire team was out on a mission they'd been planning for weeks. Dex was in the compound somewhere, but he'd made it clear that he was not to be disturbed unless Cecily was actually on fire.

Her section of the Armory was ghostly silent for hours and hours, plenty of time to realize that Rothgar's request was beyond reasonable. These guys had a purpose here, a life, and a family. She'd felt part of this world when she was with Shane, but now she just felt out of place and awkward. A distraction, and not even anybody's welcome one.

This unpleasant sensation was amplified a thousandfold when Cecily stepped out into the hall with her hair in a ponytail sprouting from the top of her head, wearing Missy's stupid reject jammies and holding an empty mug destined for the hot cocoa machine.

Because . . . Shane.

Oh, how fitting, Cecily thought miserably. How goddamn fitting that it was finally going to play out in person . . . with monkey pajamas and bad hair.

As she stood frozen in place, Shane walked forward, his eyes on the ground, the click of his dress shoes accompanied by the cheerful clinking of car keys held loosely in one hand.

Black suit. White shirt. Tie untied. Hot pink smeared along that jawline, in the undone collar of his starch-heavy dress shirt. An uncharacteristic misstep as he saw her, his shoulder brushing the wall, the slight tang of bourbon in the air.

She flushed as he saw her and stopped short, his muddy reflexes processing her appearance. One, two, three. Confusion. Amusement. *I'm so glad I can still make you laugh,* thought Cecily grimly.

"You settle on a class?" Shane asked awkwardly. Not *How's it going? How are you doing?* Or, perhaps, a wild card: *I love you madly, and I'm an idiot.* Probably because he knew her answer would involve her heaving a large ceramic mug at his head.

Cecily stared into her empty mug and then looked straight at him. "Yeah. Picked one."

His head jolted up. "Any type of contact from James?"

"Nope. I think your message got through." Her voice sounded robotic in her own ears.

"That's great," he said absently, nodding, losing eye contact. "Yeah, you should go do that. You should get on with your life."

Cecily looked at him sharply, her eye returning again to the pink smears. "What is this shit? This is the first time I see you, the first time we really talk after you act like I'm your woman and we have sex, and this is how you think it should go?" She was either going to cry again or get pissed. She figured she'd done enough crying. "Why didn't you just go back to your room, avoid this hall, avoid Missy's room? Did you *want* me to see you like this?"

Shane blinked. "This is my reality."

"That doesn't mean anything to me anymore. Your reality is whatever you want it to be. That's what I learned from you and the rest of the Hudson Kings. And I think it's a fantastic way to live," Cecily said.

She longed to say more, ask him for more, like *Do you really want me to leave? Am I just a distraction? A disruption? Is it true that I'm not what you really want after all? Was it all just a lie? Do you honestly still believe we don't make sense in each other's worlds?*

He didn't offer a thing. Just stood there.

"I got your message, remember? You broke up with me. So what are you doing here?" Cecily asked. Her heart was absolutely pounding. Her head starting to spin. She thought she really had a grip on all of this, but her heart felt like it was absolutely shattering. Why on earth had she waited to see him, just to make sure the break was complete?

"Want to make sure you're okay."

She cocked her head and stared at him. "Do you mean James? Already told you he hasn't tried anything. Or do you mean given that you dumped me? Do you have any new thoughts on that?"

Shane looked brilliantly blank, and then he said in a resolute voice, "No new thoughts."

The pain in Cecily's heart was just excruciating. "The impression I'm getting is that you want me to tell you to go to hell so you can feel better about what you did." Oh, god, this was a really stupid idea. Coming back to the Armory. Waiting for Shane to come back. She'd told Missy she wanted to see him, and now that she saw him, she knew she never wanted to lay eyes on him again. *I've got to get the hell out of here. This isn't my place.*

"Not gonna feel better. Just wanted to—"

In a voice she made sure sounded frozen solid, Cecily said, "Wait. I don't actually give a shit about what you want anymore." Before the tears came, she just turned on her heels and lifted her empty mug, saying without even turning around, "Good night, Shane. Glad you got home safe."

She couldn't tell if he watched her walk all the way back down the hall, but she figured he had, and it was all she could do not to haul flannel-clad ass.

Cecily got back to her room, her taste for hot chocolate gone, wanting nothing more than the oblivion of sleep.

Missy was glued to a computer game, totally absorbed in another world as Cecily grabbed her suitcase and started packing up her meager possessions.

After a moment, Missy's fingers went wild on the keyboard and then braked suddenly before she swept off the headphones and yelled, "Boss kill!"

She saw Cecily closing the locks on her suitcase, and her face fell. "Oh. You're going." She caught Cecily's gaze. "Gonna miss hanging out with another girl. You sure you don't want to stay?"

Cecily nodded. "Yeah. Thank you so much for everything, Missy. It's been great bunking with you, and I totally appreciate it, but Ally's apartment is really nice. Are *you* sure you don't want to come with *me*?"

Missy's answer was exactly what Cecily expected: "This is family." The girl looked at her hopefully and added, "It could be your family too. You could join, stay."

Before Cecily'd been confused by the intense loyalty the team members dedicated to the Armory; now she just felt wistful.

Cecily was surprised at how incredibly lovely that idea sounded. An idea that she once couldn't imagine at all, before her definition of what "real life" could be had blown wide-open.

But she couldn't be at the Armory without being with Shane, and he'd confirmed "they" were not going to happen.

Cecily shook her head, managing a small smile. Then she got into bed and stared up at the ceiling, praying she'd fall asleep fast.

Missy got herself ready for bed and then turned off the lights. In the dark, from her own bed, she asked, "You know you can't tell Ally any details about the mission we're working on. She left. She's not inside anymore. We trust her to a certain extent, but she can't know about James's role as a handler for the sleeper agents we've been working on. You're clear on that. Right?"

"I'm clear on that," Cecily said. "Believe me when I tell you that I'm going out there for the normal. The mission stays here when I go."

"Good." After a pause, Missy asked, "You tell Shane you're going?"

"Why would I tell Shane?"

Cecily knew Missy wouldn't answer, and the girl didn't.

Cecily pulled out her phone and set the alarm. Then she sent an e-mail replying to Allison's follow-up from earlier in the day: Tomorrow's perfect. Will bring deposit.

And then, after holding it together, she very quietly broke.

CHAPTER 29

The bar was an Armory original, a part of the structure Rothgar hadn't completely ripped apart to upgrade for security or comfort. Clusters of big leather chairs sat among relics of the past, including an old clock from the Civil War era—which Flynn had probably rewired—and a wall stacked with barrels once used for moonshine.

Shane found Romeo at the bar swathed in a red blanket falling off one shoulder, looking like a depressed superhero. The big man himself was dressed down in gray sweats, and if he was sick, he was, nonetheless, drinking gin on the rocks.

Nick sat next to him, a chiseled Adonis in a suit, downing something fancier involving olives and a swizzle stick. He lifted his drink to Shane in greeting.

Shane went behind the bar, grabbed a beer from the fridge, and took a seat across from the guys. "You'd better be *really* fucking sick," he said to Romeo.

Romeo gazed at him with hooded eyes. He actually looked in pretty bad shape. "You do her?" he asked.

Shane took a giant gulp of beer. "I don't know how you do what you do. On call. Just like that."

"I like pussy," Romeo said.

"I like pussy too," Shane said. "I just like having a say 'bout what tail I'm gonna pursue."

Romeo stuck a piece of ice in his mouth and crunched down. "Sometimes having a mission on the line just makes it hotter."

"You like having Rothgar in your ear while you fuck?" Shane asked.

Laughter all around on that one.

"Kinda have to side with Shane," Nick said. "But mostly because those Russian chicks need more meat on the bones for my taste. I like a bigger canvas on which to do my art."

"Been Anya's 'driver' a couple of times," Romeo said with a cocky grin. "She's lonely, she's got a boyfriend who doesn't do it for her, and she likes to fuck the help. Probably because she's tired of being bossed around, wants to call the shots. She give you head?"

Shane drank his beer and stared across the bar at a point over Romeo's head. In his peripheral vision, Romeo grinned and elbowed Nick. "Rumors look to be true."

"What rumors?"

"That the lights have gone on at last. A man's not gonna complain about Anya Gorchakov sucking his cock unless he's got someone serious on his mind."

"She's sweet on the eyes," Nick said across the bar. "Dex's sis, I mean."

Shane's gaze shot to Nick. "You treat her with respect," he barked.

All that got Shane was another grin shared between his brothers across the way, there. "Seems like you're the one going scorched earth," Romeo said.

Shane put down his beer. "How's that exactly?"

"You're the one who told Dex you messed around with his sister, that she wanted it, and now you're done."

"Ouch," Nick said, with a laugh of disbelief.

"That interpretation has some serious spin, man," Shane said, getting up for another beer and realizing on the way that he was a little drunker than he'd previously thought.

"And you're the one with your face between another woman's legs," Romeo continued.

"Didn't give, didn't take," Shane said.

Nick and Romeo went silent.

"Started out, thought I could, thought I would. Kissed, yeah, hands all over the place, yeah," Shane said, taking his seat again. "And it was definitely heading downtown, but I put a stop to it. I know I told Cecily it wasn't going to happen for us, so I guess I was in the clear, but in that car, with that beautiful Russian chick . . . I wasn't going there. Just wasn't. Didn't want her. Couldn't do it with Cece in my brain, couldn't do it to her, even if we're done." He leaned his head on his hand and sighed, more exhausted than he could remember feeling in his life.

Nick let out a low whistle.

Romeo stood up, a little wobbly, a lot pale. "Just for the record, I really do not feel well."

Shane shot a look of irritation toward him for the benefit of Nick, who was smiling around the red straw he was chewing.

"He's gonna boot," Nick said.

"Saying that just might make me," Romeo managed, moving quickly and very unsteadily. "I bid you two a good . . . oh, man . . ." And he was out the door.

"Who drinks gin on a sick stomach?" Shane asked.

"Old family remedy, I'm told."

"*I* need a fucking remedy," Shane said.

Nick slid one of the olives off the pick and chewed. "You're thinking too much. I realize you've probably been blindsided and all, but you're thinking way too much. I've seen you two together. It looks right to me. Why are you fighting it?"

"She's not Armory material."

"Nobody expects her to clip bomb wires or steal a briefcase in a crowded restaurant. Why does she have to be?" Nick asked.

"You never think about what kind of woman might fit into your life?" Shane asked.

Nick grinned. "All the time, but, like I said, I need to get back to normal first."

"How's that coming along?"

"If it was coming along, I'd still be living in my sweet penthouse instead of shacking up like a fraternity brother in a war compound. Not that the breakfasts aren't worth it, but still. I like my own space. And I'm worried about my fish." Nick downed the end of his drink, tossed the swizzle stick and toothpick into the trash, and slid the dirty glass lightly enough for it to zoom down the bar and end just short of the sink. "Put it in park, Shane. You were happy with her."

"You giving Shane relationship advice, Nick?" Rothgar slid onto the bar stool next to Shane's.

"Wouldn't dream of it, boss," Nick said with a wink before making himself scarce.

"Can't remember the last time I saw you in the rec room," Shane said to Roth.

The boss looked tired. "Me neither," Roth said. "Been building this business a long time. Work never ends."

Shane ran his finger along the wood grain of the bar. "I know my head's been . . . I don't want to say messed up . . . let's just say I know I'm not giving what you normally get."

"Wanted to talk to you about that," Roth said. "It occurred to me that maybe I got things wrong. Still not the hell sure, but I'm rethinking some things."

Shane hooked an eyebrow. "Something happen?"

"Yeah, something happened. A man I thought was iced over wasn't. Found I was taken by surprise. Didn't like that I was surprised. Did some thinking. Things change, and this job, what I do running this place, I can't make assumptions. Gotta watch for changes. Gotta adapt. That's how you survive. That's how you keep talent. That's how you keep the family strong . . . I shouldn't have put you in that car with Anya, Shane."

Shane stared at Rothgar. "It's my job, Roth. I owe you—"

"You paid that debt long ago, brother. If you want to be here, be here. I want you here. And I need your skills. But you don't owe me shit anymore. Not in that way."

"If it wasn't for you, I'd be in prison. I'd have nothing but bars the rest of my life. I owe you—"

"Nothing," Roth said. "You've been on the team ten years. You know it's true. You're a good man. You figured out how to be a good man, and you found a woman who wants to love you, and if you care about her, then I gotta change, and I gotta adapt our game plan so that you don't have to cross a line that threatens what you're gonna build with her. You know we've already got her back because she's Dex's sister, but if she weren't, I'd take her back because she's with you. You got me?"

"Jesus," Shane whispered. He just shook his head in wonder.

"We have all this," Rothgar said, gesturing with arms wide. "We have this because we had nothing else. We built our own world with rules we like and people we care about. Now you got something else you like and someone else you care about. I hope to hell you don't leave our team for it, but, brother, I've watched you go from iced over with dead eyes to the dictionary definition of happy. Nick is right."

A hint of a smile washed over his face. "Don't think I don't see all. You want to try and have it all, as long as I believe it's the real deal, I'll do what I can on my side. Fact is, you got someone, and I'm happy for you. Tomorrow morning, you wake up, you clean yourself up, you take the happy you deserve." Rothgar pushed away from the bar and headed for the door. "'Night, Shane."

CHAPTER 30

Shane didn't sleep much that night. A hundred times he thought about knocking on the door—*fuck the time*. A hundred times he told himself to let her sleep.

She'd asked him why he had to come see her if he had nothing new to say. All he knew at the time was that he had to know she was okay.

He finally went under himself, Rothgar's words ringing in his ears.

By the time he woke up, got himself straightened out, and knocked on Missy's door—he had headed for Missy's office, figuring he'd rather try there than Dex's—it was 10:00 a.m. and the room was silent.

Missy was up as usual, pounding a set of plans into her computer. Shane poked his head through the doorway. "You know where Cecily is?"

Missy waved him in but kept typing.

Shane strode in, impatient and refusing to sit down.

Missy pressed "Print" and pushed back. "What the hell are you doing?"

"Come again?"

"Why are you messing this up?"

"Why are you getting personal?" he shot back.

"Because you obviously need someone to tell you when you are fucking up."

"Have you even turned eighteen yet, Missy?"

She rolled her eyes. "Fine. Whatever. She's already gone, Shane. Went to go do normal. Left this morning. It's not like she had a lot of stuff to move."

Shane's breath hitched.

"What's the matter, big guy?" Missy asked. "Are you feeling something?"

"Is Dex on it?"

"On what?"

"Does Dex have surveillance on her?"

Missy raised an eyebrow. "If he thinks she needs it, I'm sure she'll get it."

"Tell him she needs it right away, not after something happens."

"I'll be sure to pass him a note in science class." Missy looked up and saw from Shane's face that he was not in the mood for snark. She sighed. "Sorry. But you and Dex need to patch things up."

"We're on our way," Shane said.

"I guess it takes a little time after you fuck somebody's sister and then give her the cold shoulder," Missy said evenly, peering into the empty barrel of her stapler. "Maybe that's bothering him a little."

"Fuck, Missy. Maybe it's bothering *you* a little."

That got her full attention. She went silent for a moment and then said, "She was in love with you. I think you're in love with her. I wish I had that. I don't understand how it went wrong. I don't understand why you think that's okay." The tips of Missy's ears were red. Shane couldn't ever remember Missy getting embarrassed about anything. "I'm sorry if I've been a dick about it, though. Really."

Shane nodded. He thought about defending himself. He thought about explaining how he thought for a second he could do normal things like take his girl to dinner and live that kind of life. How tailing Anya that day and having his car messed up without his having a clue broke something in him. Well, showed him that he was already broken, probably forever. How he'd realized that by loving Cecily she would always have a relationship with danger, and he couldn't always be there to protect her. How Rothgar had essentially given him his blessing last night. He didn't need it, but, damn, it was nice to have. How he tossed and turned all night thinking how he was going to explain to Cecily why he was all stop-and-go with her and how he only wanted to be "go" from here on out. How he couldn't wait this morning for her to open the door to her room so he could explain himself.

And then he remembered how it always came back around to this: *I just don't see how it ever ends without us standing in an alley staring at each other like we just can't understand what the hell the other person was thinking.*

"She was right to go. She can do better," Shane finally said.

Missy's hands froze on her keyboard. "What the hell kind of *better* do you think we want?" she asked.

"What?"

"If you have to ask, never mind. Now, can you get out of my office so I can finish ordering the twenty thousand pounds of beef you boys go through in a week? I'm not your fucking therapist. Go find Dex. Sort it out."

"She with Ally?"

Missy's jaw tightened. "Of course."

"You and Ally need to patch things up."

"It's too late, Shane. Really. I don't think we have anything new to say to each other that's going to make a difference," Missy said. "Better to let it all stay in the past."

"I know exactly how you feel."

Shane closed the door and stood in the hall for a moment. It was so silent he could hear the second hand ticking on his watch. Another planning session with Roth, a couple of jobs for the team, Anya would be in the can, and then he'd hit the road until Roth needed him again. Maybe he could leave sooner. Because Missy had the right idea. He wanted Cecily when he wanted her, when his body was going crazy for her and his mind wanted to pretend they could have some sort of future, but then he wanted her to let him go. For her own sake.

She deserved better than that kind of emotional whiplash, especially with James on her rap sheet. Shane would make her fall in love with him knowing he'd eventually just break her heart, never come back.

But out of sight wasn't out of mind.

He headed up to the dining hall. It was after hours, deserted, but the refrigerator was packed with leftovers. He brought the food back to his room and ate off the tray, alone.

CHAPTER 31

Thankfully, Shane had plenty to keep him occupied since it turned out they weren't done with Anya Gorchakov. Rothgar described the take from Anya's home computer as lackluster, one of several words the boss liked to use when he wanted to convey something was catastrophically disappointing.

Nobody's fault. It was what it was. But the intel they'd retrieved from her house wasn't going to be enough. Shane absently wiped the back of his hand against his mouth, thinking about the circumstances under which they'd retrieved it in the first place.

So, here they were, a week later. Rothgar'd moved on to a new plan, explaining the strategy to gain entry to and sift the so-called fashion co-op Anya shared with several other models. It was a warehouse loft in the Garment District, where a bunch of those pretty, lonely girls who only ate salad took photos of themselves for portfolios and social media accounts.

Precision timing wasn't the focal point this go-around, and thank fuck Shane's piece didn't involve playing dress-up this time. He'd get the drop-off directly from Nick this time, a handover through the window. Easy enough.

The war room was humming. And not just because the team was working out the details of Anya's takedown.

It was also humming because of the palpable tension between him and Dex, who was still holding a grudge over Cecily.

"If you don't let it go, I sure as hell can't let it go," Shane murmured over his shoulder. He'd never get over Cecily—wasn't even sure he wanted to—but, man, he'd surely love a vacation from thinking about how it had all gone so wrong and the ways in which he'd screwed things up.

Except Dex wouldn't let him forget. "I still don't know what's worse. You sleeping with my sister and then getting clear of her, or you sleeping with my sister and not getting clear of her," Dex whispered back.

"Damn it," Rothgar hissed, raising a palm to stop Missy from passing out the plans. Every head in the room snapped up. Roth was glowering at Dex and Shane. "I'm about five minutes short of ordering the two of you into the ring."

Shane looked at Dex. Not a bad idea. He wouldn't mind taking a swing, truth be told. "Not a fair fight." He gestured to Dex's leg.

"Then I guess you'll have to talk it out. Starting now."

Shane hated it when Roth played Dad. The sooner this was over, the better. He sighed and then laid it out. "Listen, Dex. I'm sorry I messed with Cecily. Sorry about how it played out. You know I'm not a player, and what happened wasn't some random shit. But I shouldn't have touched her in the first place, and for that I apologize."

Shane was already pretty tapped out on patience, and the too-interested expressions on the faces of the rest of the guys who'd gophered up to get a piece of the apology didn't help. "We good here?" he asked Roth.

Rothgar's arms crossed against the massive barrel of his chest. His mouth remained hard-set, and only his eyes swiveled to Dex. "You. Go."

"Just leave her alone. She's not good for games. She's the real deal." Dex's voice rose. "I need everybody to just leave her the fuck alone."

Shane cocked his head. "'Scuse me, but it's been a week since I even saw her. James bothering her again?"

209

"Nothing specific, thanks to the message you sent him," Dex allowed. "Cecily just feels uneasy. At this point, I'm trying to figure out if he's left town." He glanced at Rothgar, still waiting, still grim-faced, before turning back to Shane. "But it's not your business, and it's not your problem. Just need to know you're going to leave her in peace."

"Thought I'd done that." Shane felt a wave of possessiveness sweep through him. He hated the idea of Cecily feeling unsafe. "And I know it's not my business anymore, but, believe me, it's still my problem, since I seem to be in love with her."

The room went dead silent. Dex's eyes widened. "You're not very good at it," he finally said.

Someone laughed and got shushed.

"Yeah, and don't I know it," Shane said.

From the look on his face, Dex apparently didn't know whether to laugh or throw a punch. "You realize you just admitted that in front of everybody," he said.

Shane ran a palm over his face, feeling the exhaustion set in. "Welp. I guess it happens to the best of us. She's moved on, and she's living the nice, normal life with Ally you always wanted for her. Speaking of which, Cecily living with Ally means you're good for surveillance there."

Missy cleared her throat. "There hasn't been surveillance on Ally's place for at least a year. She cut the—"

Shane's, Roth's, and Flynn's heads swiveled around. "There's no surveillance at Ally's?" Shane asked in total disbelief.

A wave of dark, dark anger rolled out from the front of the room; Rothgar's expression alternated between fury and some kind of really intense pain. "I thought we overrode that decision."

"We talked about it, but she—"

"We overrode that decision," Rothgar roared. "You are not telling me we don't have eyes on Ally, are you? You are not fucking telling me that."

Missy's jaw set. She got up, her chair hitting the back of the desk from the force. "I'm telling you that. I understood that was the—"

"Even if Allison wants to go dark, she's not gonna go dark. You get that? She never goes dark, not until we find out for sure that Apollo and Graham are one hundred percent gone for good."

Missy blinked, desperately trying to hold back tears welling in her eyes. "Well, she *is* dark, and—"

Roth looked around at the men, his eyes settling first on Shane, then switching to Flynn at the back of the room. "Flynn, get over there and fix it," he barked.

"Stop interrupting me, Roth," Missy yelled. "I'm not just some stupid girl who lives in your house."

"I don't understand how this fell through the cracks," Roth replied, his voice scary-low.

"Apollo is *my* brother."

"How does something like this fall through the cracks?" he thundered.

Not a sound came from the rest of the room as tiny Missy went toe-to-toe with Roth towering over her in a complete rage.

"It was obviously a miscommunication," she tried out.

"Was it?"

"It's hard to remember everything that happened," Missy whispered, still holding her own. "It was a long time ago."

Rothgar nodded slowly. "But it's not over, you understand. It's never over until we see the bodies. Apollo was your brother. Graham was Allison's. But they were part of *this* family too. They were ours." His head turned slowly to the spot where Flynn was now standing. "Flynn, get Ally back into the light as fast as you can." He looked over at Dex and Shane. "If Ally's in the light, so is Cecily. Two birds. And then maybe we can get some fucking work done, right? We'll pick this up as soon as you're back."

Flynn nodded and headed out. Rothgar and Missy stared at each other. "She doesn't want anything to do with us," Missy whispered. "She'll never forgive and she'll never forget."

"I don't give a goddamn if she forgives or not. I don't care if she curses my name every night before bed. I just care that she's safe. Don't let there be a next time you keep Kings business from me." Rothgar stuffed the latest plans in a folder and headed out, the door slamming behind him.

CHAPTER 32

When the Hudson Kings were whole, Allison and Missy must have made an adorable odd couple. Missy was all tomboy, Allison the ultimate girlie girl who had entire closets filled with high-end craft supplies, sewing embellishments, and party dresses.

In fact, she worked as a buyer for one of those fast fashion apps, and the apartment was decorated like an article about turning out your apartment for designer tastes on an economy budget.

The living room featured bold black-and-white stripes kicked up a notch with a hot-pink coffee table and super-fluffy pillows that looked like they could conceal a kitten for an hour or two, and you'd never notice the difference.

It wasn't so done up that it was uncomfortable, though. On the contrary. Ally had made it ultimately about being comfy, and at the present moment she and Cecily were entombed in those furry throws, kicking back on the sofa, comparing the perfume strips pulled from a massive stack of fashion magazines.

It never felt like you weren't supposed to touch anything. It just felt like someone made it nice enough to stay home so that you might think twice about going out—particularly, as Allison suggested, if there were no good men left in Manhattan who could compete with the warm embrace of a cashmere throw, a good movie, and a slice of pizza.

A buzzer sounded. "That was fast," Allison said, getting up and heading for the intercom. She pressed a button and just said, "Come on up."

Then she rummaged through the pocket of a coat hanging on a hook by the door, pulled out a few dollars, and said, "Hope you like pepperoni. I got an extra large 'cause I like it for breakfast."

She opened the door, yelped, "Oh, shit," and slammed the door.

Cecily leaped up from the sofa, her heart pounding. "Not the pizza?"

"Not the pizza," Allison whispered, every molecule in her body appearing to be on high alert.

"Open the door, Ally," a man's voice said. "If you were going to open it without even checking it was the pizza guy, you can open it for us."

"Nobody likes a cold pie," said a second very familiar voice. Cecily's heart started pounding.

Allison kind of stood there, staring at the closed door, wringing her hands.

"Allison?" Cecily prompted. No response. *You can do this. It will be the good-bye you wished you'd had.* She stepped forward and looked through the peephole. Shane and Flynn waited outside, a pizza box between them. She took a deep breath and opened the door.

"Christ, Ally, have you forgotten everything you ever learned?" Flynn asked, barreling in and tossing the box on Ally's coffee table. "Are the cameras to the front door of this building even on?"

Allison stared at Flynn for a minute and then seemed to wake up. "I have no idea, since I never think about them. I put all that stuff behind me."

"Except you never turn away Missy's strays. That's not cutting ties, and you know it."

"I guess some part of me thinks that if you ever find my brother's bones, I want to make sure you know how to reach me," she snapped.

Cecily sucked in a startled breath and then looked back at Shane, still standing outside the door.

He tipped his head, clearly taking her measure. His eyes moved down her body, pausing on her clothes. She'd only worn a dress around him that once, on their date. He obviously liked her in dresses. She shouldn't have cared, but the blue floral she was sporting was one of three new summery dresses she'd picked up for peanuts at Century 21, with Ally as her personal shopper, and it fit perfectly, which meant he was taking in everything he'd thrown away: cleavage, curves, and legs. "Missy says you're doing okay," he said quietly. "You settling in, kid?"

Oh. That doesn't sound like regret. "I'm great," Cecily lied enthusiastically. *Thud, thud, thud. I'm great, other than that just seeing you again is giving me a heart attack and you've already made it back to "kid."*

Shane's fist clenched and unclenched. "Good. That's good. Gonna help Flynn with Ally's situation here." He picked up a tool kit waiting by his feet and stepped past Cecily into the apartment, the warmth of his arm brushing hers. She closed her eyes for a second and then shut the door behind him.

"Jeez, well, hello, Shane. Come on in. By all means. Yeah. So, here's the thing. I no longer have a situation. Haven't had a situation in a long time," Ally said. "If I wanted to live a life that included *a situation*, I'd have moved into the Armory when I had the chance."

"You never lost the chance," Flynn said. "The offer stands."

Allison licked her lips, her body language awkward, her gaze steadier on the floor than on anything else. "You realize how much time has passed, right? I barely even recognize you."

"You should see my good side," he said, turning his profile sharply to the other side.

It was obvious that Flynn had been a really gorgeous-looking guy before he'd taken an explosive to the face. Cecily couldn't know what he thought, but she thought that the mess on one side couldn't detract from the overall picture. Maybe it was his self-confidence, and certainly the accident hadn't lessened his natural charisma, but he still had it. Seeing the sleeves of his navy Henley rolled up, you got a sense of what else might lie beneath the rest of it, his cargoes, and the heavy boots: Muscle. Mass. Man. Cecily studied Allison and knew she wasn't alone with this. The girl just wasn't going to let the men see whatever she was really thinking and feeling.

Allison sucked in a quick breath and then pressed her lips together tightly for a moment as she processed a full view of Flynn's messed-up face. "People who hang out with the Hudson Kings don't seem to last as long as people who don't."

"Truth be told, as a team, Roth makes us last a lot longer than we would on our own."

Allison snorted.

Shane pointed to the foyer ceiling, and Flynn looked up at a jagged area in one corner. "You rip those wires out?" Flynn asked.

"I sure did," Ally said.

Cecily felt Shane's eyes on her; she forced herself not to look over. One touch of his arm was one touch too many.

"I'm gonna put them back," Flynn said. "You gonna do it again?"

Ally paused and then belligerently asked, "You gonna watch me walk around in my underwear if I don't rip them out?"

"Well, you look real good to me, honey, but I'll have to say no. I don't sit at my desk and watch a live stream of our tagged friendlies getting off and eating breakfast. I actually have things to do. If we have reason to believe the threat level's up, we'll let you know and take it from there."

"My threat level hasn't been up since Graham disappeared. Not once. It's over, and there's nothing left to say about it." She said this bitterly enough to grab everybody's attention, and Cecily felt the loss of Shane's gaze.

Flynn turned to Shane. "You take the front of the place; I'll take the back, yeah?" Shane nodded and moved away, but Ally stood her ground in front of Flynn.

He sighed. "Would it be asking too much for a glass of water?"

"If you want to look around, you're gonna look around. Get your own damn water if you're actually thirsty. You don't need to fake it."

"Not with you, for sure," Flynn said, looking Ally up and down.

"Are you flirting with me?" Ally asked in disbelief.

"So, can I look around your place and install some new wires?" he asked by way of a complete nonanswer.

Allison just stared at Flynn's ravaged face.

"Faulty equipment," he said tightly. "A freelancer who wasn't as good as he said he was. You should see *his* face."

A look of pain crossed Ally's face. "'Tagged friendlies,' huh," she muttered, just under her breath.

"The guys miss you," Flynn said. "There's always a job for you there too. We don't have anyone there good with languages. Using freelance now."

"Thanks, but fashion risks are the only risks I'm interested in taking." Her voice was flat.

The smile on his face vanished. "Water and then the install?" Flynn pressed. "I'm actually thirsty."

"Yeah," Ally said, oddly defeated. They disappeared into the kitchen.

Cecily turned to Shane, but he was already off on his own, stalking around the apartment doing a repeat of what he'd done at the hotel, and more, poking at various wires, getting showered with dust, and the like.

Within minutes he was standing on one of Ally's dining room chairs, protecting the upholstery with a *Vogue* and doing something clever with a screwdriver in the light above the dining room table.

Cecily watched him work, feeling her composure begin to slip. She remembered the scent of his skin when she tucked her face in his neck. She thought of his mouth taking hers and the sensation of those slow strokes when he—*holy crap, you need to stop thinking about that!* Wiping away sweat from the back of her neck, she grasped at normalcy, asking, "How's Dex? You guys back to normal?"

"We'll get there," Shane said. He pulled a small black object from his pocket and began installing it in the light fixture. "Anything weird going on? Any gut feelings or weird electronic shit I should know about? James get in touch?"

"I wouldn't keep that to myself. It's been quiet since I left," Cecily said, hating every second of this measured, friendly, too-polite conversation. She watched his muscles working as he tweaked the fixture one last time and jumped off the chair.

"I guess things are back to normal for all of us." She had no idea why, but she curled her fingers around the bulk of his bicep and gave him a squeeze.

Shane looked down at her hand on his arm, something yearning sparking in his eyes. "I wish . . ."

A thread of hope curled around Cecily's heart.

But he just smiled and said, "I wish I hadn't jerked you around so much. Wasn't intentional. I wanted what I wanted. I wanted to have it all, but I guess nobody gets to have that. We had some good moments. Nah, some *fantastic* moments that I'll always have with me."

Shane pulled away and put his tools back in the kit. "You're going down exactly the right path. This is all right. You're gonna do that arty stuff you like and mix it up with some arty kids at school, and it's all going to make sense. And you can rest easy knowing that Dex and I will be waiting to beat the crap out of anybody who does you wrong, and you'll never have to worry again about some douchebag turning your life upside down. You're gonna rebuild. And I'm gonna rebuild. And life is going to be better for the time we spent together. And that's really all there is to say."

Before Cecily could get a single word out, Flynn's face popped around the doorframe. "I'm done."

"Likewise," Shane said.

Cecily followed them to the door being held open by a sullen-looking Allison.

Flynn spun around. "Listen, Ally, I know you have a direct line to Rothgar you've never once used, not even when you ran into money trouble last year—"

"I figured it out—" Her eyes suddenly narrowed. "Hey, how did you know?"

Flynn paused but then said, "If it's because you don't want to bug the big guy, bug me instead. Or Shane. Or whoever you want. But call."

"I don't need to bug any of you," she said resolutely. "I can call Missy if something comes up."

"Except you never do," Flynn said.

Allison was silent for a moment. "Nope, I never do," she finally said. "Apparently nothing ever comes up. Nothing that could possibly make me want to call any of the Hudson Kings."

She and Flynn stared at each other to the point where Cecily looked at Shane in alarm; he was carefully blank, as usual. Which meant, Cecily knew, that whatever was going on between the lines here wasn't nothing.

Flynn finally broke contact and reached for his wallet.

"I don't want your money," Ally said.

Cecily smiled at Shane before she remembered they couldn't really have any in-jokes anymore. But he smiled back, which was the worst thing he could possibly do. He remembered. And he cared. Pain clutched at her heart. Normal was going so well. Normal was working. Normal didn't have any drama. But normal also didn't have any Shane. *God, I miss you.*

Flynn took out a business card and set it down on the table. "Time's been real good to you, Allycat," he said, his eyes on hers. She didn't say a word, and he grinned. "Don't feel like you need to return the compliment." He walked over the threshold and looked back for Shane. Allison released an audible sigh of . . . Cecily wasn't sure what.

"Take care of yourself," Shane said.

"You too," Cecily said. "It was good to see you." Without thinking, without taking a moment to control her impulses, she stood on her tiptoes and brushed her mouth against Shane's mouth. Absolute heaven. *Good-bye, Shane.*

His body tensed. "Shit, Cecily, I was doing so fucking well." All of a sudden he pushed her against the front door so it slammed shut with Ally and Flynn on the opposite side.

He crushed his mouth down on hers, the banked fire exploding into flames between them. Cecily closed her eyes and savored the sweep of his tongue, the tension in his body as he held her in his arms. The skirt of her dress ruffled up against the wall, and his hand swept her bare thigh.

But just as suddenly as it began, it ended. They faced each other, arm distant, breath coming in fits and starts, eyes wild. Cecily stood there trembling. In a daze, Shane slowly wiped the back of his hand across his mouth more like he was branding himself than taking anything away.

From behind the door—and likely behind the peephole—Ally said, *"Damn."*

And finally Shane spoke. "You happy in your new life, Cece? You happy living here with Allison, doing normal?"

"Yes," whispered Cecily.

"'Cause I found out I like meeting you halfway. I think part of me came to you that night to see if you could handle the worst of the things that get thrown my way. I don't know what I was thinking, exactly. But my timing was off. Went to fix it the next morning, I was too late." His eyes met hers. "Wondering if our timing is still off."

Oh, god. Oh, god.

But she couldn't do it. She couldn't handle Shane changing his mind again. She couldn't take the risk that he'd realize he'd made a mistake again. She couldn't see living through another end, so this time, she wasn't going to offer a beginning. "I'm happy doing normal, Shane," she whispered.

He held her gaze. "Got you." After a moment of silence, during which Cecily fought a war in her head, he added, "Just remember I've got your back." He rapped sharply on the door and then just hit the stairs, Flynn following at his heels with a quick salute as he passed.

Cecily went inside and closed the door behind her, and the two women stood there staring at the wood frame until Allison said, "At least we have beer."

They looked at each other and burst into stunned laughter and then headed for the fridge, where Ally grabbed a couple of cold ones and handed one to Cecily, who took a long, cold swig and swiped at the tears in her eyes. She stared at the bottle remembering Chase and Shane goofing off in the Armory garage, Shane stripping down and doing a dance, Shane's body covering hers, entering hers, making love to her . . .

"You'll be, okay," Ally said, a look of commiseration on her face as they moved from the kitchen to the living room. "It takes a while to shake a man like that, but you'll be okay."

Cecily nodded, gripping the bottle extra hard so her hand wouldn't shake.

Ally took a couple of pulls of her beer and then said breathlessly, "What happened to Flynn?"

"I don't know. He wasn't like that when you knew him before?"

"Shit, no! I mean, he had his whole face." Allison flopped back on the sofa. "I hate the Hudson Kings. I fucking *hate* them all."

Cecily took the seat next to her. "Ally," she said gently, "I think we've both got some stuff we need to share with each other. They weren't just here because of your past; they're here for mine too."

"I know. Missy doesn't send me people without pasts," Allison said with a laugh. "I don't mind if you know about mine." She took a deep breath. "Missy and Apollo and Graham and I grew up together," she said, pointing to a framed picture on the bookcase. "That was three years ago. Probably the most normal thing we ever did."

Cecily reached for the frame. Two couples at a prom. Allison with a guy who looked like Missy; Missy with a guy who looked like Allison. "Apollo and Graham," she murmured.

"Yeah, that's my brother," Allison looked at her with steely eyes. "It was the perfect plan. We were all gonna get married someday, and Missy and I would be sisters forever. It's amazing how stupid kids can be. I even thought when the guys disappeared, Missy and I would help each other through it, but she looked to Rothgar and the rest of the men. They all just reminded me of what we lost. It's easier for her to hole up in the Armory and pretend there's still a search on, but Graham and Apollo are dead. They'd never go silent like this knowing we were waiting for a word. Never."

Allison chewed on her lip. "Wow, I've never had anyone to talk to about it until now. Someone who knew about the Armory and stuff."

"I don't know all that much," Cecily confessed.

"You've been inside there," Allison said. "That's saying *a lot*."

"I got the impression Missy would love to talk to you, but—"

"We're not friends anymore," Ally said ferociously.

"Then why would she send me here? And why would you let me come?"

Ally crossed her arms over her chest. "You were the third time I've gotten an e-mail asking if I can house someone. I never answer, which she takes as a yes. She sends you with a key."

"Why don't you say no?" Cecily asked.

Ally affected a look of uncaring. "A week after you move in, I get a check for rent."

Cecily studied her face. "But it's not just the money."

Different emotions warred across Allison's face. "I don't know why I don't say no," she finally whispered. "Maybe just to keep that connection, just in case, like I said."

"That was the first time you've seen one of the guys in *years*? Why *did* they come now?"

"They still fancy that I'm Hudson Kings property. Probably will until I die. This is either just them making the rounds or . . ."

"Or what?" Cecily asked.

A smile blossomed across Allison's face. "Or Shane Sullivan's finally found the one thing he'd be willing to trade in his BMW for, and he wants to keep it safe."

Cecily pressed her hand against her heart. *Did I do the right thing? Did I just blow my last chance? But . . . we just couldn't make it work.* She looked down at her nearly empty beer. "I wish . . ."

"Me too," Ally said cryptically, before downing the last of her bottle. "I really, really wish."

CHAPTER 33

After the drop-in from Shane and Flynn, things got pretty quiet. Cecily focused on her classes, although she found herself more interested in designing fake driver's licenses and packaging for surveillance devices than in the glossy corporate brochures and shampoo bottle designs created by her classmates.

She and Allison fell into the sort of pattern Cecily wished she'd had right out of college, before things started to go off the rails with James. Ally was a great roommate and was turning out to be a great friend. They never, ever talked about the Hudson Kings, and the only thing Cecily noticed was that Ally liked to listen in on Cecily's phone calls with Dex.

Cecily was really proud of pulling herself together—if only the constant nagging of her heart calling out for Shane would leave her alone. But it was a tough road, and as she pushed through her school's doors, she wasn't thinking about the color wheel; she was replaying her last conversation with Shane in her head for the thousandth time in the week since she'd last seen him.

In this version of the fantasy conversation, the answer she gave him was "Yes, let's try again," which was why she had an enormous smile on her face even as she exited the building and stepped out into a blast of the summer season's first really unpleasant humidity.

That smile didn't last.

James Peterson stood in the central square next to a massive mirrored sculpture that made it look like he was carrying a thousand bouquets of flowers instead of just the one. He was working at a smile that flickered on and off like a faulty fuse, and his eyes said he didn't know how she was going to take this.

She took it worse on the inside, where he couldn't see, and automatically touched her jeans' back pocket, confirming her phone was there.

"Hi, Cece," he said quietly, coming toward her. "I know your brother doesn't like me, but I had to explain myself."

She blinked, a silent scream going off in her head. A scream full of anger and embarrassment and confusion and fear. "Hi," she managed. "I think it was made pretty clear what would happen if you came around again. And my brother's supposed to pick me up again. He'll be here any second." She looked desperately around for Shane, but he wasn't there. *He'll come. He always comes.*

Neither of them moved closer, but James awkwardly thrust out the mixed bouquet. Cecily eyed the flowers and forced a smile back on her face, trying not to panic as her pulse began to race. She wished to god her voice didn't shake when she said, "It's really not necessary. Thanks, but I'd rather not. How did you know I'd be here now?"

James shrugged. "Figured I'd just wait."

Oh, god.

"It was made pretty clear what would happen if you talked to me again," she said, forcing herself to stay calm, be smart. "It's not going to be just words."

"Look, Cece, I messed up. I messed up big-time. But you should know that I thought about what I did, how I acted."

James's reminder of all that helped steel her spine even more. *You're a liar. You don't care about me at all. You only "messed up" because it was too hard pretending to be a decent guy for so long. You were never my boy-friend. You were acting. But if I say it, I'll give everything away.*

Cecily stared at James's pretty-boy looks, his slender frame, his pricey banker clothes. So different from Shane in every way. "I had to run away from you, James. I literally had to take a suitcase and run to get away from your head games and your moods and your threats. You *hit* me, remember?" The details were snowballing back. The memory of James faking everything, isolating her in a Minneapolis suburb while he asked her a curious number of questions about what her brother said on the phone and wrote in e-mails, and becoming obsessive about what she did and how she spent her time, suddenly made her want to be sick. Once upon a time he seemed and looked like such a nice person, a golden boy—"You're *not* a nice person," she blurted.

James blanched. "I want you to know that I'm in counseling. I was taking pills—you didn't know that. I stopped drinking, I stopped the drugs. I'm in counseling." His voice was low, careful, his eyes never leaving her face. "I know how I treated you was wrong, and I'm sorrier than I could ever say. I want to make it up to you . . ."

He went on and on, but all Cecily could think was that he probably had a gun on him, just like Shane. Maybe something else too. Cecily didn't know what she was going to do if she couldn't shake him.

"Stop," Cecily said softly. "Stop right there. I can imagine accepting your apology, but I need more time to decide what I want, if I can ever imagine being with you again."

Biggest lie ever. She never wanted to see him again; she was terri-fied of him, because she knew that everything she went through was him acting with restraint. James without restraint must be off-the-charts scary, and she could see he was getting desperate now. She could see it. Oh, man, her cell phone felt like it was burning a hole in her pocket; she *had* to get a message to the Hudson Kings. "Will you please just . . . leave. Leave me . . ." *Alone.* "To think?" she asked, hearing the strain in her own voice.

Something flickered in James's eyes before leveling out again. Something not sorry. Something not nice.

Cecily gripped her laptop hard to keep her hands from shaking. She hadn't seen this particular act, this level of contrition, but she'd been on the receiving end of his apologies before, enough to recognize the whiplash that played inside his brain, making him contrite and then rebuilding the flame of bitter anger if she didn't accept his humility with gushing smiles and hugs. There was definitely going to be anger, and she sure as hell didn't want to be around when it struck.

God, there was more she'd like to say to James, but she was too afraid. Too much of a show of strength, and his instinct would be to prove he had more. Anything that sounded even vaguely like a threat, and his instinct would be to prove he could get around it.

Did he really think they would ever get back together? Did he think he still had a chance to get information about Dex and the Hudson Kings from her? Did he truly not know his cover was so blown it wasn't even funny?

I wish Shane were here. But he was gone, back to his regular-scheduled programming, his real life, with Cecily not more than a pixel in his rearview mirror. "I have to go," Cecily said, turning away from James and starting across the courtyard toward her subway stop.

"Cece!" James was right on her tail.

She stopped and looked over her shoulder. "I—I'll think about it. Okay?"

James stood there with an expression that was more grim than sorry, a trail of petals in his wake, the flowers forgotten but still gripped in his hand. Cecily fought the urge to panic. "Please don't follow me, James. Really, don't."

"Cecily, I love you!"

Those three words weren't supposed to sound scary. Cecily ran down the subway steps and swiped in, ran toward the closing doors of a 2 train, jammed her purse inside to make the doors open again, and sandwiched herself into the standing crowd. Sweat plastered her clothes to her body, and she could scarcely breathe watching James jump the turnstile.

The subway doors were still open.

He saw her. And he came for her.

CHAPTER 34

For the first time in a long time, Shane was in a good rhythm with work. He loved this feeling, this dance the Hudson Kings were so good at. Each man knew the choreography, and it was a thing of beauty to do your part to perfection knowing the guys on the other end were doing theirs too. And they were. The men of the Hudson Kings were the best.

Shane couldn't help thinking, though, about what might have been. He could have laughed. He could have loved. Things were going well with the Hudson Kings, but he could have had so much more.

Cecily.

God. The feelings he had for her should have started to fade by now. He should've been back in his shell. He wasn't. Not by a long shot.

"Moving," Nick murmured into Shane's ear.

"Go" time.

Blanking all other thoughts, Shane made a calculation about Nick's time and distance. He pulled away from the curb at Spring and Sullivan, where he'd kept a low profile behind a bunch of tourists lining up for Cronuts at a famous French bakery. Both windows were rolled down, his steering elbow resting on the sill, eyes ahead.

From the corner of his eye, he saw Nick in motion. Nick crossed the street and headed directly for him, an anonymous businessman hurrying, crumpling an empty pastry bag while he juggled a cup of coffee.

Nick stepped into the street to cross again, appearing to head for the subway; Shane cut him off—typical New York driver asshole turning in front of a pedestrian.

As he passed, Nick looked pissed and flung his garbage toward the trash; at least that's what it looked like on one side of the street; on the other side, anyone watching would see an annoyed businessman tossing a white piece of trash at the jerk who couldn't respect a pair of newly polished wing tips.

The crumpled bag landed in the passenger-side foot well. Shane flipped him the bird and kept driving. *Nick, you fucker. Nice touch with the trash in my car.*

A subtle glance in the rearview mirror showed Nick drinking the dregs of his coffee before vanishing from sight.

Shane headed home, on high alert with the goods in his vehicle. He'd just called in the drop to Roth when a hell of a surprising name popped up on his phone.

"Shane? It's Ally." It was loud, with lots of ambient noise in the background, but the tension in her voice was unmistakable.

Shane tightened his hand around the phone. "Don't hang up."

"I won't."

"Are you in trouble?"

"I don't know," Ally said.

"Where are you?"

"In the bathroom at Grand Central Station. Food court level. I don't know where to go. I tried to get into that safe room in Midtown. Did all the usual stuff to get there in secret. But I—I don't have the combination anymore."

"We'll fix that. What do you need?"

"It's about Cecily's boyfriend. Ex-boyfriend. His name is James. He came to my *work*."

Fury. Just red-hot fury. *Shouldn't have waited to finish this job to teach that bastard a lesson. Now the lesson is going to be a world of hurt like he's never seen.* He kept his voice even when he answered Ally: "Are you in danger right now?"

"I don't think . . . I don't know."

But you're scared shitless. "Are you in a stall?"

"Yes."

"Did you sense anybody watching, following? Anyone see you go into the bathroom? Into the station?"

"I don't think so. But I don't know."

"I want you to leave the bathroom and go hang out by the main clock in the terminal, be around people while you tell me what happened."

The sound of a door swinging open and some crackling while Ally maneuvered and her voice came back on the line. "He came to my *work*, Shane. He was waiting, hanging around outside when I went to pick up lunch. He wanted to talk to me about Cecily. Asked me how to get her back."

"Did he have a weapon?" Shane asked.

"No."

"Did he threaten you in any way?"

"No. He was sweet. Really nice. Explained how he'd messed up. Sounded like the real thing. Wanted advice. Asked if jewelry would work or spa certificates."

"What scared you, Ally?"

"He was smiling when he asked me to get in touch if I thought of anything. Gave me his business card and smiled. Really sweet and soft-spoken. I said I'd take it, you know, just to make him go away, but I think he knew I was lying. He said thank you all sugarlike, you know, but then I heard him. He whispered something really low I'm sure he didn't think I'd hear or understand."

Ally's breath was coming in fits and starts now.

"But you did," he confirmed.

"Good all-American boy. Wall Street banker type."

"Yeah?" Shane prompted.

"Perfect accent." She sounded like she was about to cry.

"What do you mean?"

"Perfect accent." She was *really* trying not to cry now.

"Talk to me, Ally. I'm headed your way."

"He called me a cunt, Shane. *In Russian.* He's not who he's pretending to be. I don't know what you're working on over there, but I'm scared for Cecily. She's not at the apartment."

Shane's stomach just fucking dropped.

"I went over there after he left my office," Ally was saying, "And I was waiting for a really long time at home, and then I saw this car waiting out front. A guy, he had, like, chicken pox scars all over his face. I took a picture of him. A tough-looking guy. Like I told you and Flynn, there's been nothing for years, nobody on me. And now this. Something's off. So I went out the back . . . just . . . went. And I called you. And I don't know . . . I don't know, Shane, but if I were you, I'd be really worried about Cecily."

CHAPTER 35

"Got anything new?" was the first thing Shane uttered when he walked into the war room with Ally at his side.

The roar of activity dulled. Shane handed Ally's camera over to Chase, who blurted, "Man, she looks just like Graham."

"Cece's not answering her phone," Dex said from behind him.

Shane whirled around and stared at Dex for a minute. The guy looked wrecked. So wrecked Shane couldn't go there. He steeled his heart, absolutely steeled himself. "Ally, keep trying her. Maybe she's screening."

Ally nodded and pulled out her phone.

Nick reached past her to hand Shane some papers. "Made copies of James Peterson's file. Hey, Ally, girl." He held out his hand; she stared at it for a minute and gave him a shake, her eyes not meeting his.

Shane dropped the folder on the desk next to Chase and opened it to reveal a series of pictures of James and Cecily dressed up on the town somewhere, probably in Minneapolis. Under that "happy times" picture were pictures of James solo, James with a gun, James in clothes looking decidedly un-bankerlike with a decidedly un-bankerlike attitude, and more. "Cecily's in trouble."

"Roth's all over it. Nice piece of glue, Ally," Flynn said, pointing to the photos of James now open on Chase's screen. Ally backed up to the wall, phone to her ear, free hand pressed against her chest. She managed a flick of the corner of her mouth and then looked away.

One by one, the rest of the guys entered the room. Nobody took a seat.

Rothgar entered with a copy of the same folder, and his eyes immediately found Ally against the wall. She stared defiantly back at him. "Glad to have you safe," Roth said. Ally's stony expression didn't change.

Time was standing way too still. "Roth," Shane said. "He's got my woman."

"She answering, Ally?" Dex asked, even though the answer was obvious.

Ally shook her head.

Shane let out a breath. "Gonna find her, Dex. You know this. You fucking *know* this."

Dex looked gratefully at him and then reached out with his fist. Shane tapped it with his own, and they looked back to Rothgar.

The boss leaned against the edge of the table and pulled a photo from the printer.

Details and data from different jobs covered different parts of the walls in the room; he moved to the wall they kept for the sleeper agent mission. It was already covered with photographs, clippings, and notes. Roth added the pockmarked henchman to the wall next to James. "Freelancer. Russian-born. Been in this country for years. Same guy who chased Shane earlier this month. Same guy who tried to muscle Chase and Flynn as well."

He then walked to the wall covered with data from the sleeper agent job they'd been working on earlier in the day and stuck two more pictures up: the one Shane had taken of James and Anya in the restaurant, and a different one of James in a bar doing shots of vodka with a younger, blonde Anya Gorchakov and another couple, unknown.

Shane remembered the memory stick he'd picked up from Nick and handed it to Roth. "From this morning," he murmured.

Rothgar nodded and pocketed the stick. "Talked to my contact in the government. Asked for more color on James. We already know James is a handler for Russian agents. Contact confirmed he's also a climber looking to move up with his Russian bosses. His sleeper agents get outed, he's fucked. So, he finds out the Hudson Kings have a contract to go after his stable. If we're successful, he looks bad. He's got to cut us off at the knees, find out what we know, and change the game. Figures he can do this when he finds out our newest team member has a cute little sister. James puts on a show for Cecily, hoping to get intel on the Hudson Kings. Pillow talk and all that. Keeps her in Minnesota to isolate and dominate, while he pretends to be going back and forth to New York for an investment banking job."

Shane made a sound, loud and angry enough for one of the brothers to squeeze his shoulder.

"Apparently didn't have the patience to keep up the facade of 'loving boyfriend.' She shook him, and Shane went to pick her up." Roth gestured with his chin to Dex. "Dex says he never told Cecily about the Hudson Kings while she was with James, but at the moment, that's irrelevant. Because James either figured she was still his best shot if he could convince her he was a changed man—or he's figured out she's deep with the Hudson Kings now and is more valuable than ever. Either way . . ."

Rothgar tapered off, clearly not wanting to vocalize the obvious: Cecily was in the hands of a Russian operative, a man who would not hesitate to kill her if he decided she was worthless. A man who would not hesitate to try to wring information out of a vulnerable, untrained woman if he thought it would help his own crumbling situation.

Cold dread threatened to swamp Shane's ability to think. "What's our last data point on Cecily?" Shane said, forcing himself to think of this as just another problem to solve, another mission to plan. If he let it get personal in his mind, he was not going to get through this in one piece.

"Still not answering her phone," Dex said, his voice robotic, his eyes staring straight ahead.

"I saw her before work," Ally said, coming forward. "She was going to class. I think she ends at two thirty. I don't know if she had plans after. Haven't seen her since morning coffee, and she didn't call, although I didn't necessarily expect her to. When James came to me, I don't know if he'd already talked to her or not."

The door opened; Missy bustled in with a bunch of printouts, which she held out to Rothgar along with a cell phone. "O'Neill," she said, her eyes big. Rothgar hesitated. "Sixth Ward," she said urgently. It was pretty unusual for Rothgar and O'Neill to coordinate on anything. Rothgar took the phone, and then Missy saw Ally behind him and froze.

The room went silent.

Missy looked at Allison, Allison looked at Missy, and then Ally broke the moment and stared down at her phone like Missy wasn't even there. "It just keeps going to voice mail," she said hoarsely.

Missy blinked and turned to the computer.

Shane speed-dialed Cecily on his own phone for what seemed like the thousandth time. No dice. That look on Dex's face was a look he was pretty sure was breaking through on his own face.

"Don't like it," Shane murmured. "Don't like it."

Rothgar took the call at the back of the room. Shane watched his face. *Jaysus.* If he was talking seriously to the Sixth Ward, he was putting his big guns in the game. No small thing to ask O'Neill for a favor.

When Rothgar came back, he took a moment, staring down at the papers and files and photos scattered across the desk. "Good news is she's not missing," Rothgar said grimly. "Courtesy of O'Neill, we know he's got her. We can't be sure what his plans are, or if he's inclined to hurt her."

Pure dread moved down Shane's spine. Rothgar put up a hand before he could speak and added, "We know he was willing to hit her once, and that was when he still thought she was on his side. So let's get a plan together and get her back."

"You have to give O'Neill a marker for that?" Shane asked.

"Yep," Rothgar said.

Respect.

The two men stood toe-to-toe. Shane could feel the blood pounding in his veins. "Where is she?" he asked quietly.

Rothgar eyed him. "We work as fast as we can to still work smart. So, first thing is let's create a plan . . . and then *you've got to respect the team plan.* If Dex can do it, you can too."

Shane looked over at Dex, whose good knee was compulsively bouncing up and down. Cecily's brother was beyond pissed, his fingers flying over the keyboard as he started pulling up on the screen closed-circuit security cameras pointing all over Manhattan. "Need coordinates," he muttered.

"Where is she, Roth?" Shane repeated in a measured voice. *Contain yourself. Gotta contain it until you get her back.*

"I'm gonna ask you to respect the team plan."

Closest he'd ever come to punching Roth square in the face, and he still wasn't sure he'd avoid it. Shane pressed his fingers into his temples. "We know where she is, we know who's got her, then which one of us is helping her if I'm sitting on my ass respecting the team plan?"

"I called Geo after I talked to the Sixth. Geo's tracking her down in the field, courtesy of their intel."

"I see," Shane said carefully. "*Geo's* in the field."

"You don't have a clear head."

"I'm clear."

Rothgar folded his arms over his chest and looked at the ground for a minute, before he raised his gaze back to Shane's face. "Are you part of this team? Do you want to keep being part of this team?"

Shane felt like he was breaking apart inside. *Contain, man.*

"You're in love with this girl, brother. Gone for her. We've got plenty of reasons to get Cecily away from James, but I don't even need more than the two sitting in this room. We're on it, and we're getting a plan together. The best way to put that plan in motion is probably to send you and Dex to his room to hold hands so you don't fuck things up. Since I'm feeling generous, why don't you hang out here in the war room."

"Roth," Shane said, doing a shit job of keeping emotion out of his voice. "I need to be in my *car*."

Rothgar stared into his eyes. Unmoved.

"I need to be in my *car*, Roth. Wheels to the ground. Cecily coming up in my sights. I need this more than I've ever needed anything in my life. I'm asking you to do this service for me, brother. I've been loyal to you. I'll always be loyal to you. Don't bench me."

Rothgar stared at Shane some more. Then he looked around the room, pausing at Allison's face, his own devoid of expression. Then he looked around the room some more and stopped at Missy.

They just looked at each other, and then she tipped her head just slightly to the side. And he read whatever the fuck she'd meant by that and finally came back to Shane. He shook his head, the toe of his boot working against the ground.

Shane felt the urge to yell at the top of his lungs. Instead, he pressed his palms together as if in prayer. Every second was a second that Cecily was in danger. Rothgar was the best. He had to know what he was doing. But, *for fuck's sake*, could he just do it already.

And then Rothgar said, "Missy goes with you, Shane."

Everybody in the room, Missy included, looked at Rothgar liked he'd gone bat-shit crazy.

Jaysus. In for a penny, in for a pound? "I don't want her in danger too."

"Then her being present should keep you from doing anything stupid," he said tightly. "I'll expect regular check-ins. Dex is watching the screen. Geo's already in the field. Flynn stands by in the room, here. Chase is on deck for any support we need outside." Roth turned to

Chase. "Get your bike out front and your leathers on in case we need something more nimble than a car."

He turned to the room at large. "Team plan: Ransom to get her back, full arsenal if that doesn't work. Deets to follow."

Shane looked at Missy. "Put your body armor on, grab a weapon, and meet me in the garage."

She stared at him. And then at Rothgar. "You're letting me go on the *front* line?"

Rothgar looked blasé. "You got a problem with that?"

"No!" Missy's eyes were huge.

"Call in from your vehicles. I'll be in touch with details. Now let's get this job done," Roth said with a nod to Shane, who nodded back. They bumped fists and everyone scattered.

Roth pulled something from a desk drawer and tossed it to Ally, who managed to catch it.

"Shane," Dex called from the computer bank. "My fucking leg."

"I know. Don't worry. I'll take care of it."

He shook his head, that despair threatening to pull him under. He looked back at Shane and said, "Safe. Get her home safe, yeah?"

"Yeah," said Shane. He lifted his chin to Dex and saw Ally staring in confusion at the box of Band-Aids Roth had thrown over. After a moment, she looked down and realized some blister on her foot was bleeding on her silver stiletto.

Shane let the door close behind him. Rothgar never did miss a thing. Hopefully, that included Cecily.

CHAPTER 36

James was not James with a very perfect upper-crust, rich American accent. James was Yakov Petrenko with a Russian accent, and Cecily now knew this because he'd told her himself in his natural accent. Right after he'd grabbed her off the street and forced her into the passenger seat of his car.

The good news was that she was alive. The bad news was that James said he was taking her to see his boss. The boss of a Russian operative seemed like the sort of person Cecily did not need to have a discussion with.

Given that Cecily's wrists were bound in front of her with duct tape cutting into her skin, this turn of events seemed net negative.

Having a guy fake a relationship with her for nearly a year was pretty gross and awful, especially when she thought about how many times she'd slept with him.

Having that guy not care that your circulation was getting cut off and blood was dripping down your fingers really meant that all pretenses were gone.

And if they weren't pretending to care about each other, then James probably wasn't too worried about what was going to happen when she got where you go when your fake ex-boyfriend wants to use you to get "intelligence" about your brother's mercenary team to please some Russian bigwigs.

So Cecily was shaking—that was uncontrollable. But she was determined not to lose it completely. Ally and Dex would talk eventually and realize she'd gone missing. And Dex would tell Rothgar. And Shane would find out.

It then occurred to Cecily that Ally might not expect her by dinner, Dex didn't call every day, and James was unpredictable to say the least. She took a deep breath.

James had buckled her into the passenger seat, with a warning that if she clued other drivers into her predicament, he'd use the gun now sitting in his lap. She wasn't sure what exactly that meant, but with a little luck, the car in front of them would stop short and he'd jam on the brakes and accidentally blow his balls off. In lieu of that unlikely though spirit-raising thought, Cecily decided to do everything he said until a better idea came along.

The way her hands were bound, she couldn't open the door, much less open the locks. For now the best she could hope for was that the Hudson Kings had a way of tracking her down. And that they'd figure out something was wrong sooner rather than later.

She looked at James's profile; strange she'd been with him for so long, was his girlfriend for almost a year, and now he seemed like a complete stranger. Not only that. Even when she thought of him at his best, all she could think was that he wasn't Shane. *Shane came back to me. He came back to me to see if there was a chance. There was a chance . . . but I didn't take it.*

She raised her shoulder and swiped away the sweat on her face. James leaned over and slammed her arms back down. "Don't even try it."

Try what? God.

Cecily didn't answer. For the first time, all the blacks and whites were gray. Marvelously, deliciously bed-blanket-BMW gray. Bending the law didn't seem so cut-and-dried. Shane and his jobs and his "dirty" money didn't seem so clearly categorized into what was wrong and what was right, because at the end of the day, the Hudson Kings were the guys who were going to look after you.

The duct tape around Cecily's wrists was definitely too tight—she could see her fingers turning patchy purple and white. Luckily, it was a little floppy at the corner; worse came to worse, she could nudge or maybe rip part of it off. Did duct tape rip off? Maybe not. *Shit. I can't even think.* She was losing it a little, starting to let the panic creep in. For now she tried to be invisible.

James was sweaty now too. He smelled like fear. This would have surprised her a couple of months back, when she'd still thought of him as strong. But that was before she'd learned what strong really was. That was before Shane.

James furrowed his brow, muttering something under his breath.

"Are you going to hurt me?" Cecily asked in a small voice.

"Can you just not talk?" he snapped.

"I thought you wanted to be friends," Cecily mumbled.

James rolled his eyes. "Cecily, obviously that was a line. Don't be idiotic. I honestly don't know what they are going to do with you, but I suggest you prepare yourself."

Ice-cold fear raced down Cecily's spine. James had hit her before. She knew what that was like. One guy hitting one girl. That was bad. But the idea of a "they." That sounded worse.

"I never should have gotten into this shit," James was saying. His lack of confidence did not make Cecily feel better. It just meant someone else besides James had the power to decide what to do with her. Not to mention, one of James's big push buttons was feeling emasculated. She knew he liked having a woman around to make him feel like more of a man; now Cecily could see how weak he truly was, now that she understood that you already had to be a man. No one else was going to make you feel strong. You just either had it or you didn't.

God, she would have done anything to be sitting next to Shane right now. Shane with his cool head and fiery heart.

"It would have been fine, if you'd just given me a fucking crumb or two, but you gave me nothing," James muttered. "You're pretty enough, fun, good in bed . . . all you had to do was *talk* about them, and we'd have had it made."

"I didn't know anything. I don't know anything."

"Bullshit." His gloved hands convulsed around the steering wheel. "Can't believe how much time I put into you—you made me look like an idiot. They gave me one job, Cecily. One job, and I was on my way up. Then your fucking brother and his fucking band of mercs got in the way. Now I've got to do *this*."

"They should have asked you to kidnap one of the Hudson Kings if they actually want to know about them," Cecily said.

James got a weird look on his face. "Probably should have," he muttered.

She stared over at him. "You do know what you're doing, right?" she whispered.

When he didn't answer, that's when Cecily really started to panic.

CHAPTER 37

Rothgar was furious. Thank fuck for the find-my-phone feature Dex had installed on his sister's new phone, but that didn't make him any less furious. Nobody fucked with his people. The Russians knew this, and they understood this because they felt the same way about their people. Therefore, it was tough to understand why they'd be this stupid.

Dex's fingertips flew across his keyboard as he tracked the device moving south through Manhattan traffic. "My guess is he's heading for a bridge or tunnel," he said.

"Bridge," Rothgar said firmly. He scanned the various videos on Dex's monitor. Twilight was descending over the Brooklyn Bridge. Lights twinkled, mixing with the one or two stars bright enough to puncture the city sky. The span itself was deserted, given over to the construction cones set up for a middle-of-the-night construction project and a couple of massive lights from the cranes shining like movie spotlights.

Now and then one of the videos would show the East River's inky water crest: first, a line of silver and then a bit of muddled foam, and gone again.

Shane's car came into view and stopped. He waited, patient as ever, his car the only car on the bridge to ignore the construction closure signage, until a single set of headlights blinked into view.

"I want in Shane's ear and in Shane's car," Rothgar ordered. The sort of personal-space invasion Shane would normally balk at big-time, but this was a special occasion, to say the least.

Dex hacked into the comms system in Shane's car and gave himself administrative privileges. Two lights on Dex's screen went green. Video and audio.

Shane looked down at the hijacked screen, saw HQ in multiple video mode, and swore loud and blue.

"Nice to know the audio's coming in clear," Roth muttered, punching the microphone button. "Shane, it's Roth. Turn your earpiece . . ." His voice trailed off. "Where the hell is Missy?"

"Backup works best when you're not in the same vehicle," Shane said tightly, putting in an earpiece.

Rothgar discovered a new level of furious. "We'll have plenty of words about that once Cecily's safe. Now call James on videophone. Use the speaker. Dex will keep your earpiece pointing to HQ. We're here, but he doesn't know that."

"Understood." Shane plugged his personal phone into the dashboard comms and dialed. After a ring, James's face appeared on the screen, a thin sheen of sweat plastering his cowlick to his forehead. Cecily sat next to him in the passenger seat, a small smear of blood at the corner of her mouth.

At Rothgar's side, Dex sucked in a quick breath.

Shane didn't make a sound, didn't change his expression. He had to be losing his mind. Because Cecily looked unbelievably lovely and lost in a strappy little white sundress. And she was in the wrong car with the wrong guy.

"Use it, don't lose it," Nick muttered from behind Rothgar.

"Hi, James. Nice to see you, Cecily," Shane said.

The video in James's car must have opened with a delay, because Cecily looked blank for a moment before her eyes widened and her mouth crooked in a tentative smile.

"It's you. Fantastic. What do you want?" James asked.

Rothgar studied the screen with dispassionate expertise: Bravado. Lots of it. Really fucking sweaty. Desperation? Or just nervous? Desperation. Blood on Cecily, in spite of the warning James'd gotten from Shane. That didn't bode well. Desperate and violent.

"I'd like you to stop your car, open the door, and let Cecily out," Shane said.

"Can't hear you very well," James said. "Audio's tricky." He reached forward with a brown leather glove and pretended to fiddle with the volume.

"Those Armani?"

James's eyebrow went up. "Yeah. The best."

"Not quite the best," Shane remarked.

James's jaw tightened.

"Needs to be the alpha dog, doesn't he?" Rothgar said quietly. Dex nodded.

"Think he's going for the Brooklyn Bridge," Ally called out. Rothgar's eyes shot to her. *Ally, in the zone. Monitoring the GPS like it was old times. Christ.*

"How you doing, Cecily?" Shane asked.

There was a pause. "Answer him," James said.

"I—I . . ." She glanced at James and then looked into the monitor, her eyes and tone trying to say a thousand different things when all she actually said was "I miss you . . . guys."

Shane's expression remained unchanged, but his Adam's apple convulsed as he swallowed. *He's going cold,* thought Rothgar.

"I'd tell you guys to get a room," James said, glancing in his rear-view mirror. "But I'm taking her to mine."

Again, just a tiny fraction, Shane went colder.

"That's good," murmured Rothgar. "He's in the zone. Not letting the emotion get in the way. He was right to ask for the field."

"Doesn't matter," Dex said through gritted teeth. "Shane's in his car, and Cece's in James's car. He's got to get her *out* of there."

"So, James," Shane said. "You already fess up to your superiors that *you've* been made? That must create a shitstorm of a problem for all those sleeper agents you're supposed to be handling. You've got a helluva problem now, I should think."

James's gloved hand squeezed the steering wheel. "Not anymore," he said, tipping his chin toward Cecily. "It'd be better if she were taller, but my bosses like the waifish type. Especially since her looks come with a lot of information about the Hudson Kings. Pretty to look at, and with thin, little bones. I have the feeling she'll break pretty easy."

That didn't sit well with Rothgar, and it had to be a thousand times worse for Shane. But Shane stayed in control. "Hmm . . . you didn't think this through. The girl doesn't know the dirt on us, so the real question is, once your Russian bosses realize they can't use you anymore and find out she's no good, what's your backup plan?" Shane asked. "'Cause I can help you with that."

"Nice," Rothgar murmured.

James didn't say anything for a moment, then: "Don't worry about me. I'm extremely good at pretending to be someone else. I can go solo anytime I want. Just like you. I can literally disappear."

"Well, I am worried about you. Cecily's got *blood* on her *face*," Shane said, his tone like steel. He let that sink in, and both cars drove in silence until he repeated, "She's *bleeding*. You have to know you take her in like this, you're not going to get a pat on the back and a promotion. You're going to get a smackdown for revealing your identity to the Hudson Kings and for jeopardizing the entire sleeper cell. So pull over, leave Cecily by the side of the road, and go disappear." It sounded like less of a request and more of an order.

"It would take a lot more than your kind suggestion to get me to do that," scoffed James.

"I've got more than a kind suggestion. I've got two hundred fifty K in my trunk that says you can disappear in first class instead of coach."

"You've got two hundred fifty K in your trunk," James repeated.

Getting through, thought Rothgar.

"You wouldn't believe what I have in my trunk," Shane said.

Cecily smiled.

Dex let out a shaky breath.

"So, show me," James said. His voice was breezy, but the look in his eyes said that he liked what he was hearing.

"Reel him in. You've got him," Rothgar whispered. He unmuted the earpiece in his other ear. "Chase, you close?"

Chase confirmed.

"I'll show you mine if you show me yours," Shane was saying.

James pulled his car to the side of the bridge and came to a stop. *Perfect. Gives both Dex and Chase time to catch up.*

Except then James got even more stupid by pulling out a gun and pressing the muzzle to Cecily's head.

Dex slammed a fist down on the desk.

Rothgar slowly folded his arms across his chest. Furious. *Furious.* "The bridge has surveillance video," he said gently to Dex.

Dex ran a hand through his hair and then went back to the keyboard, tapping into the video stream guarding the Brooklyn Bridge.

In James's car, Cecily sat with the gun to her head, her eyes clenched shut, her entire body shaking. She bit her lip so hard she started bleeding again.

"Okay, *show me the money,*" James said.

"We've got eyes," Rothgar said into Shane's ear. "Go ahead, and I'll let you know if you need to turn back."

Dex was breathing hard now, his eyes glued to the array of videos splayed across his monitor.

Shane hesitated, staring into the video.

"Focus, Shane," Rothgar murmured. "You'll get the girl. Trust me to be your eyes."

Shane went off video for about five minutes, returning with an armful of cash he shoved at the video camera.

"That can't be two hundred fifty K," James said.

"I'm not digging it out of my trunk unless it's a go," Shane said.

"It's a go," James said.

"Let Cecily out."

"You want me to let her go? On the side of the bridge?"

"Yeah. She's got legs. She can walk home."

James looked over at her. "I'll run you off the bridge, you try anything."

Cecily's expression shifted slightly, her cheeks turning redder, but she didn't make a sound.

"I'll run you off the bridge?" Shane repeated very slowly, his voice this side of incredulous.

"Shi-i-it. I know that voice. All in," Flynn said from the back.

Dex glanced over, then at Rothgar. "What about his voice?" he asked nervously.

Rothgar just shook his head, his body tense. "Shane, steady," he murmured into the microphone, trying to gentle a wild animal.

"Let me make something clear. *If you harm her*, the Hudson Kings hunt you down and kill you. *If you harm her*, the Russians hunt you down and kill you. Which is all beside the point, because *if you harm her*, you're never making it past me."

James's bravado held, but it looked to Rothgar like he was beginning to realize he was running out of options. "Let's get this over with," James muttered. "You drop the money, back up to your end of the bridge. I get out of the car with Cecily. If it's all there, she goes free, you pick her up."

"You let her out, she stays left-hand lane. You stay right-hand lane. You stay there, and you don't get close to the side of the bridge, and you don't cross over to the left-hand side, or I will accelerate and fucking grind you into the pavement. Understood?" Shane ground out. "I'm getting the rest of the money now." He opened the car door but then sat back in the driver's seat very suddenly. He looked square in the video monitor.

"There something else?" James asked, eyes narrowed.

Shane paused, then looked out the window, over the water to the twinkling lights of Brooklyn, and came back to square. "I really love my car. I just thought you should know that."

Cecily blinked. James snorted with laughter. "Yeah. That's sweet. I love my car too, man."

"What the fuck?" Dex blurted. "What's he saying?"

"Shane?" Rothgar prompted. Shane ignored him and got out of the car and went offscreen. Dex stared at the video of the inside of James's car. Cecily was holding up. He shook his head. "When did my little sister get so strong?"

Ally touched his shoulder.

They watched Cecily sitting in silence next to James. Shane needed to get the money and fast, because bleakness was settling in on James's features; he was beginning to realize he'd blown all the good options, and the last one put him on the run from the Russian mercs and, for all he knew, the Hudson Kings alongside them.

On the bridge surveillance, Rothgar watched Shane lug a duffel bag brimming with cash to the outside lane. He made a show of brushing off his hands. "Now you get her out of the car."

"You get in, start backing up. Then she gets out."

Shane got back in his car, and James pulled Cecily out of his, gun back at her head. He knelt down, counting money, his attention moving between the cash and Cecily as he went through the stacks.

Cecily looked down at James and then up at the receding image of Shane driving away in his car. All of a sudden, she started to run after Shane's car.

"Shit," Rothgar hissed.

With his car in reverse, Shane took a deep breath and said very clearly, "Missy, you're on."

Missy's voice came out of nowhere. "On it."

Rothgar lost a beat before he snapped back into focus, but he couldn't help but smile. "Make sure we've got an ear direct to Missy's piece, Dex."

Robotically, Dex typed. Rothgar could hear him chanting under his breath, "Come on, baby sister. Come on. Come on . . ."

Bridge surveillance captured headlights from a bright orange sedan coming to life in the dim parking area in the middle of the bridge reserved for repair workers.

"What, did Missy jack that ride?" Flynn murmured, admiration in his voice.

Rothgar watched James on the screen. "He's pissed. Gonna be sloppy."

James leaped to his feet, slowed by the bag of money. He opened the back door, dumped it all in, and jumped back in the driver's seat, his car door slamming shut as he accelerated.

The orange sedan sidled up to Cecily, the passenger-side door swinging open. Cecily jumped in. "You know what?" Missy said urgently, her voice a little muffled. "I think we should put our seat belts on."

The video showed James angle his car, pointing straight at the orange sedan; lights of the Manhattan skyline blurred through the glass behind him as he accelerated. "I didn't say you could go!" he yelled.

Rothgar gripped the back of Dex's chair. One of the girls screamed. Shane gunned his BMW.

The catastrophic collision that blared through the speakers of the Hudson Kings war room was Shane nailing James.

Missy's orange sedan bounced from the shockwave, then landed safely in the middle of the bridge.

James spun out and slammed full throttle through the side of the Brooklyn Bridge, jagged strips of metal railing eviscerating the chassis of his car.

Through the comms, it sounded like fingernails on chalkboard. And then a flare of orange lit up the sky, and part of the car exploded.

Shane's BMW skidded behind, tires screaming and brakes smoking.

Smoke and money shrouded the air. And then, as an eerie silence descended and a flurry of twenties fell like ticker tape, James's flaming Mercedes flipped end over end and plunged into the East River.

Shane's car was right behind, upright but balancing on the edge of the bridge above the water. The front of the car was smashed beyond recognition. The shattered windshield rained fat drops of glass into the river. A front wheel was gone, the wheel well hooked on a piece of broken barricade.

The room swelled with tension—Dex, Ally, Flynn, Nick, everybody was talking—but Rothgar heard nothing over the sound of his own calm instructions to Chase.

The video showed the doors of the orange car open; Missy and Cecily ran toward the BMW, which looked like it was hanging by a metal thread.

"She's okay," Dex choked out.

Shane's car slipped and jerked, lurching toward the tipping point. Rothgar couldn't tell if Shane was conscious.

That's my brother. And I'm stuck in this fucking room. He was nearly slain by the rare, unwelcome feeling of powerlessness, the strange, bitter taste of being safe in the war room while one of his men walked into the heart of danger.

Cecily approached the edge of the snarled barricade, two steps from thin air, her white skirt swirling around her legs.

Shane's car slipped, toppling over as it followed James into the dark. Until it hit the water, it never made a sound.

Dex's breath came out in a whoosh. Nick just nodded, arms folded across his chest. Ally clapped her hand over her mouth, her other hand digging into Flynn's arm. Rothgar put his fist on the desk and pressed very, very hard.

Together they watched Missy, in black, wearing night vision goggles and body armor, throw down her sniper gun and hold Cecily back from the edge of the bridge.

Rothgar looked away from the image of Cecily screaming down into the water to the other monitor. Shane's car was underwater. The electrical hadn't shorted yet.

"Please don't die," Ally begged.

Precious bubbles slipped from Shane's nose and mouth as he struggled against the water pouring through the broken windows. The pressure was forcing him back.

"Punch the driver's side," Rothgar muttered.

One of Shane's arms wasn't working right. His motions were disoriented. Between the white rush of the incoming water and the fact that he was running out of oxygen, he wasn't making good time.

There was a pause as he floated still for a second. As if he could breathe for him, Rothgar sucked in a deep breath.

Shane slammed his shoulder against the cracked window as hard as he could, and the video went dark.

They had to hold Cecily back. She was ankle deep in the water as Shane waded toward the shore, his shirt torn off, water and blood sluicing down his arms and chest. He moved slowly, taking oxygen from the tank strapped to Chase's body next to him.

His head was down; she couldn't see his face. She *had* to see his face.

She sloshed forward up to her thighs, trying to break free of Missy's hold on her arm.

Missy finally let go, her babbling about a first aid kit and blanket just a murmur in the background.

And then Shane looked up and saw her. Looked right into Cecily's eyes and waved everybody off, pushed away Chase's oxygen tank. He struggled to press through the water on his own, his gaze locked with hers.

They met in the middle. Cecily stopped moving, trying to find words that wouldn't come. "The car . . . the car . . ."

"Fuck the car," Shane said, hauling her into his arms. His mouth came down on hers, taking possession like he never wanted to let her go. When they finally came up for air, he added, "The only thing I want is you."

EPILOGUE

Six months later . . .

"This is it?" Cecily asked.

"Yep." Shane got out of the driver's seat and came around to the passenger side, where Cecily was peering through the window.

Cecily nodded, a huge grin on her face. She'd been waiting on the bleachers in the Armory garage because she wanted to see Shane pull up in his new car. After test-driving what seemed like an entire parking lot over the course of several months, he'd finally made a selection.

And here it was. A gray BMW sedan.

"What's so funny?" he asked.

"I adore you." Cecily stood on her tiptoes and gave him a long, slow kiss. His hands tightened on her waist, and when she moved back, he simply reeled her back in.

"Nice. Need more o' that," he muttered, kissing her again.

"Oh, wow," Cecily breathed when he moved south, his tongue streaking hot against her throat as he pressed kisses against her neck.

"Before I get distracted, c'mere," Shane said, pulling away so he could lead her to the trunk. He popped it open and stood back.

Cecily looked inside.

For a second, there just simply wasn't enough oxygen, not even in a building that had room enough for a plane or two.

"You breathless?" he said, a shit-eating grin on his face.

"Think I am," she said.

He'd rigged up the same wardrobe system he'd had before. This time he pointed to the line at the bottom of the wardrobe that was once off-limits. He pressed on a section of the panel until it popped, but it didn't open. "Open it."

Cecily opened the secret panel. Inside was a small black velvet box. Shane reached in and took out the box. He held it in his hand and looked into her eyes. Cecily's knees actually went weak.

Maybe there's an earpiece in the box. Or a small but useful vial of powder. Or a set of mission instructions.

"I love your normal," Shane said, one hand reaching out to tuck a lock of her hair back behind her ear. "I love the idea of going out for the Hudson Kings and doing this weird-ass shit I do, knowing that when the day's done, I get to go home to you in your life. I don't need you to spend your days in mine. I like—no, I *love* knowing you're safe in your world. When your normal's done for the day, sweetling, I'll be standing on the halfway line waiting for you. And I *love* knowing that if you feel like it—and sometimes I know you feel like it—if it's a day for the unusual, then I get to open the passenger door for you, and we go a little crazy together." He took a deep breath, shaking his head a little as if he couldn't quite convey all of his feelings, and said, "I love you, Cecily."

It's not an earpiece or a vial or a set of mission instructions. Oh, my god, Shane.

"So, what I gotta ask you is, are you with me in this? Because the Hudson Kings have my loyalty, but they don't have my heart. No one had that. I didn't know how to even give that. My heart was so cold, Cecily. So fucking cold before you. And, I tell you, thawing that out has been a bitch. But now it's so hot it burns. And it's the best thing I've ever felt in my life. I'm going to keep that flame burning for the rest of my life if you'll let me."

Cecily stared as he opened the box and presented her with a diamond solitaire ringed by diamond pavé.

"Will you marry me?" Shane asked, taking the ring out and tossing the box in the trunk. "Will you take that ride with me?"

Cecily had never been surer of anything in her life. "I love living on that line between black and white with you. Gray never felt so good. One of us doesn't have to cross a line if we can put our arms around each other right where we stand." She threw her arms around Shane's neck. "Yes! Totally, absolutely, yes! I will take that ride with you."

"Put it on, sweetling," he said, slipping the sparkling loop over her finger. She barely had time to admire the ring before he lifted her up in his arms and threw her in the backseat of the car.

He threw himself in next, and Cecily saw there were two blankets this time.

One beige-and-gray plaid dead-body blanket.

And a new plaid blanket: pink and white.

"Love you, baby," Shane whispered.

"Love you back," she said.

The last thing Cecily caught, before Shane's mouth drove her absolutely crazy, was the wide, easy grin on his face and the sound of him laughing. Happy.

ACKNOWLEDGMENTS

Thank you, Chris Keeslar, beloved spouse. Thank you, Megan Frampton, huckleberry extraordinaire. Thank you, agent Louise Fury, master of reinvention. And thank you, editors Alison Dasho and Lauren Plude, for taking it to the next level.

Watch for the next Hudson Kings book, coming soon!

ABOUT THE AUTHOR

Photo © 2010 Chris Keeslar

Liz Maverick is a bestselling, award-winning author and adventurer whose projects have taken her from driving trucks in Antarctica to working behind the scenes on reality-TV shows in Hollywood. Liz has written more than fifteen novels and is the creator of the *USA Today* bestselling Crimson City series, as well as *Wired*, a *Publishers Weekly* Book of the Year. She currently lives in Brooklyn, New York, and loves to stay in touch with readers via her website and newsletter at www.lizmaverick.com/newsletter.